HAPPILY NEVER AFTER

"A giggle-inducing romp that readers won't be able to object to."
—Lana Ferguson, *USA Today* bestselling author of
The Game Changer

"*Happily Never After* takes an irresistibly fun concept and expertly delivers on its promise, brimming with hilariously cheeky banter and so-red-hot-it'll-make-you-sweat chemistry between its lovable lead characters. Lynn Painter has a true gift for crafting wildly entertaining rom-coms, and this is her best one yet."
—Nicolas DiDomizio, author of *Nearlywed*

"Lynn Painter writes the rom-com banter of my dreams! *Happily Never After* is a sparkling, hilarious, sexy romance that leaps off the page and is just begging to be made into a movie."
—Sarah Adams, *New York Times* bestselling author of
The Rule Book

"Well-crafted and filled to the brim with sexual tension, *Happily Never After* is rom-com gold! We fell head over heels for the romance and the undeniably swoony chemistry. Max and Sophie are two characters so perfect for each other that you can't help but want to smoosh them together."
—*New York Times* bestselling authors Krista and Becca Ritchie

"A rom-com for the cynics . . . The supporting cast is equally funny and helps to round out an entertaining yarn that doesn't take itself too seriously." —*Library Journal*

Praise for

THE LOVE WAGER

"Painter follows up *Mr. Wrong Number* with an equally cute friends-to-lovers romance . . . Their equally filthy sense of humor makes their connection feel real, and their game of constant one-upmanship is a lot of fun. Painter's fans won't be disappointed." —*Publishers Weekly*

"A fun, flirty, and timely read from Painter . . . with likable characters to boot." —*Library Journal*

"Honestly, this book was so much fun and I can't believe it took me this long to finally pick [up] Lynn Painter. Her books are a hoot." —Culturess

"Lynn Painter . . . provides the perfect rom-com escape in *The Love Wager*, a trope-driven romance that will remind readers, as they laugh themselves to tears, why they love the genre." —*Shelf Awareness*

MAID FOR EACH OTHER

Lynn Painter

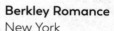

Berkley Romance
New York

BERKLEY ROMANCE
Published by Berkley
An imprint of Penguin Random House LLC
1745 Broadway, New York, NY 10019
penguinrandomhouse.com

Book design by Ashley Tucker
Title page art by Suziie/Shutterstock

Library of Congress Cataloging-in-Publication Data

Names: Painter, Lynn, author.
Title: Maid for each other / Lynn Painter.
Description: First edition. | New York: Berkley Romance, 2025.
Identifiers: LCCN 2024046841 (print) | LCCN 2024046842 (ebook) |
ISBN 9780593638033 (trade paperback) | ISBN 9780593638040 (ebook)
Subjects: LCGFT: Romance fiction. | Humorous fiction. | Novels.
Classification: LCC PS3616.A337846 M35 2025 (print) |
LCC PS3616.A337846 (ebook) | DDC 813/.6—dc23/eng/20241021
LC record available at https://lccn.loc.gov/2024046841
LC ebook record available at https://lccn.loc.gov/2024046842

First Edition: July 2025

Printed in the United States of America
1st Printing

The authorized representative in the EU for product safety and compliance is
Penguin Random House Ireland, Morrison Chambers, 32 Nassau Street,
Dublin D02 YH68, Ireland, https://eu-contact.penguin.ie.

For Kevin:
I love you more than Saturday
night spaghetti with Pappy.
I love every single thing about
you and our life together
and shall now write a haiku*
that perfectly captures my
adoration.

I love your cute face
Cute cute cute cute cute cute cute
You are the most cute

*I am not a poet.

MAID
FOR
EACH
OTHER

1

WAKING UP IN THE BED
OF A MILLIONAIRE

Abi

Is it wrong that a tiny part of me is happy to have an infestation at my apartment?

Of course it is, I thought as I sat up and stretched in the decadently soft king-size bed. But who could blame me? The luxuriousness of the million-thread-count sheets alone made it way less of a hardship, not to mention the frothy memory foam pillows. Honestly, I wasn't sure how the wealthy ever dragged themselves out of bed in the morning when it felt so good to just lie there, cocooned in expensive linens.

But I didn't have time to languish in the opulence. I needed to get the hell out of there and get to work before Benny fired me.

I carefully made the bed, ensuring it was impossible to tell I'd ever been there. I was going to wash the sheets after I came back later because I wasn't some kind of psychotic Goldilocks-coded monster who'd secretly sleep in someone else's bed without laundering away my DNA, but just in case someone happened to show up in the meantime, I wanted to remove all traces of the uninvited Abi Mariano.

I'd showered last night, just to ensure I had time to clean every square inch of the bathroom (a lot of square inches, for the record), so I quickly changed and pulled my hair into a ponytail. Five minutes later, everything I brought with me was jammed and zipped into my backpack as I reached for the doorknob and opened the bedroom door.

"Well, good morning!"

I gasped and my hands flew to my heart as I looked to my right.

Oh, God, oh, God, oh, God.

Standing there, in the enormous kitchen of the fancy penthouse, was a silver-haired man and a woman with a sleek black bob. They were smiling, but that didn't make me feel any better.

I was completely, totally, absolutely screwed.

The guy was wearing a flawless navy suit that was definitely not off-the-rack (hello, rich dude with the pocket square), and the woman was in one of those it's-just-an-oxford-and-white-jeans-but-they-cost-a-thousand-bucks ensembles. They looked like beautiful royals on retirement, perfectly put together, and they looked like they belonged in the upscale residence where I'd been squatting.

But they didn't look surprised to see me.

"Sorry, didn't mean to startle you," the man said, stepping forward to extend his hand while he smiled warmly. "I'm Charles, and this is Elaine."

"Abi," I mumbled in shock as King Charles wrapped his big hand around mine and shook it confidently, as if this was okay and I was supposed to be there.

Way to give them your real name, dipshit!

"Abi!" The woman—Elaine, apparently—beamed at me like she'd been breathlessly anticipating my arrival. "It's so nice to finally meet you."

"Yeah, um, same," I said, unsure of what she could possibly mean by *finally*.

Am I in an episode of some pranking show?

Are the cops on their way and the Chuck/Lainey duo before me is simply a distraction to keep me from getting away?

"I, um—"

"We helped ourselves to your muffins, by the way." Charles pointed toward the cooling rack on the center island, where the six face-size blueberry muffins I'd painstakingly made from scratch in that glorious gourmet kitchen the night before had now been reduced by two.

THEY. ATE. MY. MUFFINS.

I had bigger problems at the moment, but a tiny part of me wanted to rage because those muffins had been the most delicious things I'd ever tasted. They were supposed to be my amazing breakfast for the next week. I'd planned to devour one perfect little pastry every morning before embarking upon my far-from-perfect life.

Only now, two resided in the digestive tracts of these two beaming socialites.

RIP, decadent pastries, and a plague on the house of Charles and Elaine.

"They were so delicious," Elaine gushed, then added, "Declan never told us you were a pastry chef."

"Well," I said, my heart pounding out of my chest as I tried to play along, "you know Declan."

They laughed like that made sense—*what in the ever-loving hell?*—and I needed to go. I pulled my car keys out of my backpack and pasted on a huge smile. "Listen, it was so nice to meet you and I'd love to chat more but I have to get to work."

"Typical Abi," Charles said in a she's-so-adorable tone, giving me just the nicest grin. "Will you be at the Hathaway party tonight?"

Typical Abi?

"I'm, uh, I'm not sure," I stammered, doing a sideways walk in the direction of the front door, desperate to escape. Because the quicker I got out of there, the better my odds were of not being arrested for trespassing. "Probably . . . ?"

"We won't take 'probably' for an answer, Abi," Elaine said, running a manicured hand—*holy shit that's a huge diamond*—over her perfectly coiffed hair. "No going to work until you say yes. We're dying to get to know you."

"Um, yes, then." Relief shot through me when I reached the front door and felt the cool metal knob in my palm. Almost there. "I will definitely be at the party."

I would say anything to escape at that moment.

"Oh, that's wonderful," Elaine said emphatically.

"Fantastic," Charles agreed.

"I have to go now," I managed, pulling open the door and giving them what I hoped was a charming smile. "It was lovely meeting you."

The second I was in the hall and the door clicked shut behind me, I made a beeline for the stairs, ignoring the elevator completely. I wasn't usually a fan of exercise, but I full-on sprinted down all twenty flights of stairs, wanting to put as much distance as possible between me and whatever the hell that whole scene just was.

I had no idea why those strangers thought they knew me, but I definitely wasn't going to stick around to find out.

DISCOVERING THE REAL-LIFE EXISTENCE OF AN IMAGINARY FRIEND

Declan

"Good morning, darling."

"Mom." I leaned down and kissed her cheek before taking a seat between her and my dad at the round banquet table. They'd flown in late last night, so I hadn't had a chance to talk to them before giving my little welcome presentation to the Hathaway VIPs. "How was the flight?"

"Delayed," my dad said, lifting a piece of bacon to his mouth. "But uneventful. Great speech, by the way."

"Thanks." He was right—I'd fucking nailed it—but I still had the entire shareholder weekend in front of me so I wasn't about to get cocky.

The Hathaway Annual Shareholder Meeting, for which thousands of investors trekked to Omaha for a week of feeling like stock-owning rock stars, always kicked off with a Friday-morning breakfast meeting that was just for the VIPs; there was another one tomorrow morning for everyone else.

This year I'd been tapped to do the welcome address at both.

"He didn't even bore me while I ate my eggs," Warren said from the other side of the table, picking up his coffee cup. "The kid's okay."

The kid's okay.

Warren Hathaway, the richest man in America and long-term CEO of Hathaway Holdings, had just spoken those words about me. The guy had a genius brain for business and had been my hero for as long as I could remember, so I'd be lying if I said his praise didn't mean a lot.

Right after I graduated from college, Hathaway offered my family (who'd taken my great-grandmother's tiny sofa business and turned it into CrashPad, the nation's largest furniture store) a multimillion-dollar buyout. It'd been a dream come true because not only could my parents retire early and travel the world, but I was absorbed into the Hathaway enterprise and given the opportunity to work my way up in a much larger corporation.

Suddenly the MBA that my uncles had called a waste (*You don't need college to work in the family business*) was guiding me toward the career I'd always wanted.

I'd been an EVP at Hathaway for two years now, but moving higher had been proving difficult. No matter how hard I worked, the guys at the top still saw me as a "young kid," even though I was thirty.

But a disagreement at the QBR last month—where I was right and CFO Marty Mueller was nearly catastrophically wrong—put me on the map with Warren, and suddenly my career was in new territory.

The old guy and his inner circle seemed to be forgetting about my age and inexperience and actually trusting my knowledge.

Fucking huge.

"We finally met his girlfriend this morning," my mom said to Warren, and it took me a minute to catch up.

What?

"You met his Abby?" Warren set down his cup and gave my mom a grin of commiseration. "I was starting to wonder if she's real, because no one's ever seen her."

"Right?" My mom laughed in agreement.

What. The. Fuck?

She *wasn't* real.

Abby was the name I'd given to my nonexistent girlfriend.

So how had my mother met her?

For what it's worth, I never meant to make up a girlfriend. I wasn't some adolescent who was too scared of women to date, for God's sake; I was actually a big fan. But I didn't have any time to commit to all the bullshit that went along with relationships. Work was my focus for now, and I'd worry about things like settling down after I turned forty.

But when everyone in leadership had a significant other, well . . . desperate times called for desperate measures. I needed the powers that be to think I was settled and grounded and ready to lead the company, so when my personal life became a topic of conversation at the quarterly retreat, I might've offhandedly mentioned my down-to-earth-and-wanting-a-family-right-away angelic girlfriend.

MAID FOR EACH OTHER 9

Abby.

I'd literally looked at the server's name tag—Abby—and named my imaginary girlfriend after her; not a lot of forethought went into it.

I hadn't intended on keeping the Abby thing going, but it was convenient. It made my parents happy, my co-workers, my nana; everyone seemed to take comfort in the fact that I had an Abby in my life.

Only I didn't.

She didn't exist.

So what was my mother talking about?

"She's coming to the party tonight," my dad said to Warren, who'd become his pal over the past few years. "So you can meet her then."

"She . . . ," I said, squeezing the bridge of my nose as my brain ran wild trying to figure out what the hell could be happening. "She, uh, told you she's coming tonight?"

"Yes," my mom said, turning in her seat to scrutinize me. "But she looked surprised to see us in the kitchen when she woke up, Dex; did you forget to tell her we'd be staying at your place?"

"Oh," I managed, trying my best to not look shocked that a stranger had actually been in my apartment. "Ah, I didn't think she'd be there last night. I thought she—"

"I'm so glad she was," she continued, as if I hadn't even spoken. "She's the most adorable little redhead and she baked a kitchen full of muffins that were to die for."

So this was real. Someone named Abby had slept in my apartment and made fucking muffins.

"Abby can cook, that's for sure," I muttered as my mind

whirled. What the hell was going on? I lived in a secured building with a doorman. I had locks on my doors and a security system.

How could this have happened?

Who the fuck was Abby?

"I haven't had a good muffin since Ethel passed," Warren murmured, setting down his coffee. "Have your little Abby bring one tonight, okay, Dex?"

"Of course," I said, hearing a roaring in my ears as I gave him what I hoped was a casual smile. "Will you excuse me for a moment? I have to step out and make a call."

"Calling Abby?" my mother asked in a singsong voice.

"I'm definitely going to try and track her down," I said before turning away from the table full of watchful eyes and charging for the door. "Excuse me."

3

THE MILLIONAIRE MEETS HIS MAID

Abi

"Would you like your receipt?"

"No," the woman said, grabbing her Lululemon tote bag and heading for the exit of Benny's Natural Grocers without giving me a second glance.

"Have a good day," I yelled before turning to ring up the next customer in line.

I hated this job, this perfectly easy and mind-numbing job. I'd worked at Benny's since high school, so it was comfortable, not to mention necessary because it supplied me with my health insurance, but every shift just reminded me that my life was stuck in quicksand that I might never get out of.

Hence my second go-round of college.

Hence my need for this job and my three-times-a-week overnight job.

Hence my propensity for thinking stupid words like hence.

"Hi," I said robotically to the next customer, my mouth on autopilot before I noticed the person in line didn't have anything on the belt. I raised my eyes to the customer's face but then—*wow*.

I might've actually gasped aloud.

There were a lot of attractive men out there, but this man had to be The One they were inspired by.

He was tall—like six and a half feet of tall—but no one would call him lanky. They would never. Broad shoulders filled out the impeccably tailored suit, and he reminded me of a professional football player when they did the long walk from the bus to the locker room.

Expensive.

Built.

Perfect.

And not to be messed with.

His face made that point even more than his impressive physique, actually.

He had brown eyes—no, green—that were trained on me and absolutely butterfly-inducing with their directness. It was like the man was staring into my soul, I swear to God, and his lips were turned up like he wanted to smile.

I usually didn't notice mouths on men, to be honest, but the bow on his top lip—or maybe it was the fullness of the bottom— drew my eyes downward as if it were a magnet and my irises were flecked with steel.

I could picture that mouth speaking French. Or Italian. I forced my eyes back up and offhandedly thought that this well-dressed man could actually be the cover model for any romance novel about mob bosses, racecar drivers, or grumpy billionaires.

I opened my smitten mouth to say "How can I help you?" without drooling when he said in a midnight-rich voice, "Hello, Abi with an *i*."

"Hi . . . ?" I narrowed my eyes, biting my lip so I didn't smile like a lovesick schoolgirl as his eyes dipped to my name tag.

"You don't recognize me?" he asked, tilting his head.

Did I know him? There's no way I could've forgotten that face, right? I tried not to seem too flirty, but Joey Tribbiani's *how you doin'?* was totally in my tone when I said, "Should I?"

"I would think so, since just this morning you woke up in my bed and told my parents you're my girlfriend."

"Oh. Shit." *Oh, shit, oh, shit, oh, shit.*

"Oh, shit, indeed," he repeated, his eyes judgmental under slashing dark brows as he watched me like I was a bug he was about to squash.

My heart started pounding and I was hot everywhere as this man stared me down with pure disdain.

"Benny," I yelled, not taking my eyes off the guy's face. "I need to go on break."

"You just had a break, Mariano," I heard from behind me, where Benny was ordering produce at his desk. He'd been hunched over the antiquated computer for hours, rotating between grunting, sighing, and scratching his bald spot, so I knew he wasn't in the mood for this.

"Mariano," the man in front of me quietly repeated, as if memorizing that morsel of information.

"I'm taking a break, Benny," I said through gritted teeth as I turned off my aisle's light. "Whether you okay it or not."

I pulled off my Benny's apron and gestured for the guy in the suit to follow me as my pulse skyrocketed. I'd been panic-watching the door all morning, expecting the police to show up and arrest me for breaking and entering. It wasn't until an hour ago, when I ate my lunch at the table beside the big green dumpster, that I foolishly convinced myself no one would ever know it'd been me.

I'd been stupid enough to allow myself a deep breath.

"Swear to God I'm gonna fire you one of these days, Ab," Benny yelled as I walked away from my register.

"No, you're not," I yelled back as I tried not to hyperventilate. "No one else would put up with you."

"At least hurry, will ya?"

"I'll see what I can do."

I could sense Mr. Suit following behind me as I led him through the back of the store and out the door that led to the alley. Bright sunlight, warm air, and the faint smell of garbage flooded my senses as the door slammed behind us and I turned to face the guy.

Declan was what the royal couple had called him, right?

"Please let me explain. Declan."

That made his eyes narrow—oops, should not have used his name—but he didn't say anything.

"I'm not some sort of criminal, I promise. I work a few over-nights for Masterkleen as a maid—I'm actually the maid who cleans your apartment on the nights when you aren't in town. So even though I was there, I didn't break and enter or anything like that."

Good point, Abi.

I gave him what I hoped was a sweet smile, an expression that would confirm my innocence.

He frowned.

"I had a key," I said, "so it wasn't like—"

"You moved into my *bed*room." His voice was calm, but he definitely wasn't interested in understanding. His scowl made that abundantly clear as he said, "You baked muffins in my kitchen. I don't believe that's part of your job description. I believe that's called trespassing. *Abi.*"

Okay, the mocking way he said my name was straight up insulting and made my teeth hurt.

But I needed to keep my cool.

I tried again. "I know, but it was only because my apartment building has an infestation—I promise I didn't bring any critters to your place. See, the property management company—who are total slumlord jackasses, by the way—said I had to find somewhere else to stay for a few days so they can take care of it, but I don't *have* anywhere else."

My cheeks got hot as soon as I said it because it was so pathetic.

He stared at me like I was picking food out of my teeth, and any hope of him somehow showing a little empathy for my situation completely dissipated when he said, "Hotels are a thing, you know."

"I can't *afford* a hotel," I snapped, mortified. I wanted to disappear, but I forged on out of desperation. "But when I was cleaning your place last night, I thought, who would it hurt? I knew that you were in London for the week—I mean, apparently you came back early but I guess you forgot to tell Masterkleen—so I just thought I could crash for a few hours and no one would be the wiser."

His jaw flexed, but he remained quiet. I really wanted to believe he was considering my defense, but he looked like one of those über-controlled types who enjoyed keeping his mouth shut so his adversaries could bury themselves with their own words.

Which meant RIP me, because I was the world's worst rambler.

"And I'm sure you don't care," I continued, "but I'm really good at my job. I'm great at cleaning your apartment—you could eat off the bathroom floor. I mean, not that you would because that's disgusting, but you genuinely could because I'm just that thorough."

He cleared his throat and looked down at his expensive watch, the asshole, and I realized that no matter what I said, I was going to lose my job.

Oh, God.

This man was definitely going to fire me.

And I needed that job so badly.

There were a lot of jobs out there, but not many as flexible as the one I had with Masterkleen.

I inhaled through my nose, gritted my teeth, and swallowed my pride, because what other choice did I have? "I know I have no right to ask this, but please don't tell Masterkleen. I'm begging. I really need this job and literally can't afford to get fired. Please don't tell my boss."

His dark eyebrows knitted together, and he looked insulted by my request.

"Oh, I will definitely be telling your boss," he said without even blinking. "Because you trespassed in my home."

"Or," I countered, grabbing his right arm as I desperately tried to get him to understand, "I fell asleep at my job. That's not a crime, right?"

"I'm not interested in your justifications," he said, looking down at my hand so aggressively that I dropped it. "I just came here to see who the hell had broken into my place and had breakfast with my parents. Now I know."

"Please." My voice cracked and I hated it. "Can't you just forget it ever happened? Like, just pretend I never stayed there."

"I wish I could," he said, shaking his head. "But you have no idea what you've done."

"Come on." God, why was he such a hard-ass? "Who did it really hurt, though?"

"Me!" He barked out a mirthless laugh and said, "Now my parents and my colleagues all think *Abby* is coming to the most important event of my life tonight because *Abi* told them she was."

"Why can't you just tell them Abi's not going?" I paused, frowning. "And why did they act like they knew me in the first place?"

"Because they think I have a girlfriend named Abby, for Christ's sake," he snapped, his voice full of frustration. "What are the odds my maid would have the same damn name?"

"So . . ." I was missing something, something that had nothing to do with my sleepover at his penthouse. "You don't actually have a girlfriend named Abby?"

"I do not," he said through gritted teeth, his eyes on the alley just beyond my shoulder, his thoughts no longer on me but on his apparently stressful situation.

"What did you do," I said, watching him attempt to mentally formulate a plan, "make her up or something?"

His intense gaze snapped back to me and I regretted the question immediately. His voice was dangerously quiet when he asked, "Have you ever been arrested, Abi Mariano?"

"Of course not!" My cheeks were hot even though I deserved the inquiry.

"So if I ran a background check, you would—"

"Call the authorities on you for stalking? Yes," I said in a near yell, frustrated he was treating me like a criminal after I'd explained the situation. Not everyone had piles of money for hotel stays or multiple residences, damn it, and it stung that my tiny questionable decision made him behave as if I'd stolen the family jewels.

But then he smiled at me.

He smiled, and *whoa*—it was something.

That grin packed a punch, sexy and dirty from the slide of his lips to the squint of his very green eyes. Declan's voice was silky smooth when he stepped closer, so he was towering over me. "But you can't do that because you've been trespassing, remember?"

"Stop playing with me." I swallowed hard and crossed my arms. "What are you going to do?"

"I'm still working it out," he replied as his eyes went down to my chest. "What does that mean?"

"What?"

His eyebrows went down and he gestured to my shirt with his chin. "Your shirt. I don't get it."

Of course you don't. The custom T-shirt shop behind my

apartment had a clearance rack where all their mistakes were 80 percent off, so my wardrobe was full of tops that were off-center, riddled with misspellings, or downright stupid.

I didn't care when I could get a shirt for two bucks, but I'm sure that wouldn't make sense to someone like him. I raised my chin and said, "What exactly don't you get?"

The shirt—my favorite shirt, actually—had a picture of a squirrel wearing underpants. The letters above it read *Hamilton Won Chip*, and the letters below it read *Working for Underwear*. I couldn't even fathom what the attempt had been, but it made me smile every time I pulled it out of the dryer.

"Does it mean something?" he asked, seeming irritated that he didn't understand.

I made a face like he was an idiot for being confused and said, "Obviously."

"I don't have time for this today." Those green eyes moved all over my face before he said, "I'll be in touch. Answer my call."

And then he just turned and started walking away from me like a freaking king who had no more time for peasant interaction. I wanted to throw a rock at his perfect suit as he strode toward the parking lot in gorgeous leather shoes that surely cost more than my car.

"What are you going to do? What does 'I'll be in touch' mean?" I yelled, wanting to chase after him and force him to put me out of my misery. "You don't even have my number."

"I'll get it from Carl," he yelled, not even looking back at me.

"Who the hell is Carl?" I said to myself, frustration filling every molecule in my body. I didn't need this; I had enough problems, for the love of God.

"My doorman," he replied, apparently in possession of both supersonic hearing *and* privileged arrogance. "According to him, you two are thick as thieves."

Damn it, Carl.

I sighed and watched him disappear, my stomach sinking with dread as I wondered how long I had before the millionaire jerk destroyed my life.

4

WHEREIN A DEAL IS ARRANGED

Declan

I cannot believe I'm doing this.

I sat in my car—my parents were clearing their stuff out of my place so I'd been relegated to my vehicle for privacy—and pulled her up in my contact list.

Abi Mariano.

After utilizing Google to (a) make sure she wasn't an actual criminal (I believed her about the infestation), (b) ascertain whether or not she was a functioning member of society (she'd graduated with honors from UNO and had a LinkedIn profile), and (c) determine her sketchiness factor, I consulted with my buddy Roman, who convinced me to take a huge-ass gamble.

I hit the FaceTime button and waited while it rang.

And then she answered. "Hello?"

Her face popped up, her eyebrows all scrunched together like she was confused by the call. Which, I supposed, was fair since she didn't know my number and we weren't friends.

"Mariano."

"Yes?" She sighed and gave me an impatient glare before glancing at something beyond the phone and muttering an "excuse me" to someone.

"Can I have your attention for a moment?"

Her eyes shot back to me and she looked pissed, even as she said, "It is yours."

I could tell by the narrowed brown eyes that she wasn't in the mood to be messed with, which irked me because who did she think she was, using my house as her personal Airbnb and then acting like I was an ass for being unhappy about it?

She was a five-foot-nothing bundle of red hair and attitude who'd be cute if she wasn't the cause of my current headache, but alas, Abi Mariano had seemed incapable of *not* causing me difficulty. I said, "I have a proposition for you."

"Oh, joy." She was walking beside a congested street, but I couldn't tell where she was in the city. She looked at me through the camera and said, "Listen, let me stop you right there because I'm not interested in anything sexual or illegal."

"As if I am." For someone who'd squatted in my residence last night without permission, she sure had a big chip on her shoulder. I would've called her boss immediately if I wasn't so desperate to keep my career on its current upward trajectory. "Do you want to hear my offer, or should I call Ken Adams?"

That made her mouth close. *Yes, I know your boss's name, honey.*

"Please continue," she said, and I was pretty sure she was gritting her teeth.

"If you pretend to be my girlfriend at the party tonight—and do a good job without making things worse—then we're square."

"Wait, what?" She stopped walking and looked at me like I'd lost my mind. "You want me to pretend to be your girlfriend at some cocktail party?"

This was such a bad idea. "Yes."

"But I don't even know you."

"I'll give you notes so it'll be easy to fake it."

"How do I know you're not going to get me fired after I do this?"

"I won't."

She rolled her eyes. "Yeah, I'm not going to trust you on that. See previous 'I don't even know you' comment."

"I'll put it in writing."

"That means nothing. Like I'm going to hire a lawyer to sue a billionaire for going against his word to not fire me for trespassing? Nope."

"What do you want from me here?" I snapped, irritated that she was making this absurd situation even more difficult.

"Hmm." She sat down on a bench—*is that Elmwood Park?*—and was silent for a solid five seconds before snapping her fingers and saying, "I've got it. You can email Ken and tell him that you're paying me to house-sit for a week. It's electronic evidence of permission, and also an FYI so the amazing Abi doesn't get in trouble if someone saw me slipping out in the morning."

Okay, so the girl was quick on her feet; I'd give her that. "Fine, but why would I say a week? I'll just say, FYI I paid Abi to house-sit last night."

"Because you're going to let me stay at your apartment for a week, just until my situation has resolved itself."

"That is not happening," I replied, shaking my head. "I'm not letting a stranger stay—"

"First of all, we aren't strangers—I'm your girlfriend," she interrupted in a tone that made me sound like the ridiculous one. "And you will be staying at a hotel. It wouldn't make sense for me to house-sit if you're there."

"You want me to move into a hotel and let you—a stranger—stay at my house."

This girl was clearly out of her mind.

Ironically, I was already planning on staying in a hotel for the weekend. My dad had a bad back and couldn't handle shitty beds, so since I was leaving again on Monday, it'd just made sense to let my parents stay at my place.

Until Abi showed up, that is.

"Yes," she said, nodding. "And technically you let strangers come into your house all the time when you're out of town, so it won't be my first unsupervised-in-your-place rodeo. I'm there all the time."

"Absolutely not," I said.

She shrugged. "Then I'm not doing it. Count me out."

"I might consider putting *you* up in a hotel for a week," I said, not wanting to but also ready to be finished with this bullshit.

She scrunched up her nose. "Nah."

"*Nah?*" I was going to fucking lose it. "Why *nah?* I just said I'll pay for you to stay in a hotel for a week."

"Yeah, but I really want to use your kitchen."

"This is madness." I took a deep breath and tried for calm

when I had mere hours until the party. I needed to focus on that, not this ridiculous person who'd suddenly inserted herself in my life. "It was nice meeting you. Have a wonderful life—I'll tell Ken you say hi."

"And I'll tell your parents you say hi and also that you made up a fake girlfriend."

My mouth snapped closed, and I literally had no idea what to say as she watched me with her eyebrows raised. There was nothing on her face but attitude, like she was daring me to test her, and I wanted to bang my head against a wall.

"I will not be blackmailed by a maid," I said through gritted teeth, wondering how things could've gone off the rails so quickly. "Take the original offer or I'm hanging up and calling Ken."

She bit down on her lower lip, blinking fast like she was trying hard to figure the best angle. *Do the smart thing, Abi, come on.* I kept my mouth shut, waiting for her to make the right decision.

"Why, though?" She didn't look opposed to the idea, but blinked like she was trying to figure out a puzzle. "It's only solving your problem for one night and will probably make things worse in the long run."

"Look, I just need to get through this very important evening without a million questions, okay?"

She pursed her lips. "What is the dress code at this very important evening?"

Thank God—she's going to do it. I let out a breath of relief. "Do you have a cocktail dress?"

She snorted. The girl literally snorted, so I shut that down with, "Listen, I'll send everything you need—dress, shoes, the works—to the apartment, and I'll pick you up at seven."

"Wait. Your apartment or my apartment?"

"I thought yours had an infestation."

"It does."

"So wouldn't mine obviously be better?"

"Of course it would, but you threatened to have me fired after the last time I was there."

"You weren't invited the last time."

"So I can stay there?" she said in disbelief. I didn't want to give in to this person's demands, but I was also very aware we were short on time and I needed to get things moving. "Wait— your parents aren't still there, are they?"

"They're going to a hotel as we speak."

"Why?"

"Does it matter?"

"Are you going to tell me why or not?"

"They are moving to a hotel because they are paranoid their unannounced arrival is cramping your style."

"Mine?"

"Yours."

"Interesting." She sat there for another minute, eyes narrowed but staring at something off-camera, before saying, "Well, you still haven't given me a yes on the weeklong apartment stay."

"Abi—"

"But even if it's a yes, I'm going to need some time to think about this."

"How much time?" I could feel my pulse beating in my temple as this impossible girl behaved as if she had the upper hand. I trusted Roman's advice on most things, but I realized as I looked at her stubborn chin and ridiculous shirt that he was absolutely wrong in this instance.

This was a terrible idea.

"Actually, Abi—"

"I'll do it."

Is she serious? "So when you said you 'needed some time,' you were talking about ten seconds?"

"Clearly."

I rubbed my forehead and knew I needed to bail. I needed to get as far away from Abi the Maid and the ridiculous situation my lying had somehow created before it blew up in my face.

So it didn't make a damn bit of sense when I said, "Okay— here's the plan."

5

THE DELIVERY

Abi

This is insane.

I paced through the fancy living room as I waited for my delivery, wondering if I'd completely lost my mind. I still wasn't sure how it'd all happened, other than the fact that his smug rich-guy face had pissed me off and somehow inspired me to behave as if I had a leg to stand on.

I mean, I definitely needed somewhere to stay since my place was off-limits, so making a deal wasn't the insane part. He needed a favor, I needed somewhere to sleep; that had been some solid quick thinking on my part.

But his bossiness had somehow made me forget that not only had I been in the wrong to begin with, but I had no leverage. If I actually *did* go to his parents and tell them he didn't have a girl-friend named Abi (which I would never do), he could just call me an unhinged maid who was trying to milk him for a weeklong stay in his lavish condo.

Because that's literally what I was.

Yet somehow here I was, freshly showered and wearing a lux-
uriously thick bathrobe, wandering around my favorite unit
without a duster in my hand, waiting for a dress to be dropped off.

For me.

To wear to a fancy party.

With a wealthy stranger.

It was definitely the setup to something that ended with a
body being buried. I considered myself to be an intelligent person, so my current situation made zero sense.

I nearly jumped out of my skin when I heard the knock.

Calm down, everything is going to be fine, I told myself as I
pushed my wet hair behind my ears.

I took a deep breath, cleared my throat, and walked over to
the door. Channeling my inner wealthy person, I pushed my
mouth into a smile and pulled open the door.

"Hello," I said, my hands shaking just a little as three people—
and a luggage cart heaped with boxes and bags—stood in the hallway. There was a tall blond woman, a taller blond man, and a
very petite redhead with a long beard that might've given him
leprechaun vibes if he didn't have, like, ten piercings on his face
and a strong neck that was covered in tattoos.

They were dressed in black, staring like they'd been expecting me.

They looked like a kill squad.

"Are you ready for us, Abi?" asked the blond man, his voice
soft and polite.

For what, exactly? I tightened the tie on my robe, pulled it
closed a little tighter, and said, "Yes. Of course. Thank you so
much for bringing me a dress."

"Oh, we didn't bring you a dress," the woman said, not smiling. "We brought you a look."

What do I say to that?

Thank you?

And what did that actually even mean?

"Come in." I stepped back, and they moved through the door as a single three-humans-and-a-luggage-cart unit.

The blond man looked around before pointing toward the huge dining table. "Can we set up there?"

Set up? I nodded dumbly. "Sure."

Apparently the one-syllable word was all they needed, because it was on after that. I stood, off to the side, watching in awe as they went to work "setting up." In fewer than five minutes, they had the fancy dining area looking like a dressing room.

A huge three-way mirror had been erected on top of the table, and a cartful of hair-styling implements—blow dryers, curling irons, tools I couldn't name—had been unpacked and plugged in.

There was a giant tackle box full of makeup sitting wide-open on the surface, and as I watched, the small guy unfolded a director's chair and set it in front of the mirror.

The trio looked over at me, and the woman said, "Are you ready?"

"I guess I'm, uh . . . ," I said, not wanting to sound like I didn't know what was going on when I totally had no idea what was going on. It looked like they were all loaded-out to do my hair and makeup, but who was going to be paying for it? I surely couldn't afford this kind of treatment, and to be honest, I wasn't interested even if I could.

I'd never been talented with makeup, and my hair had its own unruly curls that did whatever they wanted, so I'd decided in tenth grade that the "natural look" was my jam. A little blush and mascara, a messy bun—I pretty much called it good at that.

But this? This scared me. I tried sounding unfazed when I said, "I just realized that Declan forgot to leave me his card when he left. Let me give him a call—"

"We don't need a card," the woman said. "We'll just bill Mr. Powell."

"Who?"

"Declan . . . ?" The woman's eyebrows furrowed together just the tiniest bit.

"Oh," I nearly shouted, my cheeks getting hot as I tried recovering. I hadn't even realized that I had zero idea what my fake boyfriend's/potential murderer's last name was.

Powell. Declan Powell.

I spoke quickly when I said, "I thought you said Mr. Lowell, which is my uncle's last name, so I got super confused for a second. Don't mind me. You meant Declan. Duh."

And then I fell into some ridiculous fake giggles that made me want to punch myself.

Thankfully, the trio laughed and didn't look suspicious.

The redhead gestured to the chair with his arms in a sweeping *please sit down here* motion.

"Okay," I said, pulling the robe tighter still before walking over and taking a seat in front of the mirrors. The face that stared back at me was shiny and embarrassed, and as three strangers watched me like they were waiting for a sign, the moment felt excruciating. "I'm new to . . . whatever this is, so do I need to, like, tell you anything here, or should I shut up and let you do your thing?"

"We are more than happy to proceed however you wish," the blond guy said, leaning down to grin at me in the mirror. "But if you *do* shut up and let us do our thing, you won't be disappointed."

"Shutting up, then," I said, gesturing that I was locking my lips. "What are your names, by the way?"

"I am Johnny," the redhead said from behind me, looking very serious in the mirror as he squirted some sort of hair product into his palm. "I'll be styling your hair."

"And I'm Katarina," said the blond woman, also not smiling. "Your makeup artist."

"Nice to meet you," I said, watching Johnny as he rubbed his hands together, evenly dispensing the goop to both palms while staring at the top of my head.

"When they're finished, I will dress you," the blond guy said. "I'm Edward, a stylist."

"Nice to meet you," I repeated, wondering yet again if I was dreaming. Like, this couldn't really be happening, right?

"I would like to cut this to your shoulders," Johnny said, running both hands over my hair. "What are your thoughts?"

I looked in the mirror and wasn't sure. I'd always had long hair. Always. It felt like I should refuse, because (a) it was ridiculous to get my length taken off for one night, and (b) even though he looked cool, I didn't have a clue as to how good Johnny was with a pair of scissors.

He could be the one responsible for micro-bangs, for all I knew.

Johnny Scissorhands.

But it also occurred to me, as I sat in the luxurious makeshift dressing room, that I'd never have this chance again.

A beauty team at my beck and call?

This didn't happen in the real world.

"Okay, let's do it," I said, throwing hair-caution to the wind. "But no bangs."

"With your potato-shaped face?" Johnny said with a snort. "I would never."

Potato-shaped face? I smiled like that made sense. "Okay, good."

"Quick question while he cuts," Edward said, crossing his arms over his chest. "The dresses I've curated for tonight are all black, because when Mr. Powell said you were a redhead, I couldn't comfortably select a color without knowing your skin tone. Is that okay with you, or should I call for backup? Because now that I see you're neutral, I can absolutely get some brighter options if you prefer."

Was this man seriously telling me that if I didn't like black, he could send for more dresses?

What is this life?

"Black's my favorite, actually," I said to Edward. "So no need for backup."

"Excellent," he said, looking relieved. "And I'm assuming you're okay with classic red polish for fingers and toes?"

"You're doing my fingers and toes?"

"Well, I'm not, but Kat is."

I glanced at Katarina, who appeared to be unloading all the makeup in the world from the tackle box.

Yes, I know, Kat—I'm quite a project.

"Now, Abi. This is important." Edward stepped in front of me and rested his backside on the edge of the table, giving me (finally) a friendly smile. "While Johnny and Kat work their magic, you and I will be talking through the basics of what you'll need to know for this party. Mr. Powell prepared a dossier of information for your ingestion."

My ingestion.

I felt like laughing at the absurdity of all this, but inhaled through my nose and kept it together.

"Okay," I said, nodding, surprised that this man seemed to know what Declan and I were up to. We weren't trying to rob a bank or plot a murder, but I still would've assumed that the guy who'd showed up at Benny's earlier wanted our ruse to be top secret.

He must really trust this glam team.

Which was . . . a little weird, right?

Did Declan Powell do this often? Why did he even have a team of stylists at the ready? I'd never been wealthy so I had no frame of reference, but a makeover team didn't seem like something that would be common for wealthy single guys to have on speed dial.

"Don't overthink it," Edward said, watching me with a patient smile, almost like he could read my mind. "Just channel your inner Cinderella and have fun with this, okay? It's just one night of your life."

Just one night of my life.

He was right. It was just one evening.

"Okay," I agreed, nodding and feeling a smile settle over me.

Because why not? This was a bizarre, once-in-a-lifetime situation I could either stress myself out about, or I could lean into and have a good time that I could use in a story someday.

I almost gasped when that thought hit me, because I could use it in a story *now*.

School started a few weeks ago, and it was the final year of my MFA. I had three more "packets" of written work to create and submit this semester before the thesis manuscript became my focus, and I'd been racking my brain for solid ideas. I had a notebook full of possibilities, content that could potentially work into my short story collection, but a fish-out-of-water Cinderella tale was something uniquely different from the rest.

Holy *shit*. This entire experience—meeting Charles and Elaine, Declan's appearance at my job, the makeover, the party—could become such an interesting little piece of fiction.

Like a switch being flipped, my nervousness was replaced by excitement. I looked around the room and couldn't wait to capture every ridiculous detail of this ridiculous day.

"I'm going to scooch on over to the wine fridge and fetch a nice little something," Edward said, pointing toward the kitchen. "Because we definitely need to share a toast before officially launching this transformation, don't you think?"

"Absolutely I do," I replied, noticing in the mirror that my smile was obnoxiously huge. "There's also an unopened bag of Dove caramel squares behind the milk in the refrigerator—that would pair nicely with a Riesling, don't you think?"

6

THE PICKUP

Declan

Do I knock?

I stood in front of the door—*my* door—and wasn't sure what to do. Obviously I had a key, but was it impolite to the stranger who'd forced her way into my life to use it?

The rules of etiquette were unclear on how to arrive for a date that you'd been forced to arrange.

Screw it, I'm going in.

I unlocked the door and pushed it open. "Abi?"

I said her name, fairly loudly, as I stepped inside.

"Abi, I'm here," I said, closing the door behind me. "Are you ready to go?"

I'd been away in London for the past couple weeks, so the sight of my couch and TV made me instantly wish I could just change into shorts and play COD all night, or maybe destroy a plate of nachos in front of an old episode of *Psych*.

Either option sounded fucking amazing.

But the tuxedo on my body said otherwise.

"Abi?"

Just as I thought *where the hell is she?*, I saw that the balcony door was open. I doubted she was out there, because it was raining, but she didn't seem to be anywhere else, either, so I crossed the room, tension pounding in my temple as I wondered how the evening was going to play out. Abi seemed like she had the potential to be a real pain in the ass, although Johnny's texts throughout the afternoon had given me a tiny bit of hope.

Johnny: Abi is cool as shit

Johnny: Abi looks great

Johnny: The girl is smart and knows the material—you've got nothing to worry about

"Abi?" I stepped through the doorway, onto the balcony, and there she was.

She was sitting at the teak table in a black rain jacket with a towel wrapped around her head, writing in a notebook under the patio umbrella that I rarely opened. Her bare feet were propped up on the chair across from her, and when I said her name again, she held up a finger without looking up and said, "Hang on for a quick sec."

Oh-kay. I stood there, getting sprinkled on, unsure of what the hell I was waiting for while her hand scribbled words frantically. I'd expected her to be ready and waiting by the door, not dressed like a freshly showered flasher who was immersed in fucking gratitude journaling.

On my deck.

In the rain.

With her toes out.

Her behavior didn't bode well for a calm, uneventful evening, damn it.

"What are you doing?" I asked, lifting my wrist to check my watch. "We—"

"Shhhh," she said, her Bic flying over the paper. "I just don't want to forget. One minute."

My jaw hurt from how hard I was grinding my teeth together in an attempt not to sigh or curse as I waited.

"Okay," she said, still writing. Her face was intense as she finished and muttered, "I . . . am . . . done."

With that, she closed the notebook and looked up at me.

"Wow," she said, her mouth sliding into a grin. "You look fancy."

"Thank you . . . ?" I said, for some reason irritated by how relaxed she was. Shouldn't she be nervous about our situation, or at the very least subdued? It felt wildly overconfident for her to be shoeless and smiling at me that way. "Do you know how much time you'll need to be ready? We should probably leave as soon as possible."

"Oh. I'm ready," she said, standing. She clutched the notebook and a can of Red Bull to her chest as she stepped around me and into my apartment.

Okay, then, I thought as I followed her inside, shutting the sliding door behind me.

"Give me two minutes," she said, untying the jacket while she walked in the direction of the bedroom. "I just need to put on my shoes."

I don't know what I expected, but it wasn't for her to shed the jacket as she crossed the living room. She pulled it off without slowing her progress, exposing a black cocktail dress underneath that looked very nice from the back. It was fitted, elegant, stopping at the knee and showcasing legs that were—objectively speaking—very nice.

And as soon as she had the raincoat off and tossed onto a chair, that white towel followed suit, the flick of her wrist causing a waterfall of auburn curls to tumble down and settle just beneath her shoulders.

Honestly, I couldn't look away from her fluid, nonchalant movements. They were so efficient and effortless that I was pretty fucking impressed.

Even as it bugged me.

"Do you know if it's supposed to keep raining?" she yelled as she left my line of sight and disappeared into my bedroom.

She seems very comfortable in my place.

"I think it's finished," I replied, checking email on my phone. "Except for a few sprinkles."

"Good, because my feet will get soaked in these shoes if it doesn't," she said as she came back into the room.

I glanced up and—

Holy *shit*.

The words spilled out before I could stop them.

"You are stunning," I said, my eyes drinking in a sight I hadn't been prepared for.

I'd noticed she was a cute girl, but tonight she was a knock-out. The dress was made to show off her curves—*nicely done, Edward*—but on top of that she had long-lashed brown eyes, full red lips, and exposed shoulders that looked sinfully smooth.

"Thank you," she said, her eyes squinting as she looked at me with a shy smile.

"For a felon," I added, unable to help myself. I needed to remind both of us of the reality of our situation.

"You're a very irritating boyfriend, for the record," she said, her smile disappearing as she grabbed her clutch from the counter. "No one likes when their significant other accuses them of criminal activity. Makes them very hard to love."

"Noted," I said, gesturing with an arm toward the door.

"Although maybe you've only ever had pretend girlfriends, so you probably don't know that."

"Good one," I said, pulling open the door.

"Thank you," she said as she exited. "And thank you for all this." She gestured to herself with both hands and added, "For butterflying my caterpillar."

I gave a nod instead of responding as I turned to lock the door behind us, because the last thing I needed was to be complimenting her again. We had to make it through the evening, and then she needed to disappear from my life entirely (after milking me for a weeklong stay, of course).

Nothing else mattered.

"How did you know my size, by the way?" she asked as we walked to the elevator, but before I had a chance to respond, she added, "I mean, even the *shoes* are the right size, which is mindblowing since my feet are unusually small. Like weird little middle school feet. Is that your special skill, your circus-freak talent, that you can nail sizes at a glance?"

"I had nothing to do with it," I said as we approached the elevator bank, wishing I hadn't heard her say the words *weird little middle school feet.* "I told my team what I needed, and they took care of all the details."

"*What?*" She looked up at me through narrowed eyes. "That's not an explanation. Your *team* has never met me."

She was right, but I pressed the down button and said, "Listen, do you really want to waste time disseminating the logistical details of how you came to your current appearance, or do you want to review the details of our ruse so the evening goes off without a hitch?"

"Um, definitely dissemination," she muttered as the doors opened and we stepped into the elevator, "but I guess I'll settle for ruse details."

"Wonderful." I pressed the P button, looked down at her— she was about a foot shorter than me—and said, "So tell me about yourself."

She rolled her eyes like an irritated teenager. "Is this a quiz?"

"Abi."

"Fine," she said on a sigh. "I'm Abi Green and I work in marketing at a small company called Anderson Tech. They're based out of Denver, so I have a hybrid schedule where I work remotely from Omaha for three weeks a month and in the Denver office for one. I grew up here, am an only child, I have no social media because I do so much of it with my job that I just *cannot* after five, and I run three miles with my dog every morning."

I was torn between being glad she'd memorized the details and embarrassed that over the past few months, I'd been forced to divulge random details about my fake girlfriend. I hadn't realized

how many white lies I'd told about her until I started compiling
the list for Abi to study.

The list made me feel like an idiot.

"Where did you go to college?" I asked as the elevator bell
dinged at the underground garage.

"Okay, the assigned answer is UNO, but can we talk about
this?" She stepped out into the vestibule when the doors opened,
and I gestured in the direction of my parking spot. Her heels
clicked as she walked over the cement floor and said, "Some of
your answers are just too boring. I think there's a way to make your
girlfriend sound *way* more interesting without screwing up your
story."

"I don't care if she sounds interesting or not."

"Well, you don't want these very important people to think
she's dullsville, do you? Just hear me out."

I shot her a look that she must've read perfectly, because she
held up a hand and said, "Humor me for a sec."

I unlocked my car, making its headlights flash, and she headed
in that direction as she spoke. "What if Abi Green went to Yale
for a year before deciding to move back because her parents
missed her too much? We should brain her up a little."

"Her parents are dead," I said, heading for the passenger
door to open it for her just as she beat me to it. "Killed in an accident that she doesn't like to talk about—you should know that."

"You didn't let me finish," she said as we both climbed into
my car. "I did my homework and I know that they're dead, but
we could tweak the timeline a little. If Abi goes away to Yale, that
illuminates her intelligence. If she comes home for her parents,

we're showcasing what an angel she is. Then, when they pass, she is the most tragic and beloved of all characters."

Okay, she obviously thought this was a Lifetime movie. I turned on the car and said, "No."

"Also, why did you take out my parents? Why would you add that depressing detail to Abi's backstory?"

I sighed and buckled my seat belt, offhandedly wondering what kind of perfume she wore. It was light and fresh and reminded me of summer. "My parents asked me about Abi's parents. *What does her dad do?* My mind went blank so I . . ."

"Unalived them," she said, but there was a little smile on her red lips. "Brutal."

I gave her what I hoped was a severe look because I needed her to understand. "We aren't changing anything, and this isn't a game. Stick to the script and we'll be fine."

"But," she said, her shiny lips reflecting the dash lights. "I need to understand her motivations if I'm going to nail my character."

"You aren't a damned actress, Abi." I ground my teeth together for a second, trying to keep my cool. "Just say 'Nice to meet you' when I introduce you to someone, and that's that. Don't get cute."

She stared at me for a long second, like a lot was going on in that head of hers, and then she just said, "Fine."

7

A CAR WITH NO NAME

Abi

"What kind of car is this?" I asked.

I didn't really care, but I couldn't let the silence go on any longer. It wasn't my way.

Because if I sat there in silence, I was just going to continue to rage. His fatherly *don't get cute* really pissed me off, the way he thought he could just tell me to shut up and do what he said, but I also didn't have much of a choice if I wanted to stay in his fancy condo until I could go back to my own place.

So it was better to change the subject.

"What?" Declan glanced at me out of the corner of his eye as he navigated us in and out of traffic. His car was black and sleek on the outside, woodgrain and leather on the inside. It felt expensive and sounded fast, but I'd yet to see any identifiable logo. "It's a CX1290."

"But what *make* is it?" I prodded, because it definitely wasn't a Kia.

He gave something like a shrug and said, "Oh, it's custom."

Custom?

What could that possibly mean? He'd had it custom-made? Did a car designer build him a special vehicle? Had he customized a regular car and added the CX1290 to be cool?

And wouldn't it still be a certain *make* of a car, even if it'd been customized for Richie Rich?

It's custom.

Insert one thousand rolling-eye emojis.

I knew it was a "me" thing, but I harbored a great deal of prejudice when it came to wealth.

I mean, I was fine with people working hard and rewarding themselves for their success; living well was A-okay in my book. Nice house, nice car, no money stress; hopefully I'd know what that felt like someday. My student loans pointed toward an eternal paycheck-to-paycheck lifestyle, but a girl can dream, right?

But I couldn't wrap my head around things like twenty-room mansions and six-figure sports cars. I saw it as a massive character flaw, the ability to be fine with just *collecting* wealth while most of the world struggled.

Not that I had any sort of an altruistic plan as to what millionaires *should* be spending their money on, but I just couldn't fathom being okay with things like Birkin bags and Bugattis.

And probably CX1290s.

I didn't know Declan at all so I couldn't technically judge him, but *oh, it's custom* was setting off all the alarm bells about his character.

"What exactly does that mean?" I asked, because my curiosity needed to know more than my ego demanded I protect my ignorance. "Is it a certain brand, like Tesla, but customized for you? Is that what you mean?"

"It's custom-built by my car guy, so it's not one specific brand," he said. "But we should probably discuss the story of us instead of my vehicle, don't you think? We're going to be at the restaurant in five minutes."

I wanted so badly to open a discussion about Taylor Swift's song "The Story of Us," just to irritate him, but he was actually right.

"Okay, so we've been dating for six-ish months," I said, thinking it was very bold of him to believe he could keep the same girlfriend for six whole months since he seemed pretty impossible to be with. The dossier hadn't said anything specific about Abi and Declan as a couple, so I filled in the micro-details. "You said *I love you* first and really wanted to buy me a cat but I'm allergic so you couldn't. I make you watch rom-coms even though you hate them, though I'm starting to suspect you love them and watch them without me now. I took you to get your wisdom teeth taken out and made a hilarious video of you bawling over broken Pop-Tarts while you were under the influence. I bring you baked goods every time we're together—I'm an obscenely good baker, for the record—and you secretly wonder if they're laced with something because that's the only explanation as to how you could fall for someone like me."

I knew without a doubt that it'd take some hardcore impairment for this billionaire to appreciate my . . . *me*-ness. Not that I didn't like myself; it was more that my brand seemed a thousand miles away from his.

He seemed to be all refined elegance, where I was . . . *not*.

"First of all, I had my wisdom teeth removed when I was eighteen. Second, *that* is your story of us?" he asked, and he almost looked like he wanted to smile.

Almost.

Wow, had I even seen him smile yet? He'd grinned when he was intimidating me at Benny's, but that'd been more of a wolf-like I'm-going-to-tear-out-your-throat expression as opposed to a genuine, heartfelt smile.

"Well, I mean—"

"Hold that thought," he interrupted as his phone started ringing.

"Holding," I muttered as he answered the call with a "Hi, Warren."

I sat there in the passenger seat, questioning yet again what the hell I was doing as the man behind the wheel took a business call when we were supposed to be prepping for the cocktail party. I really wanted him to tell me what the party was going to look like, who the primary characters were that I'd be meeting, and which people mattered to him the most.

The only upside of this going terribly wrong was that I could use the material.

I let my eyes wander over every inch of the car's interior, committing to memory the huge navigational screen, shiny black-metal accents, and the way the buttery-soft leather seat felt under my legs.

When his call didn't appear to be wrapping up anytime soon, I pulled out my phone and started putting details in the Notes app, just to ensure I didn't forget.

When he finally stopped the car in front of the downtown restaurant, I was instantly nervous. Yes, this didn't really matter in the overall scheme of things, but my stomach felt queasy as I looked at the impressive building.

And it got worse when Declan stepped out of the car and handed the valet his keys with the phone still attached to his ear.

Are we seriously not going to have time to share notes before the test?

I reached for my door handle, but Declan was already on my side of the car, pulling the door open. I looked up into green eyes that were a little intimidating as they focused on me, and all I could do was take his extended hand and get out of the vehicle.

But as soon as I stepped onto the sidewalk, five warm fingers slid between mine and it did something to my stomach. I swallowed as butterflies went wild, which was ridiculous when (a) he didn't even like me, (b) the hand-holding was all part of the fake dating scheme, and (c) he was still on a damn work call.

It was just so strange to be holding his hand, though.

"Declan," I whispered as he led me into the building. Palate was dark, with a huge bar just to the right of the entrance, and it was daunting in its quiet elegance. "Don't you think we should quickly go over—"

"Abi!"

My head whipped around, and the couple from this morning—Declan's parents, apparently—were walking toward us with big smiles on their faces.

Christ, had they been sitting by the door, waiting for us? It was too soon; I wasn't ready!

His mother was wearing a burgundy dress that looked like it was created for her slim figure, and his dad was wearing a gray suit with a burgundy pocket square that matched her dress perfectly.

They were ridiculously stylish in a way that only moneyed people could pull off, and I felt like a total commoner in their wake.

"Hi," I said, glad to hear Declan say "We just got here" into his phone. Hopefully that meant he was about to hang up. "Nice to see you again."

"You, too," his mother said, grinning and pulling me in for a hug.

I was not the biggest hugger, but I did my best as I dropped Declan's hand, giving her back an awkward pat, instantly relieved when she released me.

His dad tilted his head toward Declan's phone and asked me, "Is that Warren?"

"Yes," I replied, hoping he didn't require any further intel because I didn't know what or who a "Warren" actually was.

"Well, this could be a minute, then," he said with a boyish twinkle in green eyes that matched Declan's, "so you should come with us and get a glass of wine while he finishes up."

"Well, I-I don't know if Dex wants anything," I stammered, trying to give Declan *get off the phone* eyes without his parents noticing. "So I can just wait for him."

Declan looked at me, but I could tell he was concentrating on the call and barely noticed my situation.

"No, you cannot," his mom said, linking her arm with mine. "We will take you to the bar, and Dexxie can join us when he finishes."

I wanted to scream *Amber Alert!* as his parents led me away. Not only did I *not* want to go mingle with socialite strangers, but I knew nothing about what I was supposed to do or say to *anyone*, so this wasn't going to be good.

"I'm actually glad he's tied up," his mom said with a smile, "because it gives me a chance to get to know you without him butting in. I want to hear *your* side of how you two ended up together, with all the sweet stuff that he'd never share."

And as she gave me just the *nicest* grin, I couldn't help but grin back.

Because this?

This might be fun.

His mother was giving me a golden opportunity to share some anecdotal gems about the jackass who couldn't be bothered to get off the phone and take care of his fake girlfriend.

"Okay," I said, my brain exploding with ideas. "But you have to tell *me* what *he's* shared first."

"Deal," she replied, gesturing to the bartender for two of whatever had been in her empty wineglass. "That will take all of one minute. We only know that your name is Abi, you're brilliant, and I think he might've said you went to UNO."

"And we know you make incredible muffins," his dad interjected with a smile.

"Thank you," I said, still salty about losing my muffins.

That was supposed to be my meal prep, Charles!

"I'm just glad we got to them before Declan," his mom said as she grabbed two glasses of wine from the bartender and held one out to me. "He tends to eat all the sweets before anyone else has a chance to touch them."

"Did you know," I said quietly, as if I was about to share their son's deepest, darkest secret, "that he broke up with his last girlfriend because she wouldn't let him eat chocolate?"

"What?" his mom said, looking scandalized. "Who was this?"

"I can't remember her name, it wasn't serious," I said, taking the wine. "But she was worried that his sweet tooth was going to make him squishy so she forbade him from eating chocolate. I just remember him saying he'd choose Buncha Crunches over love any day."

"Declan," she said in a funny tone, like she was both amused and disappointed.

"Typical Dex," I said, raising the glass to my mouth. "Right?"

"What's typical Dex?" I heard from behind me just before two very big hands settled on my shoulders. "The way I'm charming and thoughtful?"

I ignored the shiver of awareness that slid down my spine as foreign hands rested on my body. "The way you're able to silently creep up behind someone like a stalker."

"Oh, honey," he said, and *dear God* he lowered his head and pressed a kiss to my shoulder.

It wasn't creepy—it was a chaste peck—but I nearly jumped out of my skin.

"So I don't think Dex ever told me," his mom said. "How did you two meet?"

"Come on, Ma," Declan said, and every muscle in my body was tense, defensively expecting another surprise peck attack. "We met—"

"Not from you," his mother said, holding up a hand and silencing her son. "I want Abi's version."

I had no idea what he wanted me to say, since we hadn't gotten to the part where we worked out the details of our lie. I had no idea what his daily life looked like—where he went, what he did with his time—so I was clueless about what to even guess at.

We met at his nudist club's bowling party.

We go to the same fight club.

Our dogs are dating.

I really, *really* wanted to use one of those, but as his parents stood there, staring and waiting as if this was the most important of all information, I restrained myself.

A little.

"Well get ready—it's quite a story," I said, grinning at Declan and tilting my head as he came around to stand at my side. "I was at the gym on a treadmill, and so was Dex; I always noticed him because he runs really fast."

I looked at his parents, and they were nodding and listening like toddlers with a bedtime story so I knew I'd gotten it right, that Declan Powell was a gym guy.

"So I was jogging on the treadmill directly in front of him, really self-conscious. I was trying to be cool and look good while I ran because he's so handsome, right?"

His dad chuckled, and his mom was practically bursting with enthusiasm as I praised her son.

It was a little disgusting, how much they both obviously thought he hung the moon.

I turned my gaze back to him, and Declan did not look amused. Which made me *more* amused.

"So I'm all in the zone when I hear, like, slipping. Like the sound of someone losing their footing. I turned around—*I* was smart enough to pause my treadmill first—just in time to see Dexxie fall and then get shot right off the back of his treadmill."

"Abi—" he interrupted.

"Thankfully he was in the last row, so he hit the wall instead of another person, right? I mean, he's a big boy—he could've really taken someone out."

His parents were laughing, the loud, head-thrown-back kind of laughter that couldn't be faked.

"So I jumped off my machine and ran over, asking him if he was okay as he lay there, all sprawled out like a big, clumsy puppy. His backside actually put a hole in the drywall, which must've hurt, but he was tough about it and climbed to his feet all on his own."

"Abi." He said it as a command.

"And after he hobbled over to one of the benches and stopped whimpering, he finally confessed that he'd been too busy watching me to pay attention to his own run."

"I wasn't hobbling *or* whimpering," he said in a voice that was close to a growl.

"Oh, okay, sweetie," I said, pursing my lips and smiling. "Regardless, he was very sweet and romantic and took me out for an amazing dinner afterward."

"Which was an event in and of itself," he said, his serious face suddenly brightening. "Because my little Abi here loves steak so much that she kind of forgets to chew sometimes."

I waited for the rest as his smile climbed a little higher.

That man has bad intentions.

He said, "I had to give her the Heimlich *twice* because she couldn't stop herself from just gobbling it down like a wild animal."

"Twice?" his mom said, looking shocked.

"Twice," he repeated, nodding his head. "After the first incident, she just lowered her head and got right back to it."

"I mean, I wouldn't say——"

"Abi *really* loves food," he said, looking pleased with himself, and I couldn't help it.

I laughed.

That brought his gaze back to me, and for the first time, we shared a grin. His eyes were warm, his mouth relaxed, and that look launched a thousand butterflies.

Especially when I felt him squeeze my hand.

His mom's smile dimmed just a little, and there was a wrinkle between her eyebrows when she said to me, "You should really be careful, dear."

His dad just nodded, also with a furrowed brow and concerned smile. "Dex won't always be there to dislodge your food."

That is a sentence Charles probably never imagined he'd be saying.

"Oh, sure he will," I said, shrugging. "One of these days he'll promise to love, honor, and Heimlich me until death do us part."

Instant change.

His parents immediately beamed like they'd just heard world peace had finally been achieved.

Looks like Mommy and Daddy are anxious to marry off little Dexxie.

"Or not," he said, managing to sound teasing even though I knew the mere thought of it gave him indigestion. "Should we save the rest of the stories and head to the back?"

"Yeah, it's probably time," his dad said, turning away from us to start walking in the other direction. His wife fell into step beside him, her heels making staccatoed clicks on the wood floor of the warehouse-like space of the restaurant.

We went down a hall, and at the end of it was a doorway that appeared to lead into the cocktail party. I could hear strings, as in orchestral people were wielding their bows in that very room, and everything was all darkness, white linen, and candlelight.

His parents went in, but Declan stopped just short, taking me by the hand and pulling me over to the other side of the hallway.

"So before we go in," he said, his eyes sweeping over my face. *Damn, but the man smells good.* Woodsy. His deep voice was low and quiet, like he was sharing a secret, when he lowered his head and said just beside my ear, "No more bullshit, okay?"

I couldn't speak because his mouth was just too close to my neck.

And my ear.

"Now I know you don't know anybody here," he continued, assuming I'd agreed, "so I'll stay by your side the whole time. Just let me lead the conversations, for the love of God, and this should be pretty easy for us to pull off. Okay?"

I nodded, still unable to speak as this ridiculously attractive stranger made me . . . *unsettled.*

While still holding my hand.

"Do you have any questions?" he asked, those seemingly all-seeing eyes trying to pierce my thoughts.

"What's your middle name?" I asked.

His eyebrows screwed together. "That's your question?"

I shrugged, needing to say *something* to remind my hormones that he was six and a half feet of jerk. "I might need to know."

"You won't." He stepped back, looked at his watch, and said, "Are we ready?"

"As soon as you tell me your middle name."

His fingers tightened around mine, and as he pulled me with him into the cocktail party, he muttered, "Connor."

We entered the dark, elegant room, only it felt different now; *we* felt different. He was still holding my hand, but there was more of an intimacy to us, somehow. Maybe he was a step closer to me than before, or maybe his fingers were holding mine a little more tightly.

I wasn't sure exactly what the "thing" was, but it felt like a switch had been flipped and he was now intentionally projecting our fake relationship.

The instant we walked in the room, we were noticed by everyone. I knew from googling that he came from a rich family and had an important title at Hathaway, *Vice President of Something*, but it felt like every eye in the room was on us.

And he didn't wait or blend in like I would have, settling into the social situation before engaging. No, Declan moved like he was used to being treated this way. He immediately addressed the first person who looked like they were going to say hi, a guy in his thirties wearing a navy suit and red bow tie.

"Hey, Theo, how are they mixing the drinks tonight?" Declan asked, turning into what appeared to be a really nice guy.

"Not strong enough, if you ask me, but beggars and all that," the man said, lifting his glass and not even hiding his curiosity as he glanced at me.

"This is Abi," Declan said, his hand settling on my lower back. "I can't remember—have you two met before?"

Nicely played, I thought, smiling at the man.

"No, I haven't had the pleasure," Theo replied, holding out his hand. "It's nice to finally meet you."

"You, too," I replied, taking his hand and gripping it as hard as I could. I wasn't going to do anything to ruin the evening for Declan, but since I didn't know any of these people and wouldn't be seeing them again, I was going to make sure everyone I met remembered just how firm my grip was.

Gotta find a way to make this fun.

"I've heard a lot about you, Theo," I said, immediately regretting it because what if it was absolutely implausible that Declan would've mentioned this man to his girlfriend?

But he said, "Rightfully so. If he didn't mention me after I've kicked his ass so many times on the golf course, I'd be wounded."

"From what I hear, you wound *him* fairly often," I said, and then I felt like a wild success when he threw his head back and laughed. I quickly glanced at Declan, and he was watching me like a proud father.

Like he was pleasantly surprised I wasn't burning the party to the ground.

And as ridiculous as it was, it felt a little . . . *good* to have him look at me like that. I felt a bit like a kid who was amped to have made their parent proud. I didn't know Declan Powell, and I was pretty sure I wouldn't like him if I did, but in this moment, it felt good to please the big guy in the suit.

"I'm going to go find the bartender," Declan said to Theo, "because Abi here got herself some wine but completely left me empty-handed."

"I assumed, Declan Connor Powell, that you were capable of getting your own drink," I said, teasing like I would if he were actually my boyfriend.

It felt like an actor breaking the third wall when he gave me a playful grin and said, "You actually used my middle name."

"Of course I did," I replied, grinning back.

His eyes moved over my face for an extended moment, like he was considering something about me, and then it was like he decided. I'm not sure if I earned his trust for the evening or if he was testing me, but he led me farther into the room and we proceeded to become Team Social Butterfly.

My fake boyfriend owned the room.

He helloed everyone and their brothers, smiling and back-slapping as the string quartet played Ariana Grande and I pretended to belong. He led every conversation, introducing me as if I was the love of his life before quickly guiding the attention away from me so I didn't have to answer any questions.

Every time we finished one conversation, someone else was ready and waiting to engage with Declan. It was a little nauseating, to be honest, the way everyone jostled to kiss his feet, but he had an air about him, like he was next in line for the throne or something.

"Abi!" Declan's mom appeared in front of us, grinning like she was having the very best time. I'd noticed that even though Declan's parents were retired, they appeared to still be very involved in the company. "I wasn't finished with you."

"You mean you didn't get to ask her twenty questions while my back was turned?" Declan asked.

"Exactly," she said, laughing. "I was going to hit Abi up for the details of who you really are as a boyfriend. When no one else is around."

"Gross," Declan said, and I laughed out loud at his tone.

He was kind of funny when he wasn't exuding untouchable, rich, and powerful.

"So are you looking for a cute anecdote that shows how romantic your son is?" I asked, doing my best not to grin like the cat who ate the canary as I looked at Declan.

His face gave away nothing, but I knew he wasn't amused. It was one thing for us to share a quick moment of collusion while in our act, but it was another thing entirely for me to tell lies to his parents.

I knew I should probably care, but I was so powerless in our situation that I felt the need to grasp this tiny little morsel of power.

The only power I had.

The power to *mess* with him.

"Yes, please," she replied, smiling. Then she turned to a lady in a long silver dress and said, "Come over here, Barb, you need to hear this."

The woman came over and Declan's mom said, "This is Dex's girlfriend, Abi, and she was just about to give us an example of Declan being romantic."

I refused to look at Declan. I said, "There are so many great stories, it's hard to think of just one."

And I smiled like a lovesick idiot.

"Maybe don't, then," Declan muttered.

"I'll start with my favorite," I said, lifting a hand to brush fake lint from his jacket sleeve. "One day, he wanted to buy me a kitten because I said it was cute, right? It was so thoughtful of him, but I had to be honest because I'm deathly allergic to cats. I was all *thank you, babe, but I like breathing*."

I beamed up at him, and he kind of looked like he wanted to murder me.

So I kept going.

"But instead of letting it go at that, he did all this research to find a hypoallergenic cat and surprised me with it—Little Dexxie—along with a bouquet of albuterol inhalers and EpiPens."

"You're kidding!" Barb cackled.

"She *is* kidding," Declan said with a straight face. "That is *not* its name."

"And the kitten was nice, Barb," I said, feeling like a legend as the power went straight to my head, "but the bouquet is what really swept me off my feet. I mean, asthma medicine is *not* cheap."

That made them laugh like he was the most romantic man in the world, so I gave him an eyebrow raise that said *See? I know what I'm doing.*

"And the things Dexxie says," I said, unable to stop the chuckle that wrapped around my words when I saw him literally flinch at the nickname. "Whenever I'm working in Denver, he has flowers waiting for me at my hotel with love poems *he wrote* attached."

"Poems?" his mom asked, looking surprised.

"The most amazing spicy poems you've ever heard," I said, setting my hand over my heart. "He's a legend with the desk clerks at the Denver Hilton, like a naughty Shakespeare. And sometimes when I get off the plane in Omaha, he's just there at the airport, waiting for me, because he says he 'missed me too much to wait another second.'"

"What can I say? She's easy to miss," he said with a grin, wrapping his arm around my shoulders and pulling me closer.

I looked up at him like this was normal, even though I was a little shaken by the unexpected physical contact. I said, "You really *are* a lucky guy."

His lips were still in a smile, but I just knew he wouldn't agree. I'd seen in his eyes that the naughty poetry was too far. I was pushing too much and knew without a doubt that King Declan would never bow to me.

Instead, he used his elbow to pull me even closer, nearly putting me in a headlock as he moved his mouth to my ear. To anyone watching, it looked like he was telling me the dirtiest of secrets.

But he said in that deep, deep voice, "You really *are* a little shit, you know that?"

When he pulled back, I met his gaze and grinned. "I do."

"They are so cute," his mom said to her friend, and I realized that the two ladies were beaming as they watched us, like we were two adorable baby giraffes at the zoo, on display for their entertainment.

"Come on," Declan said to me, grabbing my hand and leading me away from them and toward yet another curious onlooker.

"You think you're pretty funny, don't you?" he said as soon as we were out of their earshot, pinning a fake smile onto his face that would fool anyone.

Anyone but me.

I could see the tension in his face, and I could see the distrust that was still in his eyes when he looked at me.

"I'm just being the very best girlfriend I can be," I said with a shrug. "That's all."

The rest of the cocktail party was smooth sailing. He introduced me to person after person, and I didn't have to do anything other than look like I was enamored of him. I tried adding a few anecdotes, but he was onto me and shut it down really quick.

It was an exhausting couple of hours, but also a tiny bit fun.

I mean, how often did you get to pretend you were someone else? This was Cinderella territory, with Abi Green living the romantic life that was a world away from my *actual life*.

That being said, relief settled into every one of my bones when Declan leaned down and said, "Let's go say goodbye to my parents and then we'll take off."

"Dex," I heard from behind us as we reached them, and I turned to see an older gentleman walking in our direction. He had silver hair and glasses, and he was smiling like he was genuinely happy to see Declan. He looked sweet, so my smile came easily when he reached us.

"Warren," Declan said, reaching out a hand to shake Warren's, which made me snap to attention. So this was the Warren who seemed to require so much of Declan's attention. "I'd like you to meet Abi. Abi, this is Warren Hathaway."

"So nice to meet you," I managed, holding out my hand in spite of the shock zipping through me as it all made sense.

Declan's Warren was Warren Hathaway.

The *billionaire*.

The man was literally the richest person in the country.

Maybe the world.

"I can't believe you're real," he said, giving me a warm smile that made his eyes squint at the corners. "Dex took so long bringing you around that I was starting to think you were a Niagara Falls girlfriend that he made up."

I wanted to snort at that, but I just grinned and said, "You know Dex; he does things on his own timeline."

"Did you bring me a muffin?" he asked.

"Was I supposed to?"

Was I supposed to bring a muffin for Warren Freaking Hathaway?

"I got so busy today that I didn't get a chance to ask her," Declan said, setting a hand on my back. He looked down at me and said, "Warren heard about your amazing baking from my parents, so he kind of wanted a muffin tonight."

"Well, if your dad hadn't eaten so many, maybe Warren could've had one," I said, loving it when his father started laughing. These people didn't matter to me, and later they would never remember me, but I took pride in my work so it felt good, excelling at my fake girlfriending.

"Are you coming to the activities tomorrow?" Warren asked.

Declan jumped in and answered for me. "Unfortunately not."

He was probably desperate to ensure I didn't insert myself into his life after tonight, which made total sense.

"Aww," his mom said, pursing her lips into a pout.

"No Abi tomorrow?" his dad repeated, giving me almost the exact same expression as his wife.

"Everyone else's spouses and families are forced to endure the shareholder weekend," Warren said with a teasing smile, "so why does Abi get to miss it?"

"Obviously, I wear the pants in this relationship," I said, which made him laugh. "And I have some previous commitments."

Warren gave his head a shake and looked genuinely disappointed. "Well, that's too bad because Dex's face looks better when you're with him."

"Does it?" I asked, grinning at Declan, who looked like he hated hearing that.

"The kid's always too serious," he said. "It wouldn't hurt him to relax a little sometime."

"Oh, I don't think you want me to relax too much," Declan replied, "because then I might start ignoring your calls at three thirty in the morning."

Warren waved a hand. "I'm willing to risk it."

"Safe gamble," I said, knowing it was the truth even though I truly knew nothing about Declan and these round-the-clock phone calls.

"We have to get going," Declan said. "Because Abi's going to turn into a pumpkin if I don't get her home in time to feed the animals."

It was ironic, this lie about my having a hypoallergenic cat, because that was the one truth I'd uttered all night. I really *was* allergic to basically every animal with fur, and it wasn't just a sneezy kind of allergy, either.

My pet allergies were the kind that settled into my lungs and brought on severe asthma attacks and unwelcome hospital stays, hence the expensive medication and need for Benny's Natural Grocers health insurance.

"Well, I'll let you kids get out of here," Warren said. "But you should reconsider about this weekend, Abi. Surely you need to take a break from commitments to get some fresh air and socialization."

"With thousands of shareholders?" Declan commented with a smirk, and I found it interesting the way he was so comfortable teasing this world-famous billionaire.

"I'll think about it," I said, liking Warren even though his massive bank account meant he was probably a monster underneath the grandfatherly exterior.

We said goodbye to Declan's parents before leaving and exited the building without speaking. It wasn't tense, though. I didn't get any murderous vibes from him even though I probably deserved it for my little anecdotal surprises, but it just felt like there was no reason for either of us to talk when we were about to go our separate ways forever.

It wasn't until we were in the car and he was pulling away from the restaurant that he asked, "Was that absolutely necessary?"

His face was illuminated by all the lights of the fancy car's interior, and it probably spoke volumes about how attractive he was that I thought, *he looks good in dashboard lights*. His tie was loosened but everything else remained perfect, giving him the appearance of one of those hot guys in luxury cologne commercials.

"It absolutely was," I replied, reaching out to turn on his radio because I needed to drown out the awkwardness that was sure to accompany us on the ride home.

I scanned for songs, going around the horn over and over again because I couldn't find anything good, and his sigh told me he wasn't enjoying it.

Am I obnoxious? I wondered. I usually wasn't, but something about Declan brought out the inner shit in me, the snotty teen who wanted to push back on everything.

So I just kept scanning.

When we finally pulled up in front of his building, I was ready to bolt. I reached for the door handle and said, "So we're good now, right? I don't owe you anything else?"

He looked at me for a long moment, green eyes trying to figure me out, before giving a terse nod. "You're good. Just don't trash my place, and be out by next Friday, okay?"

"Okay," I said, stepping out of the car. I had no idea how to say goodbye to this man I hadn't even known yesterday at this time, so I just said, "Well, thanks for the date, then, Dexxie."

I slammed the door and headed for the entrance, forcing myself not to look over my shoulder as his shiny black car zipped away.

8

UPON FURTHER CONSIDERATION

Declan

My phone started ringing the second I pulled away from the building.

"What's up, Warren?" I answered through the Bluetooth connection, turning at the corner so I could slide into a street spot until the call ended.

"Did you see Abi home already?" he asked.

"Yeah, I just dropped her off," I said, very uncomfortable with the fact that Warren obviously found her to be delightful.

Hell, *everyone* had seemed to find her delightful. I mean, if I were being honest, I had, too. I hadn't a clue as to who she really was in her daily life, but she'd been charming as fuck at the cocktail party. And it seemed she was quite the creative.

"Bouquets of EpiPens," what the hell?

"I know you were both adamant about Abi having plans all

weekend, and I respect your free time." *Here it comes*, I thought. "But I really think it would be a great thing for everyone to get to know her better, and to see you behaving like a family man."

"Having a girlfriend makes me a family man now?" I countered, irritated that this was still a thing—it was such an antiquated ethos. I was the smartest person on the team, but the fact that I was thirty and single put some sort of asterisk beside my head.

And I wasn't cocky—it was a simple fact. I *was* the smartest. Not better, and certainly not incapable of learning a lot from my peers, but smarter than the close colleagues who happened to be settled down with houses and spouses.

"You're too smart to miss my point, Dex."

Yeah, I am.

Damn it.

"I'll check with her again," I said, "but she's a pretty committed person, so she doesn't like to cancel plans."

"Rescheduling isn't canceling," he said, and I honestly appreciated what he was trying to do. Warren was in my corner, I knew that, but I also knew he wasn't a genie who'd put himself out there to help me move up. He believed in trusting the process, and the process meant that I had to wait for my turn.

My turn that would probably come a little more quickly if I were attached, unfortunately.

My phone buzzed with a notification from the hotel, reminding me to check in.

"I'll run it by her, Warren," I said, "but I wouldn't hold my breath."

"Oh, but I will," he said. "I have a good feeling about Miss Abi."

"Is that right?" I said, cracking my neck, exhaustion settling over me.

"Definitely. She feels like a good luck charm," he said. "If she shows up with you tomorrow, Dex, I have a great feeling about the weekend."

Shit. Shit shit shit. "I'll see what I can do."

9

JUST WHEN YOU THINK YOU KNOW WHAT'S GOING ON

Abi

I nearly jumped out of my skin when I heard the knock.

After stopping at the convenience store in the lobby for a twelve-pack of Diet Pepsi, I came straight up and had barely removed my shoes when three very heavy knocks banged on the door.

I looked through the peephole and it was Declan.

"Who is it?" I said.

"I know you can see me," he said, looking calmly exasperated.

I opened the door. "Hi, there."

"Hi, there," he said, somehow managing to inject sarcasm into the two tiny words. "Can I talk to you for a second?"

"Sure. Come in." It was a ludicrous thing to say when it was *his* house, but my life had become ludicrous.

I turned and went into the living room, assuming that's where he'd want to talk, and after he closed the door, he followed me over.

I plopped down on the big white sofa, *very* tired of wearing the cocktail dress, and said, "What's up?"

He reached up and loosened his tie a little more, looking unhappy. "So, what would you say if I asked you to keep up this little charade with me for the shareholder weekend?"

I accidentally made a *you're nuts* noise in the back of my throat as I tucked my legs underneath me. "You're kidding, right?"

"No," he said, rubbing his forehead. "I'm totally serious."

"Oh." This was definitely unexpected. "Well, then, no, thank you."

"Come on," he said, narrowing his eyes.

"Absolutely not," I said, uninterested in more pretending.

"Why not?"

"Why *not*?" Had he not been there? "For starters, I have a life."

"Which *you* chose to drop into mine without permission."

I rolled my eyes. "And you don't even like me."

"That's not true," he said, but his face didn't support the argument. He looked like he was discussing getting a second root canal when he added, "I don't *not* like you."

"It's embarrassing when you gush like that, Powell." There was no way I was going to spend an entire weekend juggling lies and chitchat with wealthy strangers. I'd found a way to make it fun for a few hours, but as a rule, I avoided situations where I had no control. "And again—no, thank you."

"I'll make it worth your while." He rubbed the side of his neck.

"Nope."

"There has to be something you want. *Something* that would make this doable."

"Give me your car."

"Okay," he said with a shrug.

"*What?*"

He shrugged again, like it was literally no big deal, and said, "I have other cars. I'll give you the twelve-ninety if you give me the weekend."

"Oh, my God, I don't want your car," I said around an incredulous laugh. "I mean, of course I do but I don't; I was making a point. And I have to work all weekend."

"So call in sick."

His argument said just so much about how different our lives were. "I can't just call in sick. I need that money for rent."

Without giving it a thought, he said, "I'll pay your rent."

"And I don't have shareholder-quality clothes."

"Edward will bring some."

"*What?*" I kind of yelled it, but this conversation was reaching unbelievable proportions. "You really don't care about money at all, do you?"

He just shrugged again. "Does that mean you're in?"

"*No*," I snapped, feeling that my face was all screwed up. "I mean, let me think for a second. You're talking too fast and it's making my head spin."

"Okay." Something in his eyes, in his face, changed. He looked less tired and irritated and more awake and challenged, like he was an animal about to go in for the kill. "I'm going to go into the bedroom and get some things from the closet—if that's okay with you—while you just 'think for a second.'"

It was irritating, the way he air-quoted me. "Go."

He went into the other room and I tried getting my thoughts in order.

Two days. Saturday and Sunday. I only had to play with him for two days, and he'd cover my rent.

Or give me his car.

I wasn't greedy so I wouldn't ask, but I kind of thought I could get both if I wanted. He seemed to be desperate enough and also rich enough to not give a damn about the material things he'd be throwing away.

I didn't want to do it, but I'd be a fool not to, right? I could take his money for rent and put my money toward my student loan principal.

Or . . .

I got off the couch and wandered over to the windows, looking out at the downtown night sky while my brain kept replaying the thought, over and over again like a flashing neon sign.

Ask him to pay off student loans.

Ask him to pay off student loans.

Ask him to pay off your motherloving student loans!

I mean, technically, the balance that I owed was less than what his fancy car was worth, so as ballsy as it seemed to demand a stack of cash, it was less than he was offering.

Right?

The only thing was that I wasn't sure if it was possible for me to say those words. Could my mouth actually say the words and

demand forty *thousand* dollars? That felt like extortion or pros-
titution or . . . some other *-tion* that I was probably too overwhelmed to think of.

"So what are we thinking?" Declan said as he walked into the
room, and when I turned around, I was shocked to see him looking so . . . *regular.* He was wearing sweatpants and a Cubs T-shirt,
with a baseball hat on backward, and it kind of threw me.

I hadn't expected that he *ever* went casual.

This was a little mind-blowing.

I cleared my throat and crossed the room, needing to get
closer, because if I were going to say the words *forty thousand*, I
wouldn't be saying them loudly. At best, I'd be mouse-squeaking
them; at worst, soundlessly mouthing them before fainting dead
away from mortification.

I crossed my arms over my chest—I was freezing in the cocktail dress—and didn't stop until I was standing in front of him.

"So," I said, looking down at my red toenails. "I'll do it on
one condition."

"Name it," he said.

I kept my eyes on my feet as I blurted, "I'll need forty thousand dollars."

Silence.

I'd expected a laugh or a gasp, but not silence.

"Did you hear—"

"You better look me in the eyes when you're saying things like
'forty K,' honey."

My eyes shot to his, and he didn't look as insulted as I'd expected.

Or even shocked.

His green eyes were pinning me in place with their intensity, and he wasn't smiling, but his voice was absolutely calm when he said, "Maybe you should tell me what's included with this price tag."

10

WHAT A MOVE

Declan

What a fucking move.

Forty thousand dollars.

The girl who'd confessed to having an infestation in an apartment managed by "slumlord jackasses" was demanding forty thousand dollars to spend the weekend golfing, shopping, and eating.

"I will be the *best* girlfriend—we're talking next-level goddess—as I accompany you to all the shareholder events from now until Sunday at midnight."

"I find it hard to believe that you could *be* the best girlfriend," I said, remembering her bullshit fan fic about my ass getting stuck in a wall at the gym. "You're a sarcastic little shit who enjoys stirring the pot. That doesn't say 'forty K' to me."

"Well that's because you were forcing my hand tonight with your bossiness," she said, her fast blink the only tell that she was flustered. Well, that and the big swallow that brought my eyes down to the soft neck that I knew for a fact smelled good as hell. "As a volunteer, I will bring my very best work."

"You can't use the words *volunteer* and *forty thousand dollars* in the same sentence."

"Just hear me out."

"I'm listening."

"Okay." She cleared her throat and took a deep breath through her nose like she was doing yoga, then said, "You were going to give me your car, which *seems* like it's worth more than forty thousand, so the way I see it, you're getting a bargain. And I promise that I will wow you with just how perfect of a girlfriend I am."

"You have a point about the car."

"So you'll consider it?"

She said it like she was shocked, almost as if I was offering her this $40K deal out of the blue instead of it being something *she* had just thrown at me. No poker face at all. "I'd say we have a deal."

"Shut. *Up*," she very nearly shouted at me, her eyes huge. "Are you serious right now?"

"Please don't yell at me, but yes. I am."

"Holy *shit*," she said, shaking her head back and forth. "This cannot be real. Do you promise you're serious? Like, you're not messing with me and the cops are actually on the way here to arrest me?"

"Why would the cops—"

"This is insane!" Her grin was huge as she started pacing back and forth in the living room. "You are saying that you will give me forty *thousand* dollars to pretend to be your girlfriend this weekend. That is all. I just have to be sweet and enamored of you?"

"And keep the fictional stories about me to a minimum."

"Donezo," she said around a laugh.

"But I'm not paying until it's over."

Her smile disappeared in an instant. "Wait a second."

"I'd say that's fair."

"No, no, not that," she said. "That's totally fair. But how do I know you're going to pay? You could easily stiff me and there would be nothing I could do about it."

"I'm not going to stiff you," I said. If she wasn't such a question mark, I'd just give her the money now, but I'd yet to really figure her out.

And I'd be damned if I'd set myself up to be swindled out of that much money.

"I don't think you will, but here's the thing. You've got all the money and power here and you technically *could* do whatever you wanted in this situation." She bit down on her lower lip, like she was thinking. "Would you be willing to write me a promissory note and have it notarized?"

I was impressed. Abi Mariano was a quick thinker.

I pulled out my phone, slid into my contacts, then raised the phone to my ear while it rang.

"Is that a yes? Or are you having me thrown out?" she asked, her eyebrows furrowed. "What does this phone call mean?"

"Carl here," I heard in my ear as Abi continued to ramble while looking at me like *I* was the erratic one.

"Hey, Carl. Can you come up and notarize something for me?"

She stopped talking.

"Of course, Mr. Powell. I have to finish one other thing, and then I'll be right up. Five minutes or less."

I disconnected the call and took a minute to enjoy the expression on her face and the fact that I'd actually managed to render her speechless.

"Shall I write up the promissory note," I said, "or would you prefer to do the honors?"

"I'll do it." She jumped up from the couch and said, "I have a notebook in the other room. Give me two seconds."

"No problem," I said, watching her run into the other room.

"So, like," she yelled as it sounded like she was riffling through a bag, "what do you want everyone to think we are?"

Before I could answer she reappeared with a notebook and pen in her hands.

"Are we casually dating, or very serious?" she asked.

That was easy. "If we're doing this, let's make it count. Let's go with *very* serious."

"Ooh," she said, grinning, as she set the notebook on the table and started writing. "Well, I can totally turn it on, then, if you want. I'll bring the I'm-head-over-heels-in-love-with-this-man-and-want-to-have-his-babies attitude, if you think you can handle it."

She looked like a mischievous child, grinning while furiously writing in a notebook whose page she could barely see because her hair was in her face, and I realized that what I'd said to her earlier was the truth.

I really didn't *not* like her.

"Oh, I can handle it, Mariano," I said as I heard Carl's knock. "I can't wait to see what forty thousand dollars of love energy looks like."

"Oh, Dexxie," she said, raising her eyes to mine and using my nickname without sarcasm for the very first time. "Trust me, you won't be disappointed."

11

ROOMMATE

Abi

"You're sure he's not a serial killer?"

"I mean, who can ever be sure?" I said into the phone as I put the muffins in the fancy commercial-grade oven and closed the door. "But my gut tells me he's harmless. Rich and arrogant, but unlikely to wield a hatchet."

"Serial killers don't wield hatchets," Lauren said. "That's the old them. Serial killers are slick and contemporary now, Ab. Now they wield syringes that paralyze you so they can pull out your fingernails while you scream. They wield scalpels that skillfully carve into—"

"Stop it," I said around a laugh. "I don't want to hear this."

My best friend, Lauren, who was a kindergarten teacher, filled her spare time by reading books about murderers. She was a skinny brunette with the patience of a saint when it came to children, yet she was obsessed with true crime and psychological thrillers and had consumed every documentary about every terrible human who'd ever walked the planet.

Which was probably why she was equally obsessed with working out. She took boxing classes, martial arts, boot camps; she had something five nights a week, and all of them involved yelling and kicking.

I'd gone with her to boxing once, *once*, but I had to stop fifteen minutes in because I'd already taken my inhaler five times.

It was *that* intensive.

"Fine," she said, "but I'm putting a tracker on his car just to be safe."

"I have a feeling he's got a whole fleet of vehicles," I said, going over to the sink and turning on the water to let the mixing bowl soak. "Because he didn't think twice about giving me his custom ride when I brought it up."

"No worries," she said, and I knew by the sound of her voice that she liked the challenge in that. "I've got it."

And it was pointless to try to talk her out of it. My little friend was like a character in a spy movie, somehow able to figure out the what and where of what she considered her "assignment," and once she did, she just took care of business.

Lauren was one of those people who if I described her hobbies to a stranger, they'd assume she was a nut; I mean, she definitely sounded unhinged. But she was actually the sweetest, kindest person I'd ever met and everyone loved her.

She was just protective to the nth degree.

She had a code of conduct she lived by, like a bizarro set of Lauren rules she'd written for herself that never failed to make me laugh. For example, she would *never* use a tracker for her own personal gain; that would be inexcusable. In her opinion, someone tracking their significant other, even if that person was behaving suspiciously, was an egregious invasion of privacy.

When she knew that Ethan, her jerk of an ex-boyfriend, was cheating, she refused to use her skills to catch him in the act because "that would be wrong," but when my mom's last boyfriend always carried big wads of cash, she was on the case until she uncovered that he had a side hustle that involved stolen catalytic converters.

I adored my weirdo friend. I met her on the playground in first grade, when we both used to look for cool rocks instead of actually playing with other people, and she'd been my partner ever since.

Although since she'd met Derek (who I loved), I had a lot less time with her, so I cherished our weekly phone calls.

"So you're not wearing pants right now, are you?" she asked.

I turned off the faucet. "What?"

"Abi, you have a luxurious penthouse all to yourself, for free, so you're cheating yourself if you're not running around pants-less, jumping on all the furniture."

I looked down at the cocktail dress I was still wearing.

Damn it. The designer dress that now appeared to have a little blueberry muffin batter on its skirt.

I wiped it away with my finger and said, "I promise you that as soon as I get off the phone, I'll do the sans-pants runaround before diving into his room-size bathtub."

"Ooh, big tub, huh?"

"It's problematic big, actually, like a threat to the planet," I said, grabbing my favorite sponge from under his sink and running it under the water. It was weird, staying in this apartment, because I'd cleaned it so many times that it felt familiar.

Like I was staying at a friend's house.

"It's the size of a hotel rooftop hot tub, I swear to God," I said. "A team of Little League baseball players could fit in there."

"Why is that a measurement?"

"Because whenever you try to use the hot tub at a hotel there's always some stupid sports team in there . . . ?"

"Oh. Yeah," she said, and I knew she was nodding. "Why are they always there?"

"No idea. Hey, you can put bubbles in a whirlpool tub, right?" I asked, so excited to relax in the tub that I usually hated. His bathtub was the *worst* to clean because of its size, but this time I had Stephen King's latest in my backpack, so I was looking forward to reading with bubbles all the way up to my chin.

"Sure," she said. "Hey, before I let you go, are you *sure* he's not expecting something more than just *pretend* dating?"

"Positive."

"Because that is a *lot* of money for what boils down to a couple dates. It doesn't make sense."

"It doesn't, but the way he deals with money doesn't make sense because he's so rich it's inconceivable to us mere mortals. He said *okay, take it* when I said I wanted his car. He didn't blink when I asked him for thousands of dollars. Declan Powell, as a human, doesn't make a bit of sense."

"Hmm," she said. "Does he know it's for student loan debt? Maybe that's his thing, his cause."

"Nope."

"Does he know you're a student?"

"Nope," I said. "I figure the less he knows about my life, the better."

"*Now* you sound smart," she said. "Tell him *nothing*. If you can leave at the end of this weekend and he doesn't know enough to find you afterward, then you've done it right."

"Agreed." I ran the sponge over the fancified wood block countertops I loved and said, "Besides, if I'm going to use his cuckoo lifestyle as inspiration for a short story, I need to create a lot of space between us when the weekend ends."

"True."

After that we said our goodbyes, mostly because she had a workout class the next morning at five so she needed her sleep. Once the muffins were out of the oven and on the cooling rack, I filled that massive tub with jasmine-scented bubbles and jumped in with my book.

Only I quickly discovered that the jets wreaked havoc on the bubbles, as well as on my peace, because those jets inflated the bubbles to ridiculous proportions, pumping up the froth so high it was about to overflow all over the floor.

"*Shit!*" I turned off the jets but had to climb out of the tub and start bailing handfuls of bubbles out of the tub and into the bathroom sink because the bubbles kept forming exponentially. If I flooded that luxurious bathroom, any shot I had at this lottery weekend might be screwed, so I was in a full panic as I pulled the plug and kept scooping out bubbles.

I imagined I was quite a sight, running back and forth, naked, with handfuls of frothy clouds in my arms, and I couldn't stop cursing myself for being so flighty as I repeatedly attempted to corral airy puffs of bubbles into the marble sink.

"What did you think was going to happen?" I said to myself as I rushed back and forth, annoyed that I'd been so obsessed with the idea of reading in the tub that I'd failed to use my brain.

I was pretty sure this wasn't what Lauren meant when she suggested I run around without pants.

It took me nearly an hour to get the tub drained and under control, and I was going to have to clean the sink and vanity in the morning, after all the bubbles were finally gone. I was exhausted when I finally climbed into Declan's huge bed, so exhausted that I didn't even turn on the TV.

I flipped off the lights and burrowed my wet head into his pillow.

And then my phone buzzed.

"Come *on*," I muttered. When I picked it up off the nightstand, I recognized the number as Declan's.

ARE YOU STILL AWAKE?

I held the phone above me in the dark, too tired to lift my head as I texted: I don't know who this is.

He replied an instant later: IT'S YOUR BELOVED BOY-FRIEND

That made me smile and message: Oh, hey, boo.

Declan: PLEASE TELL ME YOU'VE NEVER ACTUALLY CALLED A BOYFRIEND BOO

I texted: Please tell me you don't always use all caps like this. Feels threatening. Stop yelling at me, boo.

I don't know what I expected, but it wasn't for him to *call* me. I lifted the phone to my ear and said, "Hey, boo."

"Are you always so ridiculous, or am I just lucky?"

"Hmm, I'd say both," I said, rolling onto my side. "What can I do for you, love of my life?"

"I have a problem," he said, and he sounded . . . *tired*.

"Oh?"

"Oh, yeah. It seems my hotel is overbooked for tonight, which means someone else is sleeping in my room. I've looked into it, and it also seems that every hotel in the *city* is full because of the shareholder weekend."

"Oh." I felt bad. I was in his comfy bed, and he was . . . well, not.

"So I'm sure it's going to cost me, but would you consider— with very strict rules, of course—allowing me to stay in my guest room, just for the weekend?"

"What?"

I was instantly wide-awake and reaching for the lamp. Was he asking to stay in his condo *with* me?

"Relax," he said calmly. "The choice is yours so no need to stress; if you say no, that seals it because we had a deal. But what I'm proposing is that you allow me to sleep in the guest room for the next two nights. I won't get in your way, and the second the sun comes up each morning, I will exit the premises and you'll have the place to yourself all day. I just need somewhere to sleep."

Declan Powell was going to ruin the joy of my little retreat, but I couldn't say no, could I? I mean, it *was* his place.

"Can't you sleep in one of your cars?" I asked. "I mean, one *must* be a glamorous RV or someth—"

"Please," he said, and the exhaustion in his voice got to me, especially when he added, "It's one o'clock and I literally have nowhere to crash for the night."

"Okay," I said with a sigh. *RIP, no-pants weekend.*

"Okay?" He sounded surprised. "You . . . are all right with this?"

"I mean, you aren't a creep or a murderer, are you?"

"I am not."

Lauren will be the judge of that.

"And you're not trying to, like . . . make a move on me, right?" I asked.

"Definitely not," he said, sounding horrified.

"Don't say it like that, like it's a disgusting idea. I just wanted to make sure we were on the same page. I think you're gross, too."

"Excellent. So then . . ."

He still sounded confused, like he was waiting for me to punk him or something. "Well I'm already comfy in your bed, so can you just use your key and let yourself in?"

"Of course," he said. "But what do you want in exchange?"

"For . . . letting you stay here?" Now *I* felt confused.

"Yes."

"Nothing. I mean, what are you offering?" God, I had no idea how to deal with someone so transactional. "It's *your* place, so why would you have to give me something to sleep here?"

"Because it's not what we originally agreed upon."

"Okay, well, I appreciate the thought," I said, knowing I should probably take advantage of his money-centric nature, but I was too exhausted to think. "But taking more than the already bonkers forty would be obscenely bonkers. Just don't get in my way or be a jerk and we're good."

"Really?" He cleared his throat and said, "Well, thank you, Abi."

"So . . . are we good? Can we hang up?" I didn't know how to deal with him being nice. "I need to get a good night's rest if I'm going to become a dreamboat girlfriend in the morning."

"Well I can't mess with that possibility, now can I?"

"No, you cannot. Good night, Powell."

"Good night, Mariano."

After I hung up, I had trouble falling asleep, which was shocking when I was so exhausted.

But Declan Powell, a stranger who was paying me thousands of dollars to pretend to be his girlfriend, was coming over to sleep under the same roof I was sleeping under.

Was this a fever dream?

Was I high?

Nothing made sense about this, and only time would tell if I'd scored the jackpot of a lifetime, or if I'd just made my biggest mistake.

12

WAKE-UP CALL

Declan

I tiptoed out of the bedroom, slowly opening the door so I didn't wake Abi. I'd set my alarm for 4 a.m., a godforsaken hour, but I wanted to make good on my promise to be out of her way when I wasn't sleeping.

I had my shoes in my hand, creeping in the dark toward the kitchen where I could quickly grab a coffee before disappearing from the premises, when she flew out of the bedroom and nearly ran me down in the hallway.

"Oh, my God!" she squeaked, putting a hand over her chest as I grabbed her upper arms and caught her before she fell. "You scared the crap out of me."

"Same," I said, my heart pounding. "What are you doing up this early?"

"I *always* get up this early," she said, still wearing the frazzled expression as she looked up at me. "What are *you* doing up this early?"

"I wanted to get out of here so I wasn't in your way," I said, letting go of her arms as I got a good look at her.

Her hair was sticking up everywhere, and she was wearing black pajamas that had pictures of her face all over them. I knew I should let it go because something told me she'd be pissed if I laughed at her, but I said, "I like your narcissistic pajamas."

She rolled her eyes. "Save it, I bought them for my ex."

That explains why they look huge on you. "He didn't like them?"

"We broke up the very day I gifted them."

"Because he hated them?"

"Yes," she said dryly. "We broke up because he hated the pajamas."

Was I being an asshole? I felt like an asshole. Something about the look on her face made me feel like I'd touched a nerve somehow, so I said, "It's a better story for you to wear your own face, anyway."

"I agree." She tucked her hair behind her ears and said, "And you don't have to leave this early; it's *your* house."

"I usually go to the gym around now, so it's fine," I lied, still shocked she'd been so understanding about my situation.

Although to be honest, I was pretty sure it was only a matter of time before she came up with a price for my stay. I suspected it was the surprise of my request that was responsible for her generosity, not a kind heart, because if she'd felt comfortable asking for forty thousand dollars to spend a weekend playing house, she was definitely going to come up with a fee for this request.

"Okay," she said. "Well, be careful on the treadmill."

She turned and walked toward the kitchen, her smart-ass face grinning at me from all over those ridiculous pajamas. I was tempted to follow her, just so I could deliver a verbal strike-back, but something told me that wasn't a good idea.

I'd get coffee later.

I put on my shoes, grabbed my bag, and I was out of there.

Only I'd barely finished stretching when I got a text from her.

Abi: Thank you for the clothes.

Edward must've dropped them off already. I'd told him "first thing," but I definitely hadn't meant five thirty in the morning. I sent: WILL THEY WORK?

I never texted with all caps; I'd only done it last night because I was walking while texting and accidentally clicked all caps. But after her comment, I couldn't stop myself.

She responded: Shhhhh not so loud. And yes—they're perfect.

I texted: BTW I'LL BE THERE AT 8 TO PICK YOU UP FOR THE BREAKFAST AND Q&A

Warren and his business partner, Harry, had an all-day Q&A at the convention center that was always sold out and livestreamed by millions worldwide. I was bringing Abi for the breakfast, and then she was going to "have plans" until dinner later that night.

Her response was immediate. I'll meet you in the convention center lobby at 8 instead. And FFS stop yelling.

I put my phone away and hopped on a treadmill, unable to look at the machine without thinking of Abi's ridiculous story. She was a handful, which made me a little nervous about the weekend, but she'd seemed genuine when promising to keep it together.

And even though I didn't know her, or trust her, I believed her about that.

Warren had already texted (he got up at three thirty every

morning), asking if she'd changed her mind, but I hadn't responded. It seemed like the better move to just show up with Abi, nail the speech, then make him see the entire thing as a package of the leader I could be.

Or something like that.

I showered and changed when I was done, then drove through Scooters for a couple coffees. While I was waiting, Roman called.

"Hello?"

"I'm dying to know, Dexxie boy—tell me everything."

I reached out and turned down the stereo. "God help me, but you were right. It worked."

"No shit, Abi the Maid nailed Abi the Girlfriend? That sounds like a movie I'd like to watch, by the way."

"You're a pig, and yes," I said, shaking my head because I knew he thought he was hilarious.

"Oh, come on, I'm funny. But she really killed it, eh?"

"She did," I said, *still* in disbelief that it'd gone so well. "And you're not going to believe this, but she's playing the part for the entire weekend."

"Wait." Roman was hilariously dramatic, so he was definitely losing his shit over this ridiculous situation. "Are you telling me that Abi the Maid is going to be playing the part of Abi the Girlfriend at the shareholder weekend?"

"She is."

"I was already looking forward to it," he said. "But now I am fucking losing-my-shit excited."

Roman wasn't a shareholder, but I always got him passes to the weekend events because he was a damn social butterfly who loved all of it. "Well, be cool, okay?"

"Of *course* I'll be cool," he said. "I mean, obviously since we're best friends I already know your girlfriend, so this'll add legitimacy."

"As long as you're cool."

"I'm always cool," he said, then asked, "So how did you convince her? Or did sparks fly and this fake relationship is morphing into something real?"

"Hell, no," I said, picturing her face when she told the story of how we met. *Smug little shit.* "I paid her."

"You *paid* her? Like, with money? You gave her *money* to be your girlfriend?"

"Roman—"

"I'm pretty sure that means she's—"

"A nice girl who is doing me a favor," I interrupted, not sure why I felt the need to defend her. But I did. "And being compensated for her time."

"Whatever you say," he said, his tone conveying everything I hadn't let him say. "Well, I for one think this is great. It sounds like fun and I can't wait to meet her. You said she's cute, right?"

For some reason, her messy hair and stupid pajamas popped into my head. "Very. A very cute pain in the ass."

"She sounds perfect," he said.

"Far from it, but we're moving forward anyway. Listen, I have to run because I'm in a drive-through and it's moving."

"Okay. Later."

"Later." I disconnected the call, got our coffees, and headed for the convention center.

But when I got there, Abi wasn't in the lobby.

No, she was standing outside on the sidewalk, in the morning sun, waiting for me.

And she was gorgeous.

Her hair was pulled back in a ponytail, with a few stray strands curled around her pink cheeks, and her lips were shiny. Sunglasses covered her eyes, big round movie star frames that belonged in a bubblegum commercial, and I knew without a doubt that Edward had handpicked them.

She was wearing a bright yellow sundress that hit just below the knee, showing off calves that definitely *did* visit the treadmill on a regular basis—*damn, but I am a leg man*—and she was holding a white box with a ribbon tied around it.

I saw the minute she noticed me, because her lips turned up in a grin. Without hesitation, she walked over and grabbed one of the coffee cups from my hands.

"Hey, you," she said, going up on her tiptoes to kiss my cheek. "How was your workout?"

I knew we were pretending to be in a relationship, but the move managed to shock the shit out of me. I guess I hadn't been ready for it. Her soft perfume swirled around me as she pulled back and smiled like she actually cared about my workout.

"My ass stayed out of the wall, so I'd say I killed it."

"Well, then, congratulations on the massive success," she said with a smart-ass giggle in her voice. "Ready to go in?"

"Let's do it," I replied, my fingers finding hers before I turned to head for the door.

I felt her hand squeeze mine as we started walking, and when I gave her a glance, there was a shy smile on her mouth as she reminded me, "I'm the best girlfriend ever, remember?"

"Oh, that's right," I said, very aware of the attention we were getting from the attendees we passed on the way to the ballroom.

I was used to people in my industry recognizing me, but there was definitely something extra that morning as Abi held my hand. "You're going to *wow* me this morning, if I recall."

"I am," she said. "We are mere moments from my debut, and I don't think you're ready."

"Oh, I'm ready."

But I wasn't.

I wasn't *at all* ready for the upcoming performance.

13

BEST GIRLFRIEND EVER

Abi

"So please help me welcome Mr. Warren Hathaway," Declan said through the microphone.

Holy shit, he is ridiculously gorgeous, I thought as I took a sip of my mimosa and watched as the entire ballroom started clapping. He'd just delivered a little intro speech that was intelligent and funny and definitely made him seem like a power player in this world.

I still assumed he was kind of a dick, that hadn't changed, but his look that morning was one that I personally appreciated. He was wearing really nice dark-wash jeans and a tan quarter-zip pullover, which sounded boring but looked amazing on him. The color made his eyes appear ridiculously green, and the fit suggested a very hard, very wide chest underneath that shirt.

I watched him walk back to the table, moving like a man capable of anything, and I thought, *showtime*, as I swallowed my

nerves and stood. When he reached the chair beside me, I chan-
neled my inner girlfriend and threw my arms around him.

"Nicely done, babe," I said, pulling him into an I'm-so-proud-
of-you hug. I couldn't help but notice how broad he was as I had
to go all the way up on my tiptoes and really *reach* to wrap my
arms around those wide shoulders.

"Thanks," he said, and even though I'd started it, a jolt of
shock zipped through my body when I felt his hands wrap around
my waist.

My stomach was a little jumpy when we pulled apart because
he was looking at me with intensity in his eyes.

Was he pissed about the PDA? Had I gone too far?

Let's go with very serious. He said he wanted people to think
we were "very serious," and if Declan was very seriously my boyfriend, I *would* have hugged him after he delivered such a fabulous welcome speech.

I cleared my throat and forced the nerves away, because I was
committed to being the $40K version of his perfect woman. I
brushed at an invisible something on his shoulder and asked,
"Are you hungry?"

His Adam's apple moved as he swallowed, his gaze still
packed with thoughts, but he gave a casual shake of his head and
said, "I'm good. Did you get enough to eat?"

"Well," I said quietly as we took our seats and Warren started
speaking. "I just ate my body weight in pastries, so I think it's
safe to say I won't need food again for weeks."

"The lunch is always to die for," the guy to my left whispered,
"so you need to pace yourself."

Stan Carter, fifty-two years old. Married with two sons, founder of Flye Aviation, Hathaway board member, and multi-millionaire. I gave him a teasing smile and whispered, "Why didn't you remind me of that *before* I consumed half the buffet, Stan?"

"I assumed you knew," he said with a big smile. "And who am I to get in the way of someone enjoying their breakfast?"

Declan had quickly introduced me to everyone at the table before giving his welcome speech, but it hadn't been necessary. I'd already studied the bios of everyone on the Hathaway board and performed my own extensive Google and social media searches, just to ensure I'd have my shit together.

I whispered back, "To be fair, the croissants were so good that I might've thrown a punch if you'd tried to get between us."

That made him cackle like he couldn't believe I'd said it, which made me instantly worried. I didn't know what million-aires found funny, so what if my normal behavior was lowbrow and embarrassing to Declan? Normally I wouldn't give a damn, but I was serious about this job. I might've landed this gig by do-ing something questionable, but that wasn't my default.

My default was working hard.

I sucked at a lot of things, and my life was kind of a shitshow at the moment, but I'd always prided myself on working hard and doing my best at my sucky jobs.

"You were smart to hold back, Stan," Declan said, and I felt him drape his arm across the back of my chair. "She's very in-tense about her breakfast."

When I turned my head and met his gaze, his mouth was half-cocked in a smirk that I felt low in my belly. Dear *God*, he looked good with a smile. I leaned closer, moving my mouth to his ear and saying so quietly that only he could hear, "I'm a little freaked out by how spot-on you are. I seriously inhaled three croissants before you even finished the story about when you used to take naps in the mattress department of CrashPad."

He turned his head slightly, his face so close I could've rubbed my nose against his, and then he stretched enough to say into *my* ear, "Do you seriously think I wasn't counting? And who cuts a croissant with a knife and a fork, anyway, you psychopath?"

I started giggling; I couldn't help it. My mouth was back at his ear to whisper, "I was being classy, you jackass."

"It was *incredibly* classy," he replied, a smile in his voice when he added, "The classiest."

"Good morning!"

I looked up and Declan's mom sat down in one of the empty spots on the other side of him, a little old lady beside her. The woman was tiny with a sweet face, like the poster child for adorable grandmothers, and she was staring at me.

"Hi, Elaine," I said, pulling back from her son. "How are you this morning?"

I was very aware that Declan's arm was still resting on the back of my chair and we were kind of huddled together like an actual couple.

"Wonderful," she said, "just wonderful."

"Nana," Declan said, standing. "I'd like you to meet Abi Green. Abi, this is Nana Marian."

I smiled and leaned closer, for some reason nervous all of a sudden. Or *more* nervous than I'd already been.

"It's so nice to meet you," I said, holding out my hand.

She looked at my hand but didn't take it. Instead, she narrowed her eyes behind her big round glasses and said, "I know you."

My stomach dropped and my heart started racing. "You do?"

"I don't think so," Declan said, giving his grandmother a teasing grin. "Abi hasn't—"

"I know who I know, Dexxie," she said, scowling at him, "and I know that I've met her."

I looked back and forth between the three of them while wearing a guilty smile, clueless as to what to say to this woman. "Well then, it's nice to meet you *again*."

That made Elaine smile, but the old lady pursed her lips and shook her head before turning her chair to focus on the Q&A.

"Well, that went well," I muttered, feeling like a failure.

I glanced at Declan, and his smile was gone. His eyes were narrowed as he watched his family, and then his eyes met mine. I didn't like the way he was looking at me, like he suspected me of something, so I said, "What?"

"Nana remembers everything," he said at my ear, "so you must've met before."

I stared at him, waiting for the rest, but he just looked at me expectantly.

Which was irritating as hell. "That's great that your Nana Marian is so sharp, but I've never seen her before in my life."

His jaw jumped as he watched me, and then he said, "Is there anything about your life that you need to tell me?"

"*What?*"

"Is there anything I don't know that maybe I need to know?" he asked, and the man said it like I was a child hiding the fact that I'd stolen a piece of candy he told me I couldn't have.

And I don't know why, but the fact that he was whispering made it worse.

Like I was in trouble during church.

He said, "Something you're involved in, somewhere that you frequent; I just need to know where she might've seen you, because she *will* remember. Probably within the hour."

"Why are you saying it like that, like you want to know if I'm a drug dealer or something?" Technically he hadn't insulted me, but something about his tone was insulting.

"I just want to be ahead of it if she knows you from something that doesn't work with our story."

I glanced at the rest of the table as we whisper-argued, but they all seemed enthralled by what Warren was saying, thank God.

"I mean, I *doubt* she frequents my sex club," I said, leaning close enough to smell his shampoo and ensure it looked like we were adorably sharing secrets, "and I've never seen any elderly women at the place by the airport where I dance, so—"

"Okay. Got it," he said, turning his head just a little to level me with an annoyed look from point-blank range.

I couldn't have him glaring at me, the perfect girlfriend, so I whispered, "You're cute when you're serious."

And I dropped a kiss on the tip of his nose.

His eyes narrowed, and my heart started racing because *what the hell had I just done?* I wasn't someone who kissed strangers, on the nose or anywhere else, so what the hell was that?

But then he smiled.

A slow, sliding smirk of teasing appreciation that I felt in my stomach.

He reached out a hand and touched my chin, giving it a tiny squeeze between his thumb and forefinger, and the gesture made *not* smiling back impossible.

If that man smiled more, this would be a lot of fun.

I left during the first morning break.

I was surprised by how interesting the Q&A was, because as someone not into wealth because I had no money, I'd expected to be bored out of my mind. But the way Warren talked about business and investments was so simple, so evergreen, that it totally sucked me in.

Kind of made sense that people trekked to Omaha from all over the world to listen to the man speak.

I was so into it that when it was time for me to leave, I had to be reminded.

"Didn't you say you were going to take off during the first break?" Declan asked when Warren left the stage.

"Oh. Yeah. Right," I said, reaching for my handbag and standing. "I almost forgot."

He'd offered to walk me out, but for some reason I didn't want him to see my dented old Honda Civic. Not that I had anything to be embarrassed about—it was just a car and it got me where I needed to go—but it seemed like a bad idea to remind him of the vastness of our differences.

There was already *way* too big a power imbalance in our situation.

When I got "home" (to his fancy house), I changed into sweats and went onto the balcony to write. A character had formed in my head at the cocktail party last night, and I was dying to start drafting Daphne's story.

I opened my notebook and started pinning down the details.

- *Daphne is a lonely, middle-aged woman who agrees to fake-date a billionaire for a weekend.*

- *She loathes the wealthy and inwardly mocks everything going on around her at the beginning of the first night.*

- *Gradually loathes less of it, and begins seeing the life as hers. The people are kind to her and start to feel like family.*

- *Billionaire loves her, and they sleep together.*

- *Burglar breaks in with gun and Daphne saves them all by killing him with his own gun; everyone gushing with love and gratitude for her bravery.*

- *Wakes up Sunday morning in her own house, alone—someone moved her back while she was sleeping because the arrangement is over. Knock on the door—it's the cops with an arrest warrant. She asks them to call the billionaire to vouch for her, and they inform her that HE was the one who called them.*

- *Uses her one phone call to reach him and he can't talk because he has a tee time. When she starts crying, he reminds her it was all fake.*

I was beyond excited because suddenly I had these vivid details and descriptions that I hadn't been aware existed until two days ago. Custom luxury vehicles, a team of makeover artists, doormen who were available twenty-four-seven to notarize financial papers—my writers workshop professor would probably say it was too fantastical to be believable, but I was running with it.

Daphne was getting the full treatment.

I got lost in writing for a few hours, which was so easy to do when I was on a balcony above the city, entirely checked out of life as I knew it.

But I was only checked out until my mother called.

When I saw it was her I wanted to ignore the call, but that usually meant she'd just call more often and maybe even bother Lauren.

I sighed and set down my pen. "Hello?"

"Hey, how's it going, kid?"

"Good," I said, wondering why she was calling. "What's up?"

"Do you have any moving boxes?" she asked, sounding agitated. "Daniel might be moving out and he's got shit all over the place."

I sighed and wished I would've let it go to voicemail, because the last thing I wanted was to listen to the many adventures of my mother's boyfriends. I said, "I don't—sorry. What do you mean he 'might' be moving out?"

"Well," she said, sighing loudly. "Apparently his ex-wife isn't comfortable with their daughter staying here on his weekends with her because she doesn't know me."

"Sounds fair," I said, feeling so much empathy for Daniel's daughter.

"No, it does *not*," she snapped, "because Daniel is Elsa's father, so if he thinks I'm good enough for his child, that's all that should matter."

"So," I said, wanting to divert her from her anger. "He's getting his own place, then? For when his daughter's over?"

How absolutely . . . *parental* of that man.

I'd only met Daniel a few times because I'd kind of retired from meeting boyfriends, but bravo to good ol' Danny Boy.

If only my mother had cared that much.

To be fair, my mom was a good person and had always been a good mother. I'd never doubted that she loved me, and she'd always made sure I had what I needed in terms of food and clothing.

But she was . . . scattered and selfish and utterly unable to be alone.

I don't know that I would've learned that about her if my dad hadn't died when I was in fifth grade. Before that, we'd been a happy little threesome who engaged in typical suburban things like annual vacations and daily evening dinners.

But when he passed and my mother started dating, everything changed.

It felt like, when I was a child, there was always someone new coming in and out of our lives. Boyfriends I loved who just disappeared at random, boyfriends I hated who moved into our apartment, and boyfriends with children whose homes we moved into.

My mom took care of me, yes, but she also burned to the ground any sense of stability we might've had in our lives.

Which, according to Lauren, was why I was a control freak now.

"That's what he's thinking about," she said, "but he also said

I can just move into his apartment like a month after he gets it, since she can't do much about him having friends over."

Poor Elsa, I thought, my stomach feeling heavy at the memory of my mom "having friends over."

"Listen, I have to go," I said, closing my notebook and standing. "I've got dinner plans and I need to get ready."

"Ooh, do you have a date?" she asked, perking up.

Spoiler: My mother thought being in a relationship was the pinnacle of existence.

Spoiler: I was inclined to disagree with her.

"No, just dinner with friends," I lied, because it was way easier than explaining my actual situation. "I'll talk to you later. Love you."

"Love you, too," she said as I opened the door and went back inside the condo.

Just as I hung up, Declan sent a text.

ARE YOU OKAY WITH ME COMING BY AROUND 6 TO TAKE A QUICK SHOWER BEFORE WE GO TO DINNER?

I was impressed by how conscientious he'd been about sharing his place. He was behaving as if it was my apartment and I was in charge, when in reality he could totally boss me around and there was nothing I could do about it.

I texted: if you don't stop yelling all the time I'm going to hide a catfish somewhere in your house that will slowly rot and attract vermin

He replied quickly. IS THAT A YES?

I sent: That is a yes but use your key like this is your place. How's the Q&A going?

Declan: JUST CONCLUDED, ACTUALLY.

I texted: Don't forget to give Warren his muffins.

Declan: WHAT MUFFINS?

Me: The muffins on the table next to your water.

Declan: IS THAT WHAT'S IN THE BOX?

Me: Duh

Declan: YOU DIDN'T TELL ME THAT.

Me: Sure I did.

Declan: TRUST ME, YOU DIDN'T

Me: Are you going to keep screaming nonsense at me, or are you going to leave me alone so I can shower before you get home?

Declan: I'M GOING TO LEAVE YOU ALONE FOR NOW, BUT LATER YOU'RE GOING TO PAY FOR THE NONSENSE COMMENT.

That made me pause.

Gasp.

Was he *teasing* me?

I stared down at my phone for a second before texting: ARE YOU THREATENING ME, POWELL?

Declan: Calm your ass down, Mariano. See you at six.

14

PINNED

Declan

She wasn't home.

I'd walked the entire apartment, and Abi wasn't there.

Talk about déjà vu.

Only she wasn't on the balcony this time.

Which was fine, I supposed, since we didn't have to leave for another thirty minutes, but I would've expected her to mention she wouldn't be there when we'd texted earlier.

Then again, I was a fool for expecting her to do something that *was* expected.

I took a quick shower, then as I ducked into my closet to grab a tie, I heard, "Are you in the closet?"

I turned just as she stepped in the doorway, looking stunning in a black off-the-shoulder sweater, black leather skirt, and tall black boots that made me actually forget my name for a second.

And something about the all-black outfit made her hair look like shimmery copper.

I cleared my throat, fully aware of how I shouldn't think she was gorgeous.

"Oh, my God, sorry," she said, blinking fast and turning her back to me like she'd walked in on me buck naked. I noticed her hand was holding the back of her sweater together as she rambled, "I just thought—"

"I'm wearing pants," I said slowly, because I was dressed, for fuck's sake; I was wearing the slacks that went with my charcoal Armani suit. "You're fine."

"Okay, good," she said, nodding, but she didn't turn around.

"You can turn around," I said, wanting to laugh at this unexpected shyness from my lack of a shirt. "I'm decent, I promise."

She turned around and said, with her eyes dialed in on my face, "I was just looking for a safety pin."

"Come," I said, walking over to the drawers that were built into the wall. "I've got an entire bin full of them in here."

I heard her follow me as I opened the top drawer and pulled out a container of safety pins. When I turned to hand them over, though, her eyes were on my chest and . . . well, *shit*, nothing was good about the way she looked at me and the way it made me feel.

"Do you need help?" I asked.

"Hmm?" Her eyes were back on my face, and she looked confused. She blinked fast and said, "What? I mean, with what?"

"Pinning something," I said, and I was impressed with how calm I sounded when her interest had been . . . interesting. "The part of your sweater you're holding together, perhaps?"

Especially when she looked like *that*, with those smooth shoulders out for the world to see again.

"Oh," she said. "No, I think I can do it."

"You sure?" I asked, knowing I shouldn't be offering my services but unable to stop myself.

"Well," she said, craning her neck to look at her back. "It's just a little big and I don't like when it slides, so I just want to do a little interior tuck thing to ensure it stays in place."

"I'm happy to help if it saves you from stabbing yourself in the back."

"Okay," she said, looking like she also thought it wasn't a good idea. "That'd be great. Thank you."

She turned so I was looking down at her back and the part of her sweater she was clutching, and I grabbed a safety pin. "Don't let go until I say I've got it, okay?"

The last thing either of us needed was a wardrobe malfunction. That would definitely make dinner a little awkward.

"Okay," she said.

I took the fabric between two fingers, very aware of every sound in the room as I dipped the safety pin underneath the back of her sweater with my other hand and slid it between the tuck of material.

Of course, I was even more aware of the proximity of my bare chest to her bare neck and shoulders. I don't know why, but it felt . . . dangerous. I said, "Edward's not going to be happy about this, for the record."

"Oh," she said, looking at me over her shoulder with wide eyes. "Seriously?"

Her eyes were such a unique color, brown but melted down into something lighter, and they kind of took me by surprise for a moment. I cleared my throat and reassured her, clasping the safety pin. "I'm just messing with you. He's not going to notice a pinhole in a sweater."

"Ah," she said with a nervous laugh. "Good."

"You're all set," I said, clearing my throat again.

"Thank you," she replied, turning around. "I probably *would* have shanked myself, so I appreciate it."

"Can you call it shanking when it's a safety pin?"

"You can when I'm the one wielding it."

"Note to self, hide the sharp things," I said, noticing that the perfume she was wearing was so subtle it was barely there.

Kind of made you want to investigate its origin.

If you were that type of person.

Which I was not.

"Will you be ready soon?"

"Yes," she said, nodding, her eyes doing a sweep over me before settling on some point just past my shoulders. "I'll be ready in two minutes."

"I'll be ready in five. Meet you by the door?"

"You got it," she said, then turned and disappeared from my closet.

I got dressed quickly after that, choosing to focus on the events of the evening instead of whatever had just been pinging between us in my closet. I was smart enough to know it was best to just ignore chemistry, because chemistry was a fleeting thing.

Abi seemed to know it, too, because she was all business when we left the apartment and drove to the restaurant.

"So this isn't a company event, per se," she said, looking out the window. "But just you and I having dinner at one of the restaurants under Hathaway's umbrella, correct?"

"Exactly," I said, merging onto I-80. "But the majority of the people with reservations will be shareholders. Especially when the restaurant—Immersion—is right next to Jaques Jewelers."

"Yeah, so tell me about that." She turned toward me in her seat. "I've never been to a jewelry store's 'private event' before. What does that look like?"

I personally found it to be the worst of all the events, only because it was often the most pretentious and boring. "The store is closed to everyone but those with passes. They get to enjoy cocktails, entertainment, and a generous discount on everything in the store."

"Oh," she said, not sounding impressed. "So their goal is to make rich people tipsy enough to spend more than usual."

It was clear that Abi didn't hold the wealthy in the highest regard, and I couldn't really blame her for that.

I didn't, either.

But that was a "me" issue in my world.

And hella complex when it came to my family.

Which was why I kind of led a double life, keeping the Hathaway business separate from the business I had with Roman.

"Something like that," I just said, leaving it at that.

When we got to Immersion, the hostess took us right to our table, but before we could even order cocktails, someone came up to our table, introducing themselves. And then another, and another.

I imagined an actual girlfriend would get sick of the constant interruptions that went along with being a Powell, but Abi was a professional. She smiled at everyone like she welcomed their table-crashing, and she was warm and engaging with each person she met.

Although it didn't escape my notice when she finished her second glass of wine. She didn't seem tipsy or buzzed, but her face was just a little more relaxed after the glass was emptied, like she was amused by everything.

We were finally left to ourselves when our food came, thank God.

When she cut into her filet and lifted the fork to her mouth, she said, "You know, Declan, I think perhaps it's time for a truce."

I looked at her in the candlelight and couldn't detect any sarcasm. "Explain."

"Well," she said. "I think it's silly, our battle for dominance, when we're just two people trying to get the best outcomes for our lives this weekend, right?"

"Right . . . ?" I said, waiting to hear more.

"Neither of us really expected this scenario to happen in the first place, but now that it has, why can't we behave like adults? I think it's possible for us to get along while we work together, don't you?"

"Perhaps," I said, sitting back in my chair and lifting my Manhattan. "So then, Abi, tell me a little bit about your life. What do you do with your days when you aren't fake-dating strangers?"

Abi leaned back in her seat as well, a small smile on her face, and I found myself looking forward to whatever she was about to say.

15

DINNER WITH FRIENDS

Abi

"Well, you already know that I work at Benny's and for Master-kleen," I said, swallowing my food before picking up my wine-glass while wondering what it would hurt to share a little. "I'm also in grad school—final year, thank God—getting my MFA."

His eyebrows knitted together like he was confused. "Wait, what? You're getting your master's?"

"That *is* the goal of graduate school, yes," I said slowly, cutting another piece of steak.

I wasn't sure I'd ever had a better piece of meat.

"*Not* in finance?" he clarified, then took a bite of his pesto penne with prosciutto (which looked *very* good, by the way).

Now it made sense, the confusion. He'd obviously googled me and knew I had a degree in finance, and for someone like him, it probably made zero sense why I'd want to do anything other than make the absolute most money I possibly could. I cut another piece and said, "Not in finance. I'm studying fiction writing."

I don't know what I saw pass over his face, judgment or mockery perhaps, but he recovered and said, "Explain how you went from finance to fiction."

"Well," I said, shrugging and deciding to be honest about this part of my life. I wasn't sure if it was the wine—*probably was*—but I kind of felt like opening up to him a little.

I knew he assumed I was just a grocery clerk with a crappy apartment, but I felt compelled to show him that wasn't all.

I said, "I graduated from college and got a job in finance, wherein I quickly discovered that I hated it. Like, hated it so much I could barely get out of bed every day. I decided to go back to school out of desperation, wanting to find literally anything else I could do with my life that would pay a decent salary but not steal my soul. I took a fiction writing class in the summer, fell madly in love, then discovered I could jump right into the MFA program with my existing bachelor's."

"Really," he said, looking intrigued.

"Every single writing class I've ever taken has been, like, pure serotonin for me," I said. "And my MFA advisor, Anna Vaccaro, is this accomplished lit-fic writer who is everything I want to be."

"So you want to write books?" he asked.

"No, I mean, maybe," I corrected, dipping my fork into the face-size baked potato. "But writing doesn't come with guarantees, like a salary and benefits sort of thing; it's a constant hustle. Which I'm fine with on the side, but I just couldn't live with that lack of security. No, I want to be a writing professor. I want to spend my days workshopping with students, rolling around in stories and characterization until I have tenure. Then I can write on the side and see what happens."

"Is there a lot of money in that?" he asked. "In being a writing professor?"

I shook my head, knowing this was the part of the story he wouldn't be able to understand. "No. But there is enough. If I can earn a decent paycheck doing what I love, that's all I need."

"Interesting," he said, and I felt like he meant it. He probably meant it in a *that's-interesting-that-people-don't-always-care-about-money* way, but he still looked like he was interested in what I was saying.

"So tell me, Declan, what do you like about your job? Is it *just* that you're good at making lots of money, or are there other things about it that you enjoy?"

Was that insulting? I hadn't meant to sound insulting, but maybe it'd been insulting.

"What do I *like* about my job?" he repeated. "Other than the money?"

"Yeah," I said, nodding. "For example, do you love that you get to make PowerPoint slides, or do you work with a super-fun bunch of wild-ass execs, or is it all about the joy you get in composing memorandums? What is your favorite part of the vice presidency?"

He tilted his head. "No one ever asks me that."

"About the memorandums?"

"No, about my favorite part."

"Well they should, and I'm dying to know."

He furrowed his brow and looked into space for a moment

before saying, "I like exploring the potential of an idea, I guess you could say. I like combing through data and drilling into possibilities for new directions. There is nothing quite like the buzz of coming up with a new strategy and seeing it come to fruition."

"If it *does*, right?"

He smiled. "Right."

"Did you always want to be a businessman?" I asked.

"Definitely," he said. "My great-grandmother started the business, and I grew up watching my grandmother expand all of her work. She was always looking for new and better ways to grow CrashPad's footprint and I guess I'm the same way with Hathaway."

"I can't imagine having a family business," I said, but really thinking that I couldn't imagine having a real *family* at all. It'd always just been me and my mother; that was it. "I bet you're so proud of it."

"I am," he said. "I mean, technically it isn't the family business anymore; it's a Hathaway company. But it still feels like ours because we've stuck to the same core principles."

It was confusing to my brain, listening to him talk about his job, because it *seemed* nice. I respected the way he seemed to be super committed to his family's company and now the company they'd merged with; it felt loyal and it was obvious he worked his ass off. I mean, when he wasn't schmoozing with other Hathaway people, he was constantly on his phone.

And the man wasn't checking his Instagram or playing Candy Crush.

No, he was *always* engaging with his email.

But as impressive as it was that he was a hard worker, I still couldn't write off the fact that he lived in a multimillion-dollar apartment and drove a luxury car that he'd had *created* specifically for him. His work ethic might be admirable, but he was still a man who was okay with spending millions of dollars on stuff.

And I needed to remember that.

"So did you grow up here?" he asked. "How many siblings? Give me your origin story, Mariano."

I looked down at my food and tried to come up with a way to make it sound more interesting than it was.

Tried and failed. I said, "I did. I grew up in Omaha, am an only child, graduated from Millard South."

"Do your parents still live here?"

I took a bite of potato, and after I swallowed, I said, "My mom does, but my dad died when I was in grade school. So my family pretty much just consists of my mother and me."

"I'm sorry," he said, getting a crinkle between his perfect dark eyebrows. He looked genuinely sad for me, and I imagined that for someone like him, it was the most pathetic origin story he'd ever heard. "I mean, I know a lot of time has passed, but it still has to be hard."

"It's fine," I said awkwardly, then took a gulp of wine.

Was it weird that I was a functioning adult who still didn't know how to respond to someone when they expressed their condolences about my dad who died a very long time ago?

Yes.

"I know CrashPad started here," I said to change the subject. "So I'm assuming you grew up in Omaha, too?"

"I did," he said, nodding as he scooped up another bite of pasta. "Born and raised here, graduated from Creighton Prep,

went to college on the East Coast but came back to settle down
and work."

"Where on the East Coast?" I asked.

I'd always been obsessed with that part of the country. I'd
never been farther east than Florida, and there was just something about places like Boston, Manhattan, and Philadelphia
that called to me.

"Cambridge. Massachusetts," he said.

"So you went to Harvard." Something about the fact that he
didn't *say* he went to Harvard irritated me. It felt like he was trying to get something past me; maybe I was just paranoid.

"I did," he said, giving a nod and setting his fork on his now
empty plate.

"It's an okay school," I said, "if you're into that kind of education."

His lips slid into a smirk that was hot in the way it was playful. "What kind would that be?"

"Excellent, I guess you might say," I said. "If not slightly
overpriced."

I cut another piece of steak, fully aware that he was finished
with his meal. Dexxie might be done, but I wasn't walking away
from this filet until my plate was clean.

"Yes, I guess you could say I was into an excellent-yet-slightly-
overpriced education."

I nodded. "I can see that about you."

"Is there anything that makes you less of a smartass?" he
asked, his eyes all over my face.

"Shots of tequila, but that doesn't seem like a good move on
jewelry night."

He was quiet for a second before asking, "How do you hold your liquor, Mariano?"

"Very well, Powell."

"Then let's do a shot and try to sweeten you up before the event."

I raised an eyebrow. "If you're shooting for sweet, you better make it two."

16

JAQUES

Declan

"Let's go look at engagement rings."

Normally I'd be sweating if my date said that, but before we'd left the restaurant, Abi had called her shot. "An event at a jewelry store is the perfect opportunity to show your colleagues that you're as good as married. Leave it up to me, Dexxie, and you won't be disappointed."

"Okay," I said, taking her hand and leading her to the other side of the massive showroom. "But keep it low-key."

"I've got this, Declan Connor."

The store was all decked out for the event, with music and hors d'oeuvres and trays of bubbling champagne being passed around every few minutes.

They'd done a great job, and the turnout appeared to be fantastic.

Profits were a little down for the jewelry store, so they'd put a lot of planning into this event.

We'd barely started looking at rings when Warren found us, and he had Susanna Jaques beside him. Susanna was the CEO of the jewelry store, a world-class gemologist who knew her shit.

She'd grown up in Zimbabwe and was, quite frankly, obsessed with diamonds.

I knew little about jewelry, to be honest, and I rarely crossed paths with anyone who worked within Jaques, but Susanna was an impressive lady.

Warren introduced her to Abi, completely ignoring me, and I grabbed a passing glass of champagne when the group started discussing diamond engagement rings.

Abi was right, and what she was doing made sense, but I felt like the word *engagement* pushed our little fib into another level of deceit that made me uncomfortable.

My phone buzzed, and when I pulled it out of my pocket, I had an email from Roman.

Submitting this as my official recommendation for this
month's RWDR investment.

I read through the request, saw the price tag, then sent a quick response: Approved.

My secret side hustle, RWDR Investments, had become my obsession. Hathaway was still my priority, but all I wanted to do when I wasn't at my day job was work on RWDR projects.

"Uh-oh, Dexxie, I think she's found one," Warren said, which made me jerk my attention from the email and put my phone away.

I looked up, and Abi was wiggling her diamond-encrusted ring finger and giving me a huge smile.

"You found one you like?" I asked.

"Do you see how he sweats?" she said to Warren, giving my mentor a teasing grin that made the old guy beam like he'd never been so happy. "Poor Dexxie looks like he's going to faint."

That made Warren laugh, which made the entire sales team, who'd converged upon my fake girlfriend, laugh as well. It appeared Abi had charmed everyone in that corner of the jewelry store, and I was a little proud of how good she was.

"Show me the ring, Abigail," I said, stepping closer, enjoying the look of surprise on her face as I officially entered the chat.

Susanna launched into a story about where the diamonds came from, how humanely they were mined, and who'd designed the ring, but my eyes were on Abi's face as she watched me.

It was obvious she knew she might've gone beyond "low-key."

"It's stunning," I said, holding her hand and staring down at the thousands of dollars in diamonds sitting upon her slim finger.

"I know," she replied in a near whisper. "But I think I want to take it off now."

"You don't like it?" Susanna asked, sounding shocked.

"I don't like hijacking the time of the amazing Jaques team when there are so many shareholders to assist," she said, sliding the ring off her finger. "Trust me when I tell you that we *will* be back soon, just Dex and I, to explore your beautiful selection of rings. Thank you so much for letting me try this on."

She was a talented actress for sure. The team, Susanna, Warren—everyone—appeared to be enamored of my angelic girlfriend.

While Abi was being divested of her six-figure ring, I quickly whispered to a guy on the sales team. I knew exactly what I needed, and he was going to get it for me.

"Hey," I said, grabbing her hand and pulling her away from Warren and the group. "I'm getting jealous. I'm stealing you away from this guy."

"Selfish," Warren teased, but his smile told me he approved.

"Dex," Abi said, grinning at me in a way that did something weird to my chest. "I'm trying to chat with Warren here."

"I bought you a present, though," I said, grabbing her hand and tugging her closer. "Don't you want it?"

"Bye, Warren," she said without looking back, which made both Warren and the team laugh.

When we reached a spot that was away from other people but close enough that they could see what was happening if they wanted to, I let go of her hand and held out the box that'd just been passed to me as I walked by the necklace counter.

"For the most beautiful girl in the room," I said, meaning that part of it. She was just so fucking *alive* that she very nearly glowed.

"Dexxie," she said, her smile so wide she was almost laughing. "You do know that I'd love you even if you didn't buy me jewelry, right?"

"Of course you would," I said, stepping closer to say into her ear, "*Not.*"

She let out a little breathless laugh at our inside joke that made me want to make her do it again, and I couldn't stop myself from dropping a kiss on the side of that long, exposed neck that had driven me crazy since she'd shown up in my closet holding her sweater together with her hand.

"Are you going to open it or what?" I asked, pulling myself away from her.

"Okay, okay," she said, her eyes twinkling. "But this box doesn't look like it would hold the engagement ring I picked out."

"Like I would really buy that with you in the same room and all the shareholders here. Hardly seems romantic."

"On the contrary, it seems like it would be a great way to shout out to the world how much you love me," she said.

"You might be right. Perhaps it was a missed opportunity."

"Well, I guess I will open this non-ring anyways," she said, her nose crinkling as she smiled at me. I watched as she opened it, and I knew I was totally pulling off the besotted expression I was going for because I was absolutely charmed by her at the moment.

It was all an act, and I wasn't foolish enough to think it was real, but I was having a great time pretending. It probably had to do with the shots, but this was honestly more fun than I'd had at a work-related event in a very long time.

Her mouth dropped wide open when she looked inside the box. She put her hand over her heart and said, "It's so beautiful."

"Would you like me to put it on you?" I asked. "And I totally get it if you don't want to wear it right now; I won't be insulted. There's something about your bare neck that really works with this outfit."

"You think so?" she asked in that flirtatious tone that was really starting to torture me. Was she drunk? I wasn't sure if it was the alcohol or that she was just having fun, but I was genuinely feeling this vibe she was giving off.

"Yes," I said, my voice low. "It's been driving me nuts since you showed up in my closet needing help pinning yourself into your sweater."

"Oh," she said, blinking a little faster like she was surprised I'd said that. Her voice was *also* low when she said, "Um, yes, please."

"The stones reminded me of the freckles on your right shoulder," I admitted as I moved behind her, taking the necklace out of the box and lowering it to her neck.

I wasn't lying.

When I'd been pinning her sweater together, I noticed the adorable constellation of specks, and the chocolate diamonds *almost* did them justice.

She looked at me over her shoulder, eyes searching mine. We weren't saying anything, but the look we exchanged as I clasped the necklace was me admitting to the truth, and her acknowledging that she knew it was the truth.

"Thank you," she said, her voice so quiet it was almost a whisper.

"You're welcome," I managed, my voice coming out a little raspy.

What the fuck is this?

But my *what the fuck* exploded into a thousand more when she turned and wrapped herself around me in a huge hug. A hug that felt real.

And there was nothing I could do but hug her back, right?

"Should we maybe kiss?" she said quietly in my ear. "I mean, if this was real, we would totally kiss right now."

"Well," I said, pulling back enough to see her face. "I'm all about the authenticity."

I had every intention of giving her the public-appropriate kiss of a couple who'd just exchanged a gift, but something happened.

Just as I lowered my mouth to hers, our eyes met and she whispered against my lips, "Don't disappoint me, Powell."

17

FIRST KISS

Abi

I couldn't believe I'd asked for it, but more than that, I couldn't believe what he was delivering. Instead of giving me a quick, polite kiss, Declan slanted his mouth over mine and his tongue slid across my bottom lip and into my mouth.

And not in an obtrusive, unwelcome way.

Dear Lord, it was like being drugged.

One minute we'd been two separate individuals, and the next, our mouths were fused together and it was madness inside. His teeth nibbled, his tongue went deep, his lips dragged. It was smooth and hot, like his mouth was casting spells that made mine instantly desperate to accept the offering, regardless of where we were. *Yes, sir, may I have another?*

It was overconfident and decadent, like the man himself.

His big palms were supporting my back, but they'd somehow slid underneath my sweater, so I felt the caress of his warm fingers

over my sensitive skin. When I sighed into his hungry mouth, he
answered with a low groan.

This was no chaste, we-are-in-public kiss; this was the final
kiss in a movie where the two main characters end up together.

Declan wasn't completely lost in it, though, because he was
aware enough to walk me backward while we kissed, moving us
toward a hallway. I don't know if we both forgot about pretending, or if we didn't give a damn, but we were wildly kissing in the
EMPLOYEES ONLY hall.

"What is this?" I murmured into his mouth, my hands finding
his hard jawline. "What are we doing?"

"Lust," he breathed, opening those sexy green eyes to weaken
me with his calm response of, "Innocent lust that is no big deal."

"Right," I managed. We kept kissing and I said against his
lips, "I suppose as long as we both know this is just for fun right
now, there's no harm, right?"

"That's right," he said, nipping at my bottom lip. "This is no
different than us holding hands while walking in front of the
shareholders."

"Excellent, excellent," I said, sliding my fingers up into his
thick hair to anchor him in place. "Because this is way more fun
than holding hands."

"Hey, can you guys break it up? This is a public place."

I gasped and pulled away, turning around to see a very attractive man smiling at us. I looked back up at Declan, who had
cleared his throat and smoothed his hair before his eyes flashed
with recognition.

"Roman," Declan said with a sheepish grin, grabbing my
hand and pulling me with him toward the guy.

"Hey, Abi," the guy said, smiling in such a genuine way that I was dying to know who he was and how we supposedly knew each other. "It's so nice to see you again."

"You, too," I said, my cheeks on fire as I wondered how I was supposed to play this one.

I was also mortified that he'd caught us making out in the hallway.

"How the heck have you been?" I asked with a smile, trying to sound breezy and light.

"Good," he said. "My sister was going to come with me but she's home with the baby tonight."

"Ah," I said, shrugging and going for it, laying it on even thicker. "Lucky girl."

That made the stranger and Declan smirk at each other, confirming my suspicion that this guy was fully aware of what was going on with the whole fake-dating act.

As if hearing my thoughts, Roman leaned in and said, "Thanks for doing our boy this big favor, by the way."

"Anything for *our boy*," I muttered, wondering what Roman thought of me and what *exactly* he knew.

"We were just about to head out," Declan said to his friend. "Are you bailing as well?"

"I wasn't going to, but now I feel like I must," Roman said with a dramatic eye roll. "You're the one who gave me tickets."

"You can stay all night; I don't give a shit."

Apparently permission was all Roman needed, because a minute later, when the three of us returned to the crowded showroom, he waved a hand before turning away from us and joining the shoppers.

"Let's say goodbye to Warren," Declan said, and as we approached the old guy to say our farewells, I actually felt guilty lying because I liked him so much. He seemed like a genuinely good human, which was a little confusing when he was a billionaire.

There was no way for me to make that work in my head.

"We're going to take off," Declan said. "Abi's got to let the dog out before he rips up the place."

Oh right, my dog.

Did he have a name? I couldn't remember.

"Have a great night, Abi," Warren said, giving my arm a little pat. "And that necklace looks beautiful on you; Dex did good."

"Thank you," I said, looking down at it. "He really did."

I was surprised when Warren went in for a hug.

I was equally surprised that I didn't hate it.

As soon as he let go of me he said, "You're running in the 5K tomorrow morning, right?"

Declan had explained to me that the Shareholder 5K was a big family event that Hathaway employees really turned out for. There were a lot of runners who registered because they liked racing, but there were just as many attendees who walked with kids and strollers.

He'd told me the last part as if he thought I couldn't run, which had prompted me to trash-talk about how I could actually run circles around his ass.

Even though I couldn't.

"Of course I am," I said, uneasy at the thought of it. Still, I said, "Any opportunity to embarrass Dex in public by beating him is my favorite thing in the world."

"She can't beat me," Declan corrected, shaking his head like I was adorable. "She wishes."

"We shall see," I said, feeling lightheaded when he shot me a teasing smile.

With that mouth that I now knew was incredibly skilled.

The odds of me beating him were slim. I ran every day, but I'd seen Declan with no shirt and *dear Lord*, the man must spend every waking hour that he wasn't in the office at the gym. When I'd seen him in those low-hanging pants with the buckle not fastened, I'd nearly fainted dead away.

That being said, it sounded like a fun, wholesome activity, and I was a pretty good runner so I knew I could hold my own.

We said our good nights and were approaching Declan's car in the parking lot when Roman reappeared, jogging toward us.

"Hey, Dex," he said as he ran up. "Hold up."

"Yeah?" Declan turned toward his friend, and I couldn't stop myself from stealing a glance at his profile.

Had that man really just kissed me?

I just couldn't get over it.

"Sorry, Abi—quick work question."

I shrugged. "No worries."

"I'm going to forward something that just came in like an hour ago," Roman said, looking more serious than he had since I'd met him. "But I don't want to wait. Take a look at it as soon as you get home and let me know ASAP if it's got your approval."

"I didn't know you worked for Hathaway, too," I said. It was a little impressive that they'd been friends for so long *and* worked together. "I thought you were just a personal guest."

"I don't and I am," he said. "We just have some investments together."

"Ah," I said, realizing yet again that I knew nothing about what rich people did with their time and money.

"So tell me, kiddo," Roman said to me with a grin, which was funny since he looked like he was my age. "How does this work? Does he drop you off at his building before he reports to his hotel? I just love this so very much."

"Shut up, asshole," Declan said, rolling his eyes. "The particulars of our deal are none of your bus—"

"It's just so beautiful, though," Roman interrupted, nudging me like we were in cahoots. "Please tell me you sleep on his pillow and eat potato chips in bed, Abi."

"I haven't yet, but I might have to tonight."

It was a little freeing, talking to somebody who knew what was going on, that I was basically a stranger to Declan. The honesty felt relaxing. Liberating.

Although I *was* a little embarrassed that he'd seen that kiss, and I wondered again what he thought of me.

"So were you two, like, boarding school roommates or something?" I asked, my eyes roaming over his stylish suit.

"No, we met in college; I was his poor friend."

"You don't look poor," I said, revisiting the suit.

"Compared to Declan, everyone's poor," he explained, giving me a look.

"That checks out," I said, sharing a smile with him.

We talked to Roman for a few more minutes before he left us to rejoin the event, and I realized as I watched him walk away that I genuinely liked him.

Liking Declan's people had *not* been on my fake-dating bingo card.

I got into his car, and my seat belt was barely buckled when Declan spoke up.

"About that kiss," he said, his face unreadable. "I want to apologize if I took it too far. It was all part of the act, just a fun part that I thoroughly enjoyed playing, but I would never want to do anything that made you feel uncomfortable or that you hadn't consented to."

"Oh." I was surprised by his words. "No. I was the one who started it, and hard same for me. I got into our act and just had a little too much fun with it. I think our tequila shots gave me a little boldness that usually isn't there."

"That's kind of what I assumed," he said. "But just know that I'm happy to sleep somewhere else tonight if I made you feel compromised in any way."

"No, but I appreciate the consideration." I was shocked by how concerned he was. I hadn't had *that* on my bingo card, either. "Thank you for being cool, bro."

He rolled his eyes, fully aware I called him "bro" just to mess with him.

Things were relaxed on the rest of the drive home because we'd cleared the air. It was refreshing to candidly discuss things instead of letting them fester. We'd kissed, explored why and what it meant, and now there was no reason to feel weird about it because we'd both admitted we were just having fun and it was nothing to care about.

When we got back to his place, we quickly ran through our plan for the morning, like what time we'd be leaving for the race, and then we said good night.

But after I washed my face and changed into my pajamas, I started worrying all over again. About everything. Even though he'd been nice, what if he thought I was angling for more when I kissed him? Like I was trying to wriggle my way into his life with my mouth . . . or something like that. I was already asking him to pay me a small fortune for pretending to be his girlfriend; what if he thought I was trying to deepen the relationship in order to get more from him?

I hated the thought of that. I tossed and turned for a while, unable to sleep, until finally I had enough.

18

COUCH PICNIC

Declan

I was almost asleep when my phone buzzed.

I grabbed it off the nightstand and for some reason was not at all surprised to see it was a text from Abi.

You do know that the kiss was just a spontaneous part of our game, right?

I texted: I THOUGHT WE ALREADY WENT OVER THIS

I was surprised she was bringing it up because I thought we'd settled it in the car.

Abi: I know but I started thinking about the way you're paying me a lot of money for this and I just want to make sure you know that I wasn't trying to make something happen in hopes of increasing your debt to me.

She'd been a constant surprise since I met her yesterday, and this was no exception.

I sent: IS THIS KEEPING YOU AWAKE? IS YOUR GUILTY

CONSCIENCE MAKING IT IMPOSSIBLE TO SLEEP IN MY VERY COMFORTABLE BED?

She replied: Haha nothing could keep me from sleep in this bed. It is ridiculously comfortable. Jealous?

I sent: HELL YES

Abi: Well thanks for being cool tonight

I replied: AS OPPOSED TO HOW UNCOOL I'VE BEEN SO FAR?

Abi: Yes

I turned on the lamp and texted: WELL THANKS FOR NOT BEING A PAIN IN THE ASS TONIGHT

Abi: As opposed to how big of an ass pain I've been so far?

I replied: YES

Abi: It was hard but for 40K . . .

Bullshit, I thought, wanting to give her credit for being driven by more than just money.

I texted: I'M FAIRLY CERTAIN NO AMOUNT OF MONEY COULD TAME YOUR BRAT FACTOR SO I APPRECIATE THE EFFORT

She texted: You're welcome.

Suddenly I was wide-awake again. Surely it had nothing to do with my roommate's texts and how seeing her name on my phone made me think of her mouth.

Good God, it'd been some kind of a kiss.

Her teasing words had been like a match, sparking something wild that I'd been helpless to stop. One minute I'd been fine, and the next it was like my senses were drowning in the smell of her perfume, the plumpness of her lower lip, the squinting of those amber eyes as she looked up at me.

And fucking whispered, *don't disappoint me.*

I'd absolutely lost my cool.

But I also blamed *her* for kissing like that.

The second my lips were on hers, she had been all in, kissing me back like she was starving and my mouth was the only thing she needed. Like she'd been waiting her entire life for that moment.

I swear to God I'd never experienced a kiss like that.

It was dangerous.

Especially when every cell in my body vibrated at the thought of more.

Fucking knock it off.

I texted: DO YOU MIND IF I GO TO THE KITCHEN FOR A SANDWICH?

And a tumbler of Scotch for me to use as a night-night potion because I can't stop thinking about your kiss?

She texted: Of course not—it's your house

I was still surprised she'd been so nice about my having to stay here with her.

I texted: IT'S YOURS UNTIL THE END OF THE WEEK, MARIANO

She replied: Okay, then, I will allow your presence in my glorious kitchen.

Was it weird that the sarcasm I'd *hated* when I met her was starting to appeal to me?

Yes. Yes, it was.

I'm gonna need that Scotch STAT.

I sent: OH, THANK YOU, YOUR GRACE.

Abi: I'm in love with that. Please refer to me as such for the remainder of our time, thank you.

Such a little shit.

I texted: I WON'T BE DOING THAT, AND YOU'VE ONLY GOT A FEW MORE HOURS BEFORE YOU'RE FREE OF ME.

My flight was to leave after the brunch tomorrow, and I was headed back to New York.

She texted: You won't be here tomorrow night?

Disappointed? For some asinine reason, I wanted her to be disappointed.

Probably because I wanted to know that kiss had messed with her, too. That would somehow make me feel better about the way my brain wouldn't let it go.

I sent: I FLY OUT AFTER BRUNCH AT THE HANGAR. YOU'RE ALMOST HOME FREE.

She replied: It's really gone by fast.

Yes, it definitely had.

I went into the kitchen and straight for the refrigerator. Drinking always made me hungry, though it'd been a while since I'd had a buzz like this, and I might as well have a fucking picnic because I knew I wasn't sleeping.

So I made a massive sandwich, flipped on the TV, and started watching an episode of *Psych* while I wolfed down way too much food. I sat like that through an episode and a half before my phone rang.

Of course it was Roman.

"What's up?" I said as I answered it on speaker with the volume way down, keeping my voice low as well, because it was after 1 a.m. and I didn't want to wake Abi.

"What's *up?*" he said, sounding irritated. "You still haven't responded to my email."

"Shit," I said, shocked I'd forgotten. "Sorry, I got distracted."

"*You?*" he said, sounding more shocked than I was. "*You* got distracted. That is definitely a new one."

"Cut me some slack," I said. "It's been a busy couple days."

"Was it all the kissing?" he said, sounding not exactly irritated, but not pleased, either. "Is that what made the most undistractible person I've ever met distracted?"

"No," I said. "It was the annual shareholder meeting, so spare me the melodrama."

"Dex." Roman sighed and I knew he was dragging his hands through his hair. He was the most laid-back guy I'd ever met, *except* when it came to our work. "This is in real time, remember?"

"I know," I said, opening the email. "You *know* I know. Just give me a minute to peruse and I'll be caught up."

As I finished the sentence, the bedroom door opened and Abi wandered into the room. Her hair was everywhere and her eyes only half-open as she shuffled past the living room and toward the kitchen. I would've expected the bright TV to catch her attention, but she didn't even look in my direction.

I felt like I should say something so she knew I was there—I didn't want to scare her—but it was possible she was just getting water and going back to bed, and in that case, I didn't want to wake her and make it more difficult for her to go back to sleep.

"Just send the fucking approval so I can sleep," Roman said.

Which brought Abi's attention over to the living room. She looked surprised when her eyes landed on me, then took in the rest of the room.

"Will do," I said.

"But be warned—my inbox is crazy full, so the minute I wake

up in the morning, I'm going to start going all high-speed on their asses. Expect to be bombarded."

"Got it," I said, giving Abi a chin nod from my spot on the couch.

Roman sighed on the other end of the phone. "If we're going to remain a two-man operation on this, and you know that's the only way it works, we need to be *on* twenty-four-seven, Dex."

Abi's eyes narrowed and she was definitely focused on our conversation.

"I am aware," I said, hitting the approve button at the bottom of the email. "Good night, Roman."

"Later."

I disconnected the call and said to Abi, "I hope I didn't wake you."

"No," she said, looking so fucking cute with her oversize pajamas and messy hair that I had an urge to throw her over my shoulder and carry her back to her bed like she was a toddler who'd been woken by a bad dream. "I needed water."

"Ah."

She saw my plate on the coffee table and her eyebrows knit together, like she was surprised I was eating in the living room.

"It was a good sandwich—don't judge," I said.

She shook her head and said around a tiny smile, "I'm just shocked that you're doing something so . . . common. I would've imagined you summoning a chef to serve you a sandwich in the middle of the night before I would've pictured crumbs all over your T-shirt."

I looked down and, yep—crumbs all over the top of my black Celtics T-shirt.

"Maybe I'm not the douchebag you think I am," I said, dusting off my chest.

"Let's not go crazy," she teased. "But I will say I'm impressed by your viewing choice. I love *Psych*."

"Great show," I agreed.

"Were you actually still working a minute ago?" she asked. "In the middle of the night?"

Her tone told me she was either shocked or horrified. I said, "The middle of the night doesn't technically start until after two."

"Is that true?" she asked, and yawned.

"I think so. Go to bed, Abi."

Her eyebrows went down. "You're not the boss of me."

The urge to pick her up kicked in a little stronger. "I know. May I rephrase?"

"Please do," she said, crossing her arms over her chest.

"I didn't mean to interrupt your water break with my phone call. Good night, Abi."

She rolled her eyes and muttered, "Still feels bossy, but g'night."

19

5K

Abi

"Runners, take your marks."

I glanced over at Declan and he grinned, a big wolfish smile that reminded me of the way he'd kissed me last night. *Arrogant, sinful, and seductive as hell.* I didn't care that I'd proclaimed it a fun part of the act—*oh, man, it had definitely been that*—it was impossible for me to get it out of my mind.

Because it'd been exactly what his appearance suggested—and more.

Bossy, controlling, decadent, alpha, exquisite—it'd been all those things. But it'd also been fun and hot and so full of sexual promise that it'd kept me up for hours last night, replaying it.

Thinking things like *If he kisses like that, he probably does a lot of other things really well.*

And then my brain subjected me to an endless montage of those things that I didn't need to be thinking about.

"Get set."

Focus, Abi! I looked at him again, and the dark expression on his face as he gazed at me made me assume that either he was having the same thoughts, or he could see that my brain was turned on yet again by remembering the ferocity of his mouth.

Embarrassing.

"Go!"

The man with the megaphone fired off a starter pistol, and the 5K was under way.

I'd slipped into one of the bathrooms just before we lined up to take a puff of my inhaler off-the-radar, so I felt good as we started running. I knew it was immature and absolutely a sign of my insecurities, but I just couldn't bring myself to do it in front of Declan. He was this beautiful specimen of a strong human, gorgeous and athletic and a captain of industry, and it felt embarrassing for him to see me sucking on my puffer like the nerd that I was.

But it was autumn and that was who I became this time of year: a puffer-sucking nerd.

The changing of the leaves, the ragweed, the pollen—it was the perfect storm that never failed to wreak havoc on my lungs and trigger the shit out of my asthma.

So was it stupid that I was running three miles outside today, especially when I was out of my daily Pulmicort but insurance wouldn't cover it until next week because it was too soon?

Probably.

But I was getting paid a *lot* of money to be Dex's partner for the weekend.

I couldn't just skip the event that he'd called one of the most family-centric of the weekend.

If all of Declan's peers were walking and running with their partners and children, pushing their babies in strollers, it was a fantastic opportunity for us to present a united front.

Certainly I could handle three miles.

I mean, for forty grand, I *had* to handle three miles.

My inhaler was in my sports bra, so I could hit that baby whenever I needed it after Dex pulled ahead. *You'll be fine*, I told myself, even though it didn't help the knot in my stomach. But he *would* pull ahead because not only was he in ridiculous shape, but his legs were so long that there was no way he wouldn't leave me in his dust.

And then I could puff to my lungs' content.

So it was disconcerting that he wasn't pulling away.

We didn't talk while we ran, and we both had on headphones, but he was still *right there* with me after we finished the first mile.

And as expected, I was wheezing and my chest was tight.

I needed to stop.

I *needed* to stop running.

I knew my body, and this wasn't going to get better.

I kept running, trying to figure out how to quit. I could fake an injury; perhaps pretend I tweaked my ankle. That would allow me to stop running for a bit and then just catch up to Declan at the end.

It was what I needed to do, but I kept running, nervously trying to figure out how to pull it off.

Should I make a noise?

Start limping?

How does one behave when they injure an ankle?

The whole time I was thinking through this, I was also panicking because my chest was getting tighter.

Sometimes, if I waited too long to use my inhaler, my chest got so tight that my back started hurting, and that ache was settling in.

I needed to do it *now*.

I did a fake little hop thing, then slowed to a hobble-jog, like I was trying to keep my weight off my right foot while still running.

Dex looked over at me and said, "You okay?"

Dear God, he's not even sweating. Or winded.

What a psycho.

It was hard to talk when I was breathing heavily from the run and also wheezing, but I managed, "My ankle's a little wonky. I'll catch up."

I moved off the cement path and hopped over to the grass, but much to my horror, he followed me.

"No, you go," I said, trying not to sound like I couldn't breathe. "I'm good."

"Sit," he said, grabbing my arm and guiding me down to the curb.

"I'm fine," I said, dropping to a sit while trying to catch my breath. My brain was short-circuiting between the panic that my erratic breathing always caused and the mortification that Declan was trying to figure out my fake injury while listening to me pant like an out-of-shape elephant.

"You're not fine, let me look," he said, reaching out to gingerly touch my ankle. I was rolling my eyes at myself as he did that because it was just so ridiculous—*I* was being so ridiculous.

His gentle fingers slid over my skin, searching, and I wanted to disappear.

What is wrong with me? It was so fucking immature that I had these issues with admitting to my asthma, but it still kept happening.

But even knowing that didn't help.

I'd literally sat inside friends' houses before while their dog's dander tightened my chest because I didn't want to insult them by not hanging out with their dog.

"It looks okay," he said, his eyes on my foot. "It doesn't look swollen."

"That's good," I said, and there must have been something in my voice—probably the intense rattling—because his eyes shot to mine immediately.

"Are you okay?" he asked, a wrinkle between his dark eyebrows.

I nodded, trying to gut the panting and tone it down.

But his eyes narrowed.

"Are you sure?" he asked. "Because it seems like you're having trouble breathing."

I smiled and shook my head. "I just have a little asthma and sometimes it flares up when I run. It's fine."

It wasn't fine.

"No big deal," I added.

"Um, that actually seems like a really big deal," he said, his eyes all over me, like he was trying to see inside my body.

I shook my head and explained, "I just need to take my inhaler and I'll be fine."

"Where is it? Do you need me to go get it?" he asked.

"No, I've got it," I said, my cheeks burning as I reached into my sports bra and pulled it out. "Can you just, um, not look at me for a sec?"

He looked at me in disbelief, like I'd just insulted him, when he said, "Jesus. Don't worry about me, just take the damn medicine."

His frustrated tone made me feel like a fool for getting myself in this situation. I mean, I *was* a fool for getting myself in this situation. I turned and faced the other direction as I took two puffs from my inhaler.

Unfortunately, I'd let it get past the point of resolution, so the relief would take some time.

Sometimes when I took my medicine and stopped what I was doing early enough during an attack, I'd feel completely better and be able to move on right away. But I'd pushed it too hard and had been an idiot for too long, so now it was going to be hours before I was breathing right again.

But I was good at faking it.

"I just need to sit here for a few minutes and then I'll be fine, Declan, but you need to go finish the race."

"Here," he said, grabbing my hand and pulling me to my feet. "Standing up might help you take deeper breaths. Put your hands on top of your head like this."

He set his hands on top of his head and took deep inhalations through his nose. It was ridiculous that he was showing me things I already knew, things I'd forgotten in my panic.

I followed his lead, doing what he said, feeling like a child while also appreciating him. I felt a little emotional as he looked out for me, like I wanted to hug him and bury my face in his strong chest because it felt nice having someone worry about me.

Which was pathetic and misguided.

I knew Declan didn't care about *me*; he was a decent guy and would do this for anyone. In fact, since this was a game we were playing, he was probably just trying to make sure I recovered as quickly as possible so I would be okay for the rest of the day. If I were him, I wouldn't want me wheezing around any of his important colleagues the rest of the day.

But knowing that didn't lessen how good it felt to be looked after.

"Is it getting any better?" he asked.

I nodded. "I think so."

"Do you have any stronger medicine you can take? Like a nebulizer?"

I was shocked that he knew what a nebulizer was. I said, "I have one back at the apartment, but I really *am* starting to feel better."

And I really was, thank God. I was still wheezy—I would be for hours—but I was able to take deep breaths again.

"Please go finish the race, Dex."

I hadn't meant to use his nickname, and he definitely hadn't expected it, either. I saw his jaw flex and I regretted it because I didn't want him to think I was overstepping.

I said, "Go run the rest of the race with everyone else, and I will catch up to you at the finish line."

"I don't want you walking fucking two miles right now, are you kidding?" His voice was quiet but intense, like he was trying to keep it together. "You need to just be still."

"I appreciate this, really I do, Declan," I said, tossing in a fake laugh to lighten the moment. "But I'm an adult—I can handle this. You go, and I'll see you in a little bit."

"*Can* you handle it?" he asked, frustration in his voice. "Because it seems to me that you have asthma and you're not taking care of yourself."

I was embarrassed and also confused by how pissed he seemed. I had no idea what to do, and in spite of everything else, I was worried he wasn't going to pay me if I didn't finish this race.

Maybe *that* was why he was so frustrated.

I wasn't fulfilling my contractual obligations because I let my asthma attack get this bad.

"Here's what we're going to do," Declan said, his green eyes staring into mine. "You are going to climb on my back and I'm going to give you a piggyback ride."

"*What?*"

"No argument and no discussion," he said. "This isn't up for debate. You weigh about five pounds, and it's a beautiful morning for me to take a walk. You can concentrate on deep breathing while going for a ride on your fake boyfriend's back."

Five pounds, my ass, but I'll let that delightful exaggeration slide.

I wanted to argue, but I could see on his face that there was no point.

And I was also getting so tired, the bone-deep exhaustion that always followed an attack settling over me.

I was so mad at myself for being reckless with this again. I had definite *issues* when it came to my inhaler; my therapist's theory was that it was like the physical evidence of my hidden imperfections or something. I wasn't sure if that was exactly true, but I *did* have a lot of childhood memories that included trying to hide from my mother how often I had to use it. She'd made no secret of the fact that it wasn't cheap, dealing with my asthma, and she'd also made it clear that my inability to be the healthy, athletic daughter she'd always wanted was a huge disappointment to her.

So yeah—I was a little neurotic about my puffer.

Logically I knew it was just medicine to help a relatively common health issue, but getting myself to take it in public without feeling like my insecure ten-year-old self was another thing entirely.

"Okay," I said, shaking my head because I just really couldn't believe this was happening. "But, Declan, I am so sorry."

"Don't apologize," he said, and his mouth turned up the tiniest bit, like he was trying to reassure me. "This is seriously no big deal. I'm not competitive about running and I don't feel like it's a loss that I didn't get to prove I'm faster than Gloria in accounting. Now get on."

He turned and crouched down so I could jump on his back. It was absolutely absurd, but I climbed onto his back and wrapped my arms around his shoulders. He started walking, and I started feeling marginally better as I concentrated on taking big, slow breaths.

"So how long have you had asthma?" he asked, not shying away from discussing it. There were sporadic people walking and running around us now, the noncompetitive hanger-backers who didn't care about what time they finished, but they weren't really paying attention to us.

"Pretty much my whole life," I said, not wanting to discuss it but then again, I wasn't going to be seeing Declan anymore after tonight, so what did it matter? "It wasn't as bad when I was little, and it's not this bad all the time. Most of the time I take my daily medicine in the morning and then I don't really think about it. It only becomes an issue when I'm around things I'm allergic to, like cats and dogs, and in the fall."

"So you decided to run in a race in the fall," he said, and the arms that were wrapped around the backs of my knees felt warm and strong. I don't know why I was noticing them, but it suddenly seemed like that was all I could feel.

"You're paying a lot for my services, so the least I could do was give the 5K a shot," I explained, expecting him to appreciate the sacrifice.

The frustration was back in his voice when he asked, "Did you really think I was such an asshole that if you told me you couldn't run in this race, I wouldn't pay you?"

He sounded insulted.

"No, no, it's not that," I said, even though that was exactly what I'd been worried about—minus the *asshole* part. "It's more that I wouldn't *want* you to pay me if I didn't fulfill my obligations."

He made a noise in the back of his throat, and I thought he wasn't going to comment. But after a moment or two, he said, "You know, when you stood in that stupid shirt and threatened to call the cops on *me* for stalking, I never would've believed you'd be so dedicated to our ruse."

"That's because you didn't know me," I said, remembering the way he'd looked down at me in the stinky alley like I was an annoying gnat.

"I suppose that's true," he said, and his voice was a little weird when he added, "And now I do."

"And now you do," I repeated, feeling unsettled by the acknowledgment.

"So what do we have going on the rest of the day?" I blurted, trying to reset the tone of the morning. "I think you said something about a brunch, but I couldn't find anything online about a shareholder breakfast."

"Well that's because this is not for everyone," he said, shifting to boost me higher on his back. "Also, you need to stop talking. Concentrate on those deep breaths and we can talk after you sound better."

I wanted to argue, but then I started coughing, which kind of proved his point.

I wasn't sure if it was to shut me up, but he started explaining the event.

"There is a brunch for a select group of investors at Monk Aviation, a private send-off to the shareholders who are leaving in their private planes. Everyone socializes in the hangar, Warren says a few words, and then everyone boards their planes and the weekend is over."

Private planes.

Even after witnessing the lives of the wealthy all weekend and seeing the next-level ways in which they moved about in the world, I still hadn't imagined private planes.

It was yet another reminder of how different I was than all of them.

When we got closer to the pavilion, people started noticing Declan carrying me toward the finish line on his back.

Of course.

But it was all surprised laughter, as if we were absolutely the most adorable couple. The people standing at the finish line were grinning and clapping, and I wished so badly that their misconceptions were real.

Not that we were an actual couple, but that we were just being adorable and Declan hadn't been forced to rescue me from my own terrible health management.

He carried me over to a picnic table and lowered himself so I could get down, and as I climbed off his back, I saw his parents walking over. I hadn't really seen them at the last couple of events, but he told me they didn't attend everything because they liked visiting friends when they were in town.

I was torn between being happy to see friendly faces converging upon us and feeling guilty because I genuinely liked them and was starting to really hate all the lies.

I also hated the reality that someday I might just pop up in conversation as "that Abi girl" that Declan dated briefly. I don't know why I cared—it probably had to do with the fact that I didn't really have much family in my life or very many friends of my own—but it somehow felt like a loss that I would ultimately be purged from their circle.

"What is all this?" his mom asked with a grin.

"Abi twisted her ankle," Declan said, giving me a surreptitious look.

"Well, thank goodness she had you to help her back," his dad said.

"Oh, I'm pretty sure Abi didn't need me," Declan said, smiling. Only I could sense the sarcasm in his smile and words. "I've never met anyone who takes care of themselves the way she does."

I wanted to roll my eyes.

Yes, I get it, Dex.

After his parents moved away to talk to someone else, Declan dropped to a squat in front of me.

"Listen," he said quietly, giving me serious eye contact that made something inside me go soft again. I wanted to reach out and run a hand over his jawline.

But I didn't.

"After the 5K, usually everybody socializes here at the park for an hour or two. There are mimosas and bagels in the tent, and it's a beautiful morning, so everybody will be sipping and talking about the weekend. I was going to subject you to that, but I think it might be a better idea for me to get you back to the apartment so you can get in a breathing treatment."

"No, I seriously am fine now," I said, meaning it. "I promise I'm not just saying that. As long as you don't force me to run, or bury my face in a dog's fur, I am fine to stay and socialize at your side."

"You sure?" he asked, his eyes moving all over my face like he was looking for the truth.

"I am," I said, and then I couldn't stop my hand from doing it, from touching his cheek. "Thank you."

His eyes were all I could see as we shared a look. I couldn't explain what *exactly* was happening between us as our eyes stayed locked together, but it felt nice and warm and like it *meant* something.

"Shall we go socialize, then, girlfriend of mine?" he asked, his mouth moving into a sweet smile that made my chest feel pinched.

"We shall," I said, standing up.

His big hand wrapped around mine and my eyes felt scratchy

as he pulled me to my feet. I was so soft for him at the moment, weak for the person who'd cared for me, that it was a little dangerous.

This is a job, dipshit—get it together.

I cleared my throat and lifted my chin.

This is my job.

We started walking around the tented areas of the park, Declan chatting with everybody, and I was glad I was there for him.

Because it seemed like the colleagues closest to his age and at his level within the company were all present and they all had spouses.

Most of them had children, actually, and they were happily participating in this adorable family event. Looking at it all spread out in front of me, I totally understood why he was seen as *less than* when it came to the business. All these people appeared to be fully fledged adults with their lives together. Kids in bouncy houses, dogs leashed to strollers, Volvos with car seats; they were *it*.

Declan, on the other hand, was young and attractive. Alone. It made sense that they would look at him and see somebody who might be brilliant at the moment but not necessarily a long-term leadership solution when so much of his life had yet to be carved out.

It was an archaic way of thinking, totally unfair and biased (and an absolute HR violation), but I could see why he'd feel pressured into *this*.

When I left his side to grab an apple from the refreshment table, I watched him.

He looked so comfortable talking to everyone, like there wasn't an awkward bone in the man's body. He was open and friendly as he engaged with spouses and children, and he was the same with his colleagues, though his face got a little more "business intense" when he spoke to them.

Which made me think of his phone call last night.

Were he and Roman . . . *up* to something?

I didn't know anything about what he did in his role, but since Roman didn't work for Hathaway, it seemed weird to me that they'd be on what had sounded like a pretty serious work call at two in the morning.

What was that about?

What did their "investments" entail? I'd overheard Roman say they were a two-man operation, which was absolutely bizarre, but I didn't *need* to understand.

They were two rich dudes, doing rich-dude things, clearly trying to make themselves even richer.

By the time I went to sleep that night he'd be out of my life forever, so it was of no importance to me whether Declan Powell was scheming.

I picked up a Granny Smith, watching him as he conversed with a silver-haired guy and his wife, and a feeling of pride came at me out of nowhere. We were nothing to each other in real life, but he'd still made me a priority when I'd needed him.

Which was something I wasn't used to.

When I joined him, I wrapped both my arms around his right arm and smiled up at him.

"What?" he said, smirking down at me.

"Nothing," I replied, still smiling. "You just look very handsome this morning."

I looked at the silver-haired woman and said, "He's very handsome, don't you think?"

"Oh, very handsome," she agreed, beaming as if we were the most lovely couple she'd ever met. "He looks a lot like his grandmother."

I didn't agree with *that*, because Declan actually smiled sometimes and was capable of kindness.

From what I'd seen so far, Nana Marian was the opposite of that; kind of a wealthy old battle-axe.

I spent the rest of the time at the park being a dreamboat of a girlfriend, pointing out my necklace and gushing about how thoughtful Declan was. I was pouring it on thick, but as far as I could tell, everyone believed it.

And Declan looked like he was absolutely on board.

His hands never strayed far from me, little touches to my elbow or my back, and occasionally pushing back a stray tendril of my hair when it blew across my face; all the sweet, subconscious things that somebody did to their significant other when they cared about them.

It was top-grade acting, and if I didn't constantly remind myself that the man was indeed pretending, I might've been in a little trouble.

When we finally got to the car, I buckled my seat belt and said, "Just try and tell me I wasn't the best girlfriend ever this morning."

His smile disappeared and he looked anything but pleased as he turned the key. "The best girlfriend ever wouldn't put herself in harm's way for a meaningless 5K. The best girlfriend in the world wouldn't let herself get into a health crisis because she was too nice to say anything."

"Are you mad at me?" I asked, shocked by how upset he looked.

He'd seemed concerned when I'd been having my asthma attack, yes, but he hadn't looked anything like this irritated man who was pulling out of the parking lot.

"Yes, I'm mad—are you kidding me?" he said, his voice full of frustration. "That was fucking terrifying, Abi. Why would you do that to yourself? I don't even understand."

"I don't know," I mumbled, kind of shrugging before turning to look out my window. "I'm sorry."

He didn't talk as he drove, and I was so conflicted I wouldn't have known what to say if he *did* want to talk. Because it was natural for someone—anyone—to worry about someone having a health crisis.

He was simply being a decent human being.

But something about Declan's worry, and the way he'd taken care of me, felt personal.

And it was disturbing how much I liked it.

20

DOWNTIME

Declan

I had no idea why I was so pissed off.

Abi Mariano was not my problem, so her health was not my concern.

It was stupid that I felt this mad.

But when I'd heard the wheeze of her trying—and failing—to get air in her lungs, it had scared the shit out of me. And even as she stood there, telling me she was fine, she'd looked scared as hell.

Like she wasn't sure she believed that she *was* okay.

I mean, she was kind of my employee right now, so surely that was what this was about. My annoyance that someone, while on my watch, would put themselves in jeopardy. That was the only explanation, right?

But it'd felt eerily familiar, dealing with her asthma. My grandpa used to pull that shit all the time with his COPD. He hadn't wanted to be a bother, or he didn't want to hold up what everyone else was doing, so he'd try to just power through no matter how uncomfortable it made him, which usually landed him in the hospital.

I'd watched him go from being the most active person I'd ever met to a man who struggled to walk across a room without needing to stop for air.

Obviously, Abi was young and active and healthy, so she wasn't at all like my grandfather.

But it'd felt too familiar and I hadn't liked it.

When we got back to the apartment, I wasn't sure how to behave around her. On the one hand, I felt like I needed to reassure her that I wasn't an asshole, even though I'd basically yelled at her. I knew I should explain myself and apologize.

But on the other hand, I wasn't ready to talk because I couldn't stop seeing the fear in her eyes when she hadn't been able to catch her breath.

Fuck.

"So what time does your flight leave?" she asked, and it was obvious that she was just tossing out small talk for the sake of killing the awkwardness. "Or is it whenever you want? I don't actually know how private planes work."

"I don't have a plane," I said, dropping my keys onto the counter. "I attend the hangar event, but I'm flying out of the main terminal."

"Wow, like a commoner?" she asked, slipping out of her running shoes.

"Yes, like a commoner," I said, fully aware that Abi was mocking me and pretty much everyone around me.

Which was fair.

We had too much.

I was very aware of my privilege—I always had been—but I felt guiltier than usual about it when I was around her.

"I think it's more fun to have to get there two hours early and hang out with screaming children and outlet hogs than quietly fly in peace, don't you?" I slid off my shoes and went into the kitchen, in desperate need of coffee.

"I wouldn't know," she said, shrugging. "I haven't been on a plane since I was a little kid."

"Seriously?" I couldn't imagine that. Half of my life was spent traveling, so it was hard to wrap my brain around not hopping on a flight at least once a year.

"Yeah, when I was little we went on a couple family vacations," she said, leaning on the island. "But after my dad died we didn't really do that anymore."

"And you and your friends never went on a wild spring break?" I asked, wondering what her friends were like.

Actually, I was really curious what her daily life looked like.

She told me a little at dinner, but it'd only made me more interested because it hadn't been what I'd expected. Initially, I thought she was just a girl who worked at a grocery store and cleaned apartments. Then, after I looked her up, I assumed she was someone who worked in finance and had a part-time job on the side.

But the fact that she wanted to be a writing professor, on top of all that, made her fascinating to me. I wanted to know what she wrote and what her slumlord jackass–owned apartment looked like.

Did she work extra jobs because she struggled for money, or

did she work extra jobs because she had financial goals and things she was saving for?

"No wild spring breaks for me," she said with a shrug, not giving me any additional information.

We each went to our rooms to shower and change after that. I didn't hear a nebulizer turn on, so I did what I knew she'd hate, and I texted her.

SHOULDN'T YOU BE DOING A BREATHING TREATMENT WHILE WE'RE HOME?

She instantly replied: I'm fine, Dad

I sighed. I knew it wasn't my responsibility, and I didn't want to be a control freak, but it'd only been a couple hours since she'd almost needed to take an ambulance to the hospital (even though she'd never admit it'd been that serious).

I texted: I KNOW YOU'RE FINE, BUT WOULDN'T IT BE A GOOD IDEA WHILE WE HAVE DOWNTIME, JUST TO MAKE SURE YOU'VE COMPLETELY RECOVERED?

I guess I'd expected a smart-ass response, because I was surprised to see her simple text: Thank you.

And a few minutes later—*thank you, Jesus*—I heard the sound of a nebulizer turn on.

I threw some things into a travel bag after my shower, even though I wouldn't need them. I spent a lot of time in Manhattan, so my apartment in SoHo was fully stocked with everything I could possibly need. I changed into jeans—the brunch was always casual since everyone was preparing to leave—and then I was ready.

But I didn't feel casual or remotely relaxed, mostly because I was leaving and something about leaving *her* made me feel unsettled. This was just a game and we barely knew each other, but it felt strange that it was ending when we'd only just begun.

When I walked into the kitchen, she was sitting at the island, writing in her notebook. Now that I knew she was a fiction writer, I was even more intrigued to know what she was writing. What ideas were alive in her mind, vivid enough for her to be inspired to put them down on paper?

And Edward had done a hell of a job, because somehow she looked like her future. Abi *looked* like an English professor. She was wearing jeans and a navy blazer, with a white T-shirt underneath and a pair of tortoise-shell glasses (that had slid almost all the way down on her nose as she wrote). Her hair was pulled back in a ponytail with a navy clip holding it together.

I was taken aback by how natural she looked that way. If I didn't know better, I would assume this was the everyday version of Abi Mariano.

"What are you working on, professor?" I asked, and my heart kind of stuttered when she looked up at me and smiled.

Because she was so fucking pretty.

But it didn't escape my notice that she quickly closed the notebook and a guarded look crossed her face.

"Just random thoughts that will probably equate to nothing," she said, shrugging and waving a hand to brush it off. "I do this all the time, constantly jotting things down so I don't lose the information even though I know I'll probably never use it."

"Makes sense," I said, even more curious to know what she'd been working on. "Is this for class this week?"

A crinkle formed in between her eyebrows and I could tell she'd temporarily forgotten that she shared a little bit of her actual life with me last night.

And for some reason, I didn't like the idea of her regretting it. I *liked* that she'd felt like sharing, even though I knew it essentially didn't matter since we'd be going our separate ways soon.

"Not specifically," she said. "It's the beginning of the semester, so I'm prepping, trying to figure out which story ideas will go into my capstone project. I'll have to meet with my advisor soon for approval, so I need to get it all mapped out."

"I see," I said, disappointed that I'd never know more than that. There was something about the idea of her brain running wild on paper, creating stories, that I found mildly intoxicating. Made me want to sit at her feet and listen to her talk for hours.

Shit—what the hell is wrong with me?

Obviously it'd been a long weekend and I was losing perspective when thoughts like *that* popped into my head. It was good that we were wrapping up, and that in a few hours I'd be on my way to New York.

The sooner this weekend of pretend was over, the better for my brain.

"Are you almost ready to go?" I asked. "You look nice, by the way."

"Thank you," she said, standing and looking down at herself. "I've never really been a blazer sort of person, but I feel like Edward is good at knowing what sort of person I *should* be."

"He's the best," I agreed. "But I wouldn't second-guess the fact that you know better than anyone who you are."

Her eyebrows crinkled together even harder at that, like she didn't understand my words, which was fair because I didn't, either. It hadn't even been forty-eight hours since we'd met, and now I was trying to convince her of her style or outlook on life.

I wasn't sure what was going on with me.

Maybe I was coming down with something.

"I'm ready," she said. "Let me just put this notebook in the bedroom."

She walked into the other room, gesturing to my bag as she passed, saying, "Don't you have a suitcase?"

It was strange to see her go into my bedroom like she belonged there. "No," I said. "I live in New York, too, so I have everything I need in my apartment."

"I can't believe you have a place in New York," she said—squealed, actually—as she came back in the room, a look of childlike wonder on her face. "I've always wanted to go there."

Something about the excitement in her voice made me feel . . . *guilty* again. Or just hyperaware of how lucky I was. Because to me it was no big deal. It was just an apartment, and New York was just another busy city.

But to her, it was somewhere she'd always wanted to go but had never been.

Abi hadn't been able to afford a weeklong stay at a hotel for a simple apartment building issue, yet I had multiple residences.

So, yes—here she is again, reminding me of my privilege.

"Do we have time to get coffee on the way?" she asked, grabbing her purse off the counter. "I know we're going to a brunch where they'll likely have some, but I am a person who thoroughly enjoys a Frappuccino for breakfast on the weekends every once in a while."

"Only every once in a while?" I picked up my keys, not unaware of the way they'd been sitting beside her bag like we were an actual couple who lived there together. "You mean you're not someone who gets it every weekend?"

"Are you kidding me?" she said, looking at me like I'd lost my mind. "It's like seven bucks a drink. I am not on a Frapp-every-weekend budget, but thank you for thinking that I might be."

She laughed and patted me on the shoulder as she walked past me, leaving a waft of something floral but vanilla that I was worried would be my new favorite scent.

21

TAKING OFF

Abi

It's impossible to believe people actually live this way.

I looked around the luxury hangar and had a hard time believing *this* was in any way, shape, or form related to the airplane travel I remembered. While normal people stood in security lines with donut-shaped pillows strapped around their necks and sat in crowded terminals, the privileged hung out *here*?

Unbelievable.

The Monk Aviation hangar was ridiculously cool. It had tall ceilings, shiny floors, and a wide-open warehouse feel that was the polar opposite of modern air travel spaces. The furnishings were all next level, sleek and modern and actually comfortable, and I swear to God there wasn't a speck of dust or piece of trash anywhere in this place.

Tables had been brought in for the brunch—tables that were *covered* in food. A huge buffet was laid out, but not the kind of buffet I was familiar with in my life. There were no sneeze guards dangling down in front of aluminum trays filled with precooked scrambled eggs and questionable bacon.

No, this was a carefully curated collection of exquisite breakfast foods.

A crepe station (manned by a chef, of course), gorgeous pastries heaped upon gleaming silver trays, a full-service bar, and a man in a big white hat carving prime rib—this was the shit.

And the second we walked in, we were approached by many familiar faces.

There was Warren, and Dex's parents, and I could see all his fellow vice presidents wandering around, socializing with the elite shareholders who all looked like they were on golf vacations and preparing to return home to their mansions of choice.

"I think we should get some prime rib before we do anything else," I said, sliding my arm through Declan's and pointing toward the buffet. "All of your people are going to keep you busy, so you deserve some delicious meat first, don't you think?"

"So you're hungry?" he asked, glancing down at me with a smirk on his mouth, that mouth that was *such* a distraction now that I knew what it was capable of.

"No, I'm a good girlfriend and I think you need to eat. I mean, that's kind of my love language, making sure that my man is well-fed."

"Really?" He narrowed his eyes and looked at me like he wanted to figure me out, like he was trying to see more. *I loved that look.* It was intimate and made it feel like he actually appreciated the real me. "That doesn't seem like it would be your love language."

"Sure it is," I replied, lowering my voice. "I think I know how to make three dishes, maybe even four, so I'm going to make some man really lucky someday."

"Name the three dishes," he said, grinning.

"Okay, maybe two," I said, thinking through the things that I made when I felt like preparing something not from my freezer. "I make killer spaghetti and meatballs, I slay goulash, and I also make a really great pepperoni casserole."

"So you only make pasta," he said around a laugh, and I was a big fan of the way his eyes got squinty when he genuinely smiled.

"Yeah, I only make pasta," I agreed. "Although I also make a really good Crock-Pot beef roast, too."

"Isn't that just dropping meat into a pot and hitting the power button?"

"I drop it really *well*, though."

"Fine," he said, his smile simmering down to just the slightest curve. "Let's go get my girl some meat."

We were just playing, I knew, but there was something about this indulgent side of him, when he gave me a look that meant he was going along with what I wanted, that was unbelievably charming. It was so out of character for the all-business, vice presidential version of Declan that it almost skewed romantic.

He was a control freak boss who ruled everything, so the times that I wore the pants felt really fucking delightful.

We went over to the buffet, and I entertained myself by putting food on his plate that I knew he didn't want. It felt very girl-friendy to say things like "Oh you need to try the crepes," even though I'd already seen him eat three whole-wheat bagels after the 5K so I knew he couldn't be very hungry.

But I liked the way it made his lips quirk, like he was trying not to laugh every time I plopped something unwanted on his plate.

"I should make you eat everything you're loading up," he said quietly, out of the corner of his mouth, as we walked over to a tall table.

"But it would look very unladylike for me to eat that much," I said sarcastically. "Although you're probably watching your figure and won't eat anything I put on your plate, anyway."

"Oh, I think *you're* the one who's been watching my figure," he teased.

"No, I'm not," I squealed, cringing at how much I sounded like a middle schooler. "I walked into your closet and you were half-naked; I had no choice but to look at your chest."

"Honey, I didn't say anything about that," he said quietly, a sexy smirk on his mouth. "I was just joking, but apparently your brain is still on my chest in the closet yesterday."

I didn't know what to say to that, so I proceeded to cut into my prime rib and stuff my mouth, which made him laugh.

After eating we made the rounds, and it was actually pretty nice. I'd started to come around to a lot of Declan's co-workers; I still thought they were pretentious and privileged, but I appreciated the kindness they showed me.

It was scary how much I felt like Daphne in the story I'd just started drafting. I was getting sucked into these people and their lives surprisingly quickly, my disdain morphing into something... warmer and less judgy.

I still rolled my eyes inwardly at the designer shoes and expensive handbags, but I couldn't deny that I enjoyed the friendliness that came from their owners.

Throughout the course of the brunch, there was a steady stream of departures. There was a bag-check counter by the doors, and with a simple wave to the attendant, travelers had their luggage whisked away before they disappeared out the door.

Even as I watched the crowd gradually diminish, for some reason I wasn't prepared for it to be Dex's turn.

"Hey," he said, leaning down to speak into my ear. "It's about time for me to go catch my flight."

I looked to his left and realized the shuttle driver was standing behind him, waiting to take him to the main terminal.

The plan was for me to drive his car back to his apartment, which I was so geeked out about doing, and a shuttle driver was going to take him over to the commercial terminal at Eppley.

"You have to go already?" I said, absolutely not acting. I'd been having a great time with him and found that I didn't want him to leave. It was nothing big, no emotional thing to overthink, but I liked him.

"I do," he said, looking at me with something in his eyes that kind of felt like regret.

And I don't know if it was a boldness born from pretending all day, or the fact that I felt so much closer to him since he'd taken care of me earlier, but I knew exactly what I was going to do.

"Well, let me walk you out to the shuttle," I said, giving him a look.

He must've understood, because he gave me a wink. "Let's go."

I held his hand and walked with him, which was kind of ridiculous when it was literally parked on the other side of the big glass windows, but I didn't care.

As soon as we were outside and next to the black SUV, I threw my arms around him as if he was actually my boyfriend and he was leaving me to go on a trip. He hugged me back, that big body wrapped around me as his woodsy scent found my nose, and I said, "Safe travels."

I set my hands on his cheeks and pulled his mouth down to mine, giving him the kind of kiss that I knew would be appreciated by any onlookers who might be watching from inside the terminal.

A simple press of our mouths together.

Once again, I was attempting a normal couple's kiss.

And once again, I failed.

Because I stopped thinking about kisses and terminals and actual words the second he started kissing me back.

Damn, the way that man kissed.

His mouth opened over mine and his arms tightened around my body and he kissed me like he didn't want to leave me. I felt it in the backs of my knees when his tongue stroked over mine, I felt it in the center of my body when his teeth dragged over my bottom lip.

And I felt it *everywhere* when he made a noise in the back of his throat that told me he wished we were alone.

It was the throat clearing of the shuttle driver that brought me back, that made me remember who I was, where we were, and who I was with.

Declan pulled back and looked down at me, his eyes hot.

"You make it really hard to leave, Abi Green," he said with a little smirk.

"You make it really hard to let you go, Declan Powell," I said back, reaching up to wipe my lipstick off his lips. "Text me when you get there so I know you landed safely."

"You know no one is out here but us, right?" he asked, eyebrows raised.

I pressed my lips together and admitted, "I know, but still text me when you get there so I know you made it, okay?"

He swallowed and gave a nod. "I will."

Then he turned and got into the shuttle.

Goodbye, Declan.

I stood there, wondering what the hell was wrong with me that I knew I was going to miss him. Instead of going back inside the fancy hangar and making small talk and saying goodbye to people I would never see again, I just went straight to Declan's car on the other side of the building.

It didn't make sense, the way I felt so emotional, but I wasn't going to overthink it. The bottom line was that I was still getting paid a fortune, and now I got to drive a fancy car to the fancy apartment where I was staying till Friday.

Any emotion about Declan's leaving was just silly and I needed to stop thinking about him and remember who I was and what the reality of our situation was.

But that was pretty impossible when, as soon as I got back to the apartment, I immediately got a text from him.

Dex: I'm bored. It's ridiculous to get here 2 hours early when you have TSA pre-check. I got through security in 2 minutes and now I have 2 hours to kill.

I sat down on his sofa and replied: Aren't you going to get drunk at the bar like all the other businessmen do?

Dex: I have no interest in drinking by myself at an airport. It seems too depressing.

I was about to text back with a joke but stopped mid-tap. We were done and I needed to cut this off.

So I tried; really, I did. I texted: I know we both had ulterior motives, but I had a surprisingly good time this weekend. Thank you for changing.

Dex: What do you mean "changing"?

I grinned and sent: You were kind of a dick the day I met you, but you've grown over the weekend. You have moments of delightfulness, actually.

Dex: I have never been described as delightful before.

I texted: I'm sure that's true but I had a delightful time with you at the hangar.

Dex: I had an OK time ;)

I sent: I'm pretty sure it's like Munchausen syndrome or something, the way I've grown to tolerate you after hating you so much.

Dex: (a) You never hated me, and (b) isn't Munchausen's when mothers poison their own children because they want medical attention?

I snorted because he was right. I texted: I meant the thing where hostages start to like their captors.

Dex: I knew that's what you meant. Btw I left your check on the desk in the bedroom.

I walked into the bedroom and wanted to vomit when I saw the check sitting there, on top of the desk across from the bed. The symbolism of that made me feel like trash. Now that I thought he was a decent person, the fact that he was paying me a small fortune for basically nothing felt super ick.

Like I was extorting him or something.

I'd realized at the hangar that I had a decision to make about that. I desperately wanted my student loans to be paid off, to be able to start fresh on my future without that hanging over my head, but I hadn't *earned* forty thousand dollars. I mean, I had barely earned *forty* dollars, if I was being honest.

I'd slept in a fancy apartment and went to fancy outings wearing fancy clothing that I would never be able to afford in real life; how was that something I thought I could charge someone for?

I hadn't come up with my definitive answer yet, but I was beginning to think I wasn't going to cash that check.

I walked out of the bedroom and texted: That reminds me— I'll leave your necklace on the kitchen counter when I head out on Friday.

Dex: Don't. It's yours.

I groaned and went into the kitchen, raising a hand to touch the chocolate diamonds that hadn't left my neck since he'd bought me the necklace. How was I supposed to keep my wits about me when the man was giving me jewels? I could *not* keep that gorgeous necklace that he'd so charmingly said reminded him of my freckles, which was why I'd already taken about a hundred pictures of it.

I texted: It most definitely is NOT mine. I saw the price tag. It was a great idea—Warren and the gang ate it up—but there's no reason you should be stuck for that money.

Dex: I'm not going to return it so you might as well keep it.

The man was an absolute ghoul about money. A fifteen-thousand-dollar necklace that he was going to let sit in a drawer because he didn't want to return it?

I texted: Save it and give it to someone else.

Dex: I'm not going to do that. It was fun, and if you like it you should have it and wear it.

I sighed and opened the fridge. Texted: You really don't care about money at all, do you?

Instead of texting, my phone started ringing. It was him, of course.

When I answered, he said, "I don't care about stuff."

Stuff. He considered a fifteen-thousand-dollar necklace "stuff."

I didn't want to get into it, so I said, "This is random, but do you mind if I use your kitchen implements? I'll buy my own groceries, but I would really love to bake in your fabulous kitchen one more time before I go."

"I thought you said you only know three recipes," he said.

"That's cooking." I leaned down to peer into the back of the fridge. "Baking is another thing entirely."

"Of course," he said, sounding amused. "Yeah, uh, feel free to use whatever you want and if I have the things you need, don't go buy groceries."

I stood back up straight. "Why are you being so nice? Are you so happy this is over that you're kissing my ass in celebration?"

"I suppose that's part of it," he said. "And now that I sort of know you, I guess you feel a little less like a threat."

"Did you see me as a threat before?" Was I threatening? I kind of liked that thought. "I don't know that anybody has ever called me that before."

"It was your attitude. I wasn't scared of you causing me bodily harm, but I was a little terrified about what you might do to my life and reputation."

I shut the fridge and wandered over to the pantry. "Is this the part where you're going to admit that I was fantastic?"

"This is the part where I'm admitting you didn't destroy everything."

"I guess I'll take it," I said, stepping into what was basically another room. His pantry was stocked from floor to ceiling with dry goods and ingredients, and I'd never be over it.

"So what are you doing with the rest of your day?" he asked, and I thought how weird it was that he was chatting with me on the phone like a friend. Like, what *was* that? And even weirder was that it felt so . . . comfortable.

Was Declan my friend now?

"I want to get some ideas outlined before class tomorrow, and I have to work at Benny's tomorrow morning and clean a unit in your building down on five tomorrow night."

"Is it weird that I kind of forgot you do that?" he asked.

"Yeah, it is weird," I replied. "What's weirder will be the first time I have to clean *this* place now that I know you."

"I might have to become a slob," he said teasingly, "just to ruin your life."

"That sounds on-brand with who I thought you were before." I dropped to a squat and noticed he had every single flavor of Doritos, all lined up on a shelf.

"I should probably take advantage of this time before I board and get some work done," he said. "My inbox is overflowing."

Was it overflowing with Hathaway work or with Roman

work, which was still a giant question mark? My curiosity couldn't take it anymore so I decided to throw out, "So what kind of stuff do you and Roman do, investment-wise?"

There was a brief pause before he answered.

"Why do you want to know?" he asked.

What a . . . weird way to not answer my question.

"I don't. I mean, I'm just curious," I explained. "Because it's unique to see two best friends working on investments together in their spare time."

And by "unique," I mean suspicious.

"It's kind of . . . complicated," he said, his tone warning me to butt out.

"And it has nothing to do with Hathaway, you said?" I asked.

"What are you trying to ask me, Mariano?" he said, sounding . . . defensive? Exasperated, maybe. "Spit it out."

"Okay," I said, unsure why it felt important for me to know. "Tell me *exactly* what kind of work you do with Roman, even if it's too complicated and boring for me to understand."

"No." I heard him clear his throat before he said, "I can't. It's nothing illegal or immoral, but it's confidential."

"I see," I said, wondering what that could even mean in terms of investments.

"I'd tell you if I could," he said, "but it's just one of those business things."

Like drug-running and embezzlement?

As soon as I had that thought I shut it down, because he'd given me no reason not to trust him. I might not understand what he was up to, but I didn't have to.

"So, do you fly first class?" I asked, changing the subject while trying to picture him in an airplane.

"I do today," he said.

"You don't always?"

"Okay, I do most of the time," he admitted, which made me laugh because *of course* he did. If he didn't mind buying an expensive necklace and then throwing it away, the man would *not* care about saving money on airfare.

"Do they really give you hot towels?" I wondered aloud.

"Not on short flights, and not on smaller airplanes, but more often than not, yes, there are hot towels."

"What do you do with them?" I asked, feeling yet again like the rest of the adults in the world had received a life manual that I'd somehow missed out on. "I mean, I know the obvious answer is wipe down your face, but it just seems like such an odd thing to offer."

"I guess it is, now that you mention it," he said, sounding amused, like he'd never thought about it before.

"Okay, you go do your work," I said, "and I'm going to see if you have enough in your kitchen for me to make chocolate chip cookies."

"My fingers are crossed for you," he said dryly.

"Sure they are."

"Talk to you later," he said.

Before he could hang up I said, "Text me when you land, just so I know you didn't crash."

"Are you concerned about me, Mariano?"

I was speechless for a second, unsure why I blurted that out and unsure why his voice sounded like *that*, like he was smiling and genuinely curious.

"Yes," I said, my cheeks warm even though no one was here for me to even be embarrassed in front of. "Only because if you die, I'll probably get kicked out of this place before Friday."

"I already wrote it into my will that way. You'll definitely be dragged away."

"Goodbye, Declan," I said, rolling my eyes.

This time, before I hung up, I heard his quiet voice. "I'll text you."

I smiled to myself, biting my lower lip. "Good."

After the call ended, I felt a sense of lightness as I immersed myself in a game of hide-and-seek with the ingredients in his massive pantry.

Declan didn't have any chocolate chips, but he had enough overripe bananas for me to make six loaves of my grandma's banana bread. He also had a massive industrial mixer, which was something I'd never used before, so I *really* enjoyed whipping up that batch of yumminess.

But after I cleaned the kitchen and put away the bread, I felt a little lost.

I texted Lauren, but she didn't respond. Which wasn't a surprise. She was my very best friend—my only friend aside from co-workers, if I was being honest—but she didn't have much time for me anymore. She was in love, had found her soulmate, and now he took most of her time.

Which was how it was supposed to be.

She'd found the perfect person for her and they were constantly together.

But it left me feeling lost a lot of the time.

I plopped down on the sofa and tried to see if I could find an episode of *Psych*, because I was too tired to write at the moment and I wasn't in the mood for Stephen King.

But sitting there, looking for something on the TV, kind of illuminated just how stagnant my life was.

Because here I was, in a stunning multimillion-dollar apartment, and I literally had no one to call and freak out about it to. No one but my mom, who arguably didn't really care where I was or what I was doing if it didn't affect her. Truth be told, I kind of wanted to order a pizza just so I could show the *driver* that I was doing something exciting.

But I didn't have money to waste on pizza.

God, I was pathetic.

Loneliness was a stupid word, a word that conjured images of moonfaced women crying because they didn't think anyone loved them, and I wasn't that.

I wasn't *lonely*.

It was more that I was . . . invisible. Everyone else in the world seemed to have their full and busy lives, and my tiny little existence happened outside their jurisdiction. I exchanged conversation with customers and co-workers, and they seemed to like me, but I was alone in my personal life.

And sometimes it felt like I'd been that way for a very long time.

I was fine with being by myself—good with it, actually—but I hated when the realization that no one in the world knew where I was or cared grabbed onto me at random moments.

"Screw this," I muttered, and turned off the TV.

It didn't matter how tired or down I was, I was going to make the most of this staycation. I grabbed my laptop and my notebook and went out on the balcony, forcing myself to write while I still had an inspiring view.

And after a minute, everything else melted away.

Daphne grabbed my attention and it was hers.

I started writing, capturing the way Daphne would see custom cars and luxury airplanes, and it was like the words were pouring out of me. My fingers couldn't type fast enough. Daphne was so easy to write because she was—in a way—me, or at least her observations belonged to someone with similar experiences to my own.

And there were so many things about Declan and his life that, at a surface level, functioned as amazing characterization. A millionaire who treated cars and jewelry as if they were disposable because he had so much money it'd lost all meaning. A man who was used to people behaving as if he were royalty. There was a lot more to Declan than that in real life, but the same couldn't be said for Daphne's love interest, Connor.

Yes, I am using Dexxie's middle name, I thought with a grin. He would hate that.

I sat out there for hours, a million miles away with Connor and Daphne and her fish-out-of-water experiences, and only came in when I wanted to add a few reminders to my notebook and realized I didn't have a pencil.

I popped into Dex's office—I knew he had a drawerful of freshly sharpened pencils from all the times I'd cleaned that room—but as I was opening the drawer, my eyes spotted a piece of paper on top of the desk.

I *never* snooped, but when my eyes happened to see it was a printed email message from Roman to Dex, I couldn't stop myself.

From: Roman Halder <rhalder@RWDR.com>
Date: September 29 at 4:53 PM
Subject: Invest Ops 9/29
To: Declan Powell <dpowell@RWDR.com>

Dex-
Strongly recommend the first three, your call on the 4th
      -REZAK, JONATHAN {917055} 125K
      -JOHNSON, CAMILLE {765003} 76K
      -KPH CONSULTING {891077} 2 MILLION
      -HANNIFORD, PETER {122739} 325K

I don't know what came over me, but I got out my phone and took a picture. Dex said his work with Roman was confidential, and I knew in my gut that he wasn't doing something criminal, but if I was going to be alone and bored all night, what would the harm be in some Google investigating?

I went back to my makeshift outdoor office, but it was getting a little chilly so I moved inside. As soon as I sat at the dining room table with my laptop, I opened the search window, too engaged with the idea of sleuthing to get back to work immediately.

I googled RWDR, but found nothing. A bunch of random things, in random places, that were obviously not connected to my fake boyfriend and his pal. I googled the names on the list but couldn't find information that meant anything at all. I found an RWD Consulting in South Dakota, but it looked like an IT firm that was super . . . unimpressive.

They probably made their own website using Canva, and it looked like they had three Midwestern-looking employees.

It was *not* the kind of business that millionaires were looking to invest in—or anyone, honestly—so either it was the wrong firm, or this made even less sense.

I was getting bored with my search when my phone buzzed. I jumped, feeling like I had gotten caught.

I picked it up off the table and was disappointed to see it was Lauren and not Dex.

Which was dumb; why would he even be calling me?

"Hello?" I said, closing out my search engine and opening my Word doc.

"I cannot believe the pics you sent!" she squealed. "I am so jealous that you are just hanging out like a millionaire."

"It's pretty great," I said, leaning back in the chair, looking around the room.

Tall ceilings, big windows, recessed lighting—the place was a dream.

"So what are you doing? I put a tracker on Mr. Powell's car, by the way. It looks like it's parked in a garage downtown."

I laughed in spite of myself. What would Declan do if he knew? He'd probably be pissed, but I could honestly say I knew nothing about it because I really didn't.

I didn't even know what a "tracker" was. I was assuming it was the industrial version of an AirTag, but what was I, a spy? "It's down in the garage beneath me."

"Oh, I know," she said, and I could hear how proud of herself she was. "And my initial check of your boyfriend-for-the-weekend came back clean, by the way."

"Told you," I said. "Although . . ."

"Although what?" She instantly sounded intrigued. "Did you find something, Ab?"

"No, nothing like that," I said, wondering if I should tell her. It technically wasn't breaking confidentiality when I didn't know anything, and Lauren was literally a vault. If you asked her to keep something quiet, she'd take it to the grave.

"Okay here's the thing: this is nothing I'm worried about; this is something I'm *nosy* about. I totally trust Declan, but . . . I just really want to know what one of his businesses is and he says it's confidential."

"He is a murderer," she said knowingly.

"Oh, my God, he is not!" I laughed, getting up to pace while I talked to her. I wasn't good at sitting when I was talking on the phone.

I told her exactly what I knew, and then I told her about the email that I found.

"You should send me the screenshot," she said. "I won't *do* anything, but I'm better at investigating than you are. Let me sleuth for you."

I looked down at my toes, which were still perfectly painted—*thank you, Kat*—and second-guessed telling her. He'd told me it was confidential; should I really be sharing his information?

"No," I said, walking into the kitchen. "I shouldn't have read it, much less taken a picture. I'm already done with my time playing fake girlfriend, so what he does with his life is none of my business."

"But aren't you curious?" she prodded. "Wouldn't it be fun to know? To have a secret on the millionaire that you once spent a weekend with? Ten years from now, when you see him in the paper with his second wife and third yacht, won't it be fun to feel like you know more than her?"

Why did I hate everything she'd just said? "I doubt he'll ever have one wife, much less two. He works twenty-four-seven."

"Just let me peek; I'm sure I won't find anything, by the way. If Declan Powell says it's confidential, I'm positive it can't be found by some rando cool chick on the internet."

"Okay, I'm sending it," I said with a groan. "But please delete it the second you're done looking."

"It'll be scrubbed by midnight," she said. "I promise."

She shifted gears then, telling me about her new martial arts obsession, and by the time we hung up, my stomach was grumbling. I hadn't eaten since brunch, so regardless of what time it was, I needed food.

I went into the kitchen, now fully aware of the location of virtually everything in Dex's cabinets, and it was a little mind-boggling, the way it suddenly felt like I was staying at a friend's house instead of a stranger's apartment.

As I pulled some angel hair pasta from the pantry, I wondered if he would actually text me when he landed. He could easily forget, or just not care to.

Of course, that begged the question: Was our last conversation the final one we'd have before this whole thing ended, or could it be the start of something different?

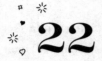

FIRST CLASS

Declan

"Are you seriously FaceTiming me?" she asked as she answered my call.

Abi's face popped up on my phone screen and she appeared very different from the young professor she'd looked like when I left her. Her hair was in a braid, she appeared to have some sort of powder—I had to assume flour—on her glasses, and she was wearing a neon-orange T-shirt that read *YOUR MO GOES TO COLEGE*. She asked, "Are you even allowed to use your phone on a plane?"

"First class has boarded but everyone else is still getting on so I've got a few more minutes."

"And you were dying to see me? I'm trying to make noodles here, Powell."

She set the phone down so I could now see that she was standing in front of my stove.

"Well, you seemed very interested in first class," I said, watching her use a table fork to stir the pasta. "So I thought I'd give you a little tour, starting with the wet towel."

"You have one?" She appeared to be half listening while she watched her noodles, which for some reason fascinated me. There was something about seeing her move about in her world—in my apartment—that I found mesmerizing.

I wanted to know more, to sit and watch what happened next.

"This is the hot towel," I said, holding it up. "And you just put it on your face like this."

I covered my face for a few seconds, then removed the towel.

"But, like, wouldn't that just smear your makeup?" she asked.

"Do I look like I wear makeup?" I replied.

"Well, no, but then that's a sexist benefit because no women could use the hot towel without ruining their face."

"*That's* sexist, assuming all women are wearing makeup when they travel."

She scowled. "You're not allowed to call me sexist when you're a man."

"Is that right?" I asked, and her nose crinkled when she smiled into the camera.

"Shut up and show me the rest," she said, shaking her head.

I turned the phone around and showed her the business class seat and how it all worked. I was so used to traveling all the time that it was inconceivable to me that there were people unfamiliar with planes.

"So you can literally lie down with a blankie and go night-night until you land in New York?" she asked incredulously.

"Well, I could, but I'm not tired," I said.

"If *I* was given a comfy bed on a plane I would absolutely sleep."

"I can see that about you," I said, wondering if she knew just how filthy her glasses were. "I really should go now, but I just thought you'd want to see it."

"That was very thoughtful of you," she said, moving her face a little closer to the phone. "Seriously. I can't believe you called just so I could see. That's really nice."

"I was bored," I lied.

"Well, thank you," she said with a grin. "You just keep surprising me with the fact that you aren't always a jackass."

"Oh, I am. I just have moments of decency."

"Well, I'm thrilled to have witnessed one of those moments."

I didn't mean to, but I thought about Abi on the entire flight to New York.

And I came to the unexpected conclusion that when I *was* ready to actually jump into dating, I might want to consider looking outside my existing social circles. Abi was so smart and real and funny, so different from the last few people I'd gone out with, and the thing I liked most about her was that she was fun.

Fun.

I hadn't had *fun* with anybody in a very long time.

After I got into the SUV that would take me to my condo, I sent her a text that simply said: landed.

I was unsure if she'd respond because we were officially done with our collaboration, but she replied with: You're probably busy working on your phone or computer, but if not and you're bored, you should FaceTime me.

I texted: Miss me already?

Abi: You wish. I just want you to turn the camera around
so I can live in New York City vicariously through you.

I didn't respond but just hit the FaceTime button.

"Yay," she said when she answered, and the way she grinned
at me made it impossible for me to not smile, too. She'd obviously
just taken a shower, because her hair was damp and wavy and she
was wearing those stupid pajamas with her face on them again.
"You have no idea how excited I am."

"Well, I live to excite you," I said, feeling a little safer about
teasing her now that we weren't together with that in-person
chemistry buzzing between us.

"Okay, so show me the city," she said.

I held my phone up to the window and pointed out where we
were as the driver headed in the direction of my apartment.

"Are you in a taxi?" she asked.

"No, I have a driver."

"Ooh, you have a *driver*. Like there is literally someone on
your payroll whose job is just to chauffeur you around?"

"That's the actual job description of a chauffeur, but he isn't
just mine. He's been the driver for my family and CrashPad employees for years."

"Not Hathaway?"

"No, Leonard started working for Nana Marian back in the
day, and he's been exclusive to our family since then."

"Does he open doors for you?"

"No, I know how to open a door," I said.

"Does he give you sage advice while looking at you through
the rearview mirror?" she asked.

MAID FOR EACH OTHER

"Quit being a dumbass," I said.

"Is it weird that the second you held up your phone and showed me a random New York City street, 'Empire State of Mind' by Jay-Z featuring Alicia Keys started going through my head?"

"Somehow this does not surprise me about you," I said, but the truth was that everything about her surprised me. She was so different from the people in my life. She chattered like that through the entire drive to my place, which was a lot more entertaining than reading email or staring out the window and barely noticing these familiar sights that were new and magical in her eyes.

When I finally reached my place, Abi squealed over the fact that it was in SoHo, that I had a doorman, at the shiny silver walls of the elevator, and the music I'd never noticed that was coming from the speakers.

Abi seemed to love everything about my place.

It was fascinating, seeing my life through someone else's eyes.

I loved New York and this apartment—it'd always been one of my favorite places—but Abi's enthusiasm was next level.

"Okay, so I need the entire tour," she said as soon as I unlocked my front door. "And you can't just say *this is my apartment* and leave it at that. I want to see everything."

"Creeper," I muttered as I dropped my keys on the entry table.

"No." She laughed. "It's not because I'm a creeper and want to see where you sleep, it's because I want to feel like I'm there."

"Like a creeper."

"Again, not because I'm a creeper but because I want to live vicariously through you."

"Still a creeper," I said pointedly, but paused and gave her a wink. "But I'll allow it for my biggest fan." I slipped off my shoes and started walking farther into my apartment.

"How gracious," she said, deadpan.

"This is my apartment," I said, turning in a slow circle so she could see it all.

"Oh, my God, look at those windows," she squealed, and she wasn't wrong. One of my favorite things about the place was that it had more windows than walls. She made a noise and said, "Declan, your house is *beautiful*."

"Thanks," I said, happier than I probably should've been that she approved.

She made me give her a full tour, then she made me take her out on the private terrace.

"I have to go to Benny's now because I got called in, and that makes me so sad," she said. "I want to force you to sit on the balcony for hours so I can just watch the street below like a dog with his head out the window."

"Sorry, kiddo," I said, walking over to the stack of mail on the kitchen counter.

"Hopefully my car didn't get towed; I parked it down the street yesterday and forgot all about it."

"Why don't you take mine?" I asked. "You've got the keys and it's in the nice, warm garage; you should take it."

"No," she said. "I'd feel like I was taking advantage of you, and I would die if something happened to it."

"It's not taking advantage of me because I'm the one who offered in the first place, and nothing's going to happen to it. And if it does, well, that's why we've got insurance."

"Please don't take this the wrong way, but I am constantly amazed by how little money means to you," she said, her eyebrows all bunched together again. "You don't care about stuff at all."

"Stuff is just stuff," I said, absolutely meaning it. "I told you that."

It drove Nana Marian crazy, the way I was unfazed by money, but the difference was that she grew up without it. She still got excited by every expensive purchase she made, even after all this time, and she loved to tell me exactly how much things cost.

My grandmother said to me on a weekly basis, *Can you believe how rich I am?*

And she didn't mean it in an arrogant way. She just literally could not believe, even after all these years, that she was rich.

I was the opposite.

We'd had money and expensive things my entire life.

I mean, my parents made me work for things I'd wanted when I was growing up, to teach me about priorities, and I'd always witnessed their generosity to others.

And I was grateful for that.

But when you grew up in a house where your father had an entire garage full of expensive sports cars, you weren't really impressed by expensive sports cars anymore.

I'm not even sure I realized that level of privilege until I met Roman.

Through a glitch in the system, I ended up with Roman as a college roommate, even though I'd signed up to have a dorm room to myself. I didn't mind because Roman was cool as shit and I had a blast with him, but he didn't play it casual like everyone else always had.

He didn't act like having money was normal, and he kind of acted like it was disgusting.

Somehow in a nonjudgmental way.

He'd been considering joining the Peace Corps when I met him, and he was super into social issues. He opened my eyes to so many things and kind of completely changed my way of looking at the world.

By the end of my sophomore year, I wanted to quit school and join the Peace Corps myself.

But then Roman said something important to me.

You can do more good with money than without it, he'd said. *Why would you leave this life and join the Peace Corps, where you could help a few people, when you could graduate and get a job at Hathaway and make millions of dollars that you could give away?*

We talked about it a lot, and by the time I was a senior, we'd formulated a plan.

He loved number-crunching and had intended on finding a job in finance or accounting with a nonprofit.

I loved business. I loved the challenge of finding new and exciting ways to grow a company and make more money. I wanted to work for Hathaway and move up in the ranks.

We found a way to merge our interests.

My career goals remained unchanged, but my plan for what I was doing with my money had changed.

On the surface, I operated like everyone else in my family. I used my income to buy and maintain two great apartments, nice cars, and great clothes.

And I'd be lying if I said I didn't like nice things.

But instead of investing all my excess income to become richer, I invested so I had more to give away. My family didn't know (Nana Marian would fucking disown me), my friends didn't know; it was only Roman and me working our asses off to distribute funds to those who needed them via our anonymous and extremely confidential partnership.

It was complicated and more time-consuming than either of us had imagined, but we also saw it as a priority. This was probably the tea that Abi had wanted and I was unwilling to share— especially not at this juncture of our efforts.

"Please, take my car, Abi," I said, gazing at her face, scrunched in worry. "I want you to."

"Okay, maybe I will," she said, and I could tell she didn't know if she was actually going to do it or not. "I promise to be super careful if I do."

"I know," I said. "Have a good night at work, Mariano."

"You too, Powell."

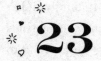 **23**

CONVERSATIONS WITH FRIENDS

Abi

I didn't expect him to text me through my entire shift.

It was a pretty quiet night at Benny's, so I had plenty of time to waste on my phone. But the thing of it was, I usually *didn't* waste much time on my phone because I just didn't have anyone to text with. Sometimes Lauren might send a quick note, but more often than not I just scrolled on my phone for a few minutes before putting it away and staring into space.

Brainstorming and getting lost in my stories.

So I didn't usually engage in conversation with another human on my phone at work.

(Well, unless my mom had drama, but that was another thing entirely.)

I quickly discovered that work was a lot more fun when he was texting all night. It was all about nothing: what he was watching on TV, what Warren had emailed him about, what his mom was texting him about.

Spoiler: She was texting him about me.

Apparently we'd done such a fantastic job as a couple that everyone he knew was blowing up his phone to tell him how much they loved me. Which made me feel really great because—see previous comment about not having many friends.

Not only was I a generally awkward person, but I didn't usually put myself out there to talk to people I didn't know. So the fact that I'd been forced to socially engage with upper-upper-class strangers and those people had actually *liked* me?

Well, that was really kind of a fantastic miracle.

When my shift finally ended and I was starting his car, I had to send him a text.

Because driving that beast to work was the most fun I'd ever had behind the wheel. That car hauled ass while still handling like a smooth luxury vehicle, and I was in love with it.

I texted: So tell me more about this custom car you had built. Like someone put it together from a kit?

He responded: No. Webb selects parts from his favorite motors and builds a customized vehicle. So the car you're driving has a Maserati engine, a Porsche body, and the interior of a Bentley Flying Spur.

Mind-blowing.

I texted: First of all, a Flying Spur is a ridiculous name for a luxurious car. It sounds like a touristy dude ranch. So where does the 1290 come from?

Dex: He registers the car when he's done, just to create a record of the finished product, and he has me choose the

numbers. 1290 are the last four digits of my grandfather's
Social Security number.

I replied: Seriously?

Dex: I swear to God.

We texted back and forth for the rest of the night, and just
before I climbed into his luxurious bed, he actually *called* me.

"Why are you calling me?" I answered, unaccountably glad
that he was. "Afraid you couldn't sleep without hearing my voice?"

"Maybe," he said, and his deep voice sounded so flirty that it
kind of curled my toes. "Or maybe I needed confirmation it actually *was* you since I gave you my grandpa's last four."

"Yeah, that was a dumb thing to do. Let's go with the second
as the official reason," I flirted back. "Even though we both know
it was the first."

"Do we?" he said, and the way he said it made my stomach
dip as I slid under his heavy comforter.

"Don't we?" I replied, then realized I was precariously close
to giggling like a lovesick middle schooler as I teased him.

"So," I said, clearing my throat and changing the subject before I made a fool of myself. "Did you know that I've never been
as comfortable as I am in your ridiculously decadent bed? After I
leave on Friday, it is going to kill me every time I clean your
apartment."

"Is it weird that I've never considered the idea that you would
go back to cleaning my apartment after this week?" he asked.

"Yeah, I just realized that a little bit ago myself."

It wasn't just weird; it was depressing. I didn't have a problem
with our differences, as far as the fact that I was a virtually penni-

less part-time maid, while he was a millionaire. I was good with the reality of who I was and wasn't ashamed to clean a toilet.

But the closure that would come with once again scrubbing his toilet was going to sting.

"I don't want you to," he said, suddenly serious.

"What?"

"I . . . don't want you to." He paused for a second, almost like he was just receiving this information himself and needed to process it. "I don't want to mess with your job, Ab, but . . . God, it just feels ick, doesn't it, the thought of you having to clean up after me now that we know each other?"

It *did*, but I had a feeling it was more uncomfortable for him because he'd probably always thought of "housekeeping" as some faceless entity, not a person he could actually be friends with.

Regardless, I didn't want to talk about the "after," not like that.

So instead I said, "It could be fun messing with your stuff and leaving things in drawers."

"What do you mean, leaving things in drawers?"

"Baby tarantulas or perhaps my new pet snake."

"You have a snake?"

"No, but I could," I said.

"Because no fur?"

"Because no fur," I agreed, for some reason pleased he remembered my allergy. It felt *nice* that he remembered this personal piece of information about me.

"Do you really want to land back in *please don't fire me* territory again, though?" he teased.

"You wouldn't do that, would you?"

"Don't push me," he said, but I knew he wouldn't. "You don't want to find out."

"Okay, well, back to my point. I'm super excited to sleep in this monster bed again. Is *this* thing custom-built? For a princess? Because I never dreamed a bed could be this comfortable."

"No, I ordered it from CrashPad. You're forgetting my family did furniture. It would be a travesty if my beds *weren't* the most comfortable, wouldn't it?"

"I guess I forgot about that," I said, rolling over and snuggling into the pillow. "Does that mean everything in this apartment is from CrashPad?"

"Of course it does—as if I could buy furniture from any-where else. My furniture here in New York was purchased at CrashPad, too."

"Man, Nana Marian would freak out if she saw the particle-board coffee table that I bought at Target. And my entire bed-room set came from Amazon. She would hate me even more if she saw those things."

"You've got her all wrong," he said. "She snapped at you be-cause she gets pissed when she forgets things. Trust me—Nana Marian is a brilliant, sweet lady who knows more about furni-ture than I'll ever learn."

I pictured her face and didn't believe him. "I still stand by my previous answer that she would hate my furniture."

"Well, she absolutely would," he said. "But not because she's a snob. It's just because she appreciates the value of good-quality, handcrafted furniture. She was actually the one to come up with the scratch-and-dent center, where people can get good-quality furniture for half off. She wanted that. She made that happen."

"That's nice," I said, wondering why I suddenly wished she liked me. Maybe it was because Declan thought she was sweet and brilliant. Obviously there was more to her than I'd seen, and it felt like a rejection, somehow, that I'd yet to see that side of her. "I'm going to bed now."

"Yeah, same," he agreed, and I heard him yawn. "Good night, Abi Mariano."

"Good night, Declan Powell," I said, my heart pinching just a little as I ended the call.

After we hung up, I burrowed my head into the big pillow, but now I even had questions about that.

Was I sleeping on his actual pillow, the one he slept on every night?

And why in God's name did the thought of that make me happy?

24

THE INVITATION

Declan

I spent the entire next day playing catch-up in the office, responding to emails I'd ignored and accepting meeting invites I'd been putting off.

It was time to go back to real life.

I didn't hate the fact that throughout the course of the day, nearly everyone I came into contact with mentioned Abi. It seemed the entire company had accepted our lie as truth, and the general consensus appeared to be that we were steps away from the altar.

Perfect.

On the other side of that coin, I didn't text Abi at all, mostly because I knew I should probably start getting out of that habit. Besides, I knew she had class, and Benny's, and was cleaning an apartment later. Our lives couldn't be more different, so it probably didn't even make sense to keep chatting.

But when I got back to my apartment after work, I got a text from her. It was short and sweet.

Hope you had a good day.

And God help me, I was glad to hear from her. I slipped off my shoes and went into the kitchen, wondering what the fuck was happening to me.

I texted: How was class?

Abi: GREAT. We mapped out my short story collection and it WORKS, Declan.

I replied: That's fantastic.

I wished I could read them all.

Abi: So what New York things are you doing tonight? I still want to live vicariously through you.

I texted: I'm actually doing nothing tonight because I'm tired.

Abi: But you're in the city that never sleeps. How can you just be sitting inside?

I grabbed a beer from the fridge and replied: I'm not a tourist, remember?

I hopped up onto the counter, still dressed in slacks and a dress shirt—I was so tired that I was unwilling to walk all the way to my bedroom to change.

Abi: You have no idea how jealous I am right now. NYC is seriously the one place in the world I'd go if I were given a free trip anywhere.

Curious, I texted: What would you want to do if you magically showed up here right now?

Abi: Walk. I think I would be happy walking the streets of New York for days. I'd walk to Central Park and go write by those famous turtles near the big rock. I'd walk to the grocery store from You've Got Mail. And maybe go to a flea market in Brooklyn.

I texted: What about the Empire State Building? Statue of Liberty? Do you want to do all the touristy things?

Abi: Nope. I see those on TV and I'm sure they're fantastic, but my goal would be to visit everything that made me feel like I lived there. Give me all the bodegas, let me roll around in honking horns. And I'd want to walk by all the publishing houses, just to manifest writing something that someday might show up in print.

It was so on-brand for Abi to want to visit "the city that never sleeps" but do something absolutely *not* exciting.

I texted: That's a very low-maintenance visit to the city. You don't even want to go to a show?

Abi: I mean, going to a show would be cool but I wouldn't want the time investment of trying to get tickets.

As we texted back and forth, I could picture it. I could picture her at a show (that she didn't have to wait in line for tickets for), petting bodega cats even though she shouldn't, writing in Central Park, and reading on my terrace.

Fuck.

I wanted her here.

I texted: You should come meet me.

The word *Delivered* just beneath the text message should have scared me, but it didn't. She was *kind of* my friend, and all the people who mattered at Hathaway had already engaged with her. So what would be the harm of hanging out with her a little more?

Just as friends.

Or.

Abi: Haha just let me fire up my private jet and I'll be there within the hour.

Laughing, I texted: A private jet wouldn't make you get there any faster, and I'm serious.

Abi: You cannot be serious

I texted: WHY NOT?

There were conversation bubbles, but it took her a couple minutes to send a response. Finally she replied: Because that's not the way life works. You can't just say someone should come hang out with you in another city on the other side of the country.

Somehow I knew she'd have to be convinced. I texted: I'll be booking your plane tix so it's free, Mariano

Abi: WHY WOULD YOU DO THAT?

I could almost *hear* her yelling that and it made me smile.

I sent: Because I'm bored and all about making your dreams come true.

Abi: Very funny. And I have to work.

Suddenly, I wanted this badly. I texted: Come tomorrow. Call in to Benny's—a relapse of your weekend illness. Just do it and fly back the next morning.

She texted: THIS IS NOT HOW LIFE WORKS.

I wasn't giving up. I replied: Tell me why this won't work. All you have to do is show up at the airport and you can come to New York like you've always wanted. We can do whatever you want while you're here, and then you go home the next day. I have infinite frequent flyer miles so it won't cost me anything if that's what you're worried about.

I saw those conversation bubbles, but I wasn't having it.

I speed-texted: And if you don't want to hang out with me when you get here, I can show you how to take the subway. Or book a hotel room if you don't want to stay at my place.

I was committed to convincing her, trying to sell my ass off.

Abi: You're really serious? Are there Hathaway people there that you want to see us together?

I wanted to tell the truth, that I wanted her there for no apparent reason, but I chickened out and gave a half-truth because I had no idea how she'd respond to honesty in this scenario.

I texted: I wouldn't hate that, but I just think it sounds fun to have my friend Abi visit.

Abi: We're officially friends now? Is that what you're saying?

I texted: Absolutely it is.

Abi: Let me think on this while I go to work tonight OK?

I was disappointed, but I knew she needed to think about it. Especially when on my end, the thinking I was doing was on whether I wanted to maybe move this past friendship.

Everything inside me was screaming to chill out and proceed with caution, but every time I looked at her, talked to her, or had a solitary thought that included her, I kind of wanted more.

So this trip might help me right the ship.

Or send me deep underwater.

I finished the rest of my beer and changed into workout clothes, but not before adding: Do me a favor, Ab. While you're working, think about how great a day in NYC with no responsibilities would be.

Abi: Trust me, I will.

25

NEW YORK

Abi

"I guess I just don't understand this reluctance."

Lauren's voice sounded loud over the speakerphone as she said, "You have always wanted to visit New York and now you have a rich friend who is going to pay for you to spend a day in the city with him. Why would this even require any thought?"

"Well, it's more complicated than that," I said as I scrubbed the grout with a toothbrush. According to my boss, the lady who lived in this unit was very particular, so I always made sure to be attentive to every detail so I didn't have trouble later.

"For starters, he just paid me to pretend to be his girlfriend for a weekend. We kissed a couple times and even though it was all part of the show, they were good enough kisses to make me unsure if I should spend more time with him."

"What exactly are you afraid of?" Lauren asked. "Are you saying you think you'll fall for him, or are you saying you think you two will hook up? Or wait—are you worried he's into you and you're not into him?"

I didn't know what to say, but I was saved from responding when she spoke up again. "None of those sound like a reason not to go, though. If you're kind of into him, why wouldn't you want to lean into this weekend? It sounds like he just wants to hang out with you, which is the perfect opportunity to explore the vibes. If you're concerned you two will hook up, either do it because it sounds fun and there are no strings attached, or don't do it because you're a grown-ass woman and you don't have to."

I hated that she was making sense.

"I understand that this is an odd situation because your relationship has been transactional so far, but this is different, right? This is entirely unrelated. This is a guy who wants to hang out with his friend, so if you like him, you should go and have a good time. Embrace it."

"Really? So you think I should go."

"I do, unless you think he might be dangerous or something."

"No—he's not. But . . ." Suddenly I was struggling to remember why it seemed like such a terrible idea.

"And I'm looking into his little side hustle with his bestie," she said, "but that Roman guy's name doesn't pull anything so I'm guessing it's a legit investment thing. I found something on one of the names on that list that I'm checking out, but if that comes back clean, they're just two boring rich dudes doing boring rich-dude things."

"I knew it. Did you delete the photo?"

"Of course," she said, sounding disgusted by the question. "So . . . ? You're dragging your feet why . . . ?"

MAID FOR EACH OTHER   211

"I don't know, I guess I saw all weekend how little he treasures things, right? He offered to give me a car, he wrote me a huge check without thinking about it, he's throwing free trips out there without a second thought. He is so rich that nothing means anything to him. So I guess I just wonder about me in this scenario."

"Do you mean romantically?" she asked.

"No, I mean even as a friend. I could totally see him wanting me as a friend until he gets bored with me and then just tosses me to the side like he does cars and money and everything else that he's finished with."

"Oh, honey, you're overthinking here," she said, her tone turning maternal. "That could happen even if you don't go visit him. You're always worrying about the future, but sometimes you need to take a chance and enjoy the now."

"I suppose," I said, wondering if she was right.

"And it's freaking New York, baby—come on."

I didn't tell her that I'd decided not to keep the $40K, because I had a feeling she'd see it the same way as New York. She was a good person with good values, but she was also very practical and wouldn't understand why I'd give up money that was already agreed upon.

"I need to get going, babe, but I feel like the only reason you would say no is if you're starting to have feelings for him and don't know how to move forward with that."

"That's not true," I said. "I legitimately just like the guy, money values aside. That is all."

"So you like him," Lauren said. "That's nice. You're not great at getting close to people, so I think it's great that you're looking to expand your posse."

Her nice way of saying I had no friends.

I dipped the brush in my bucket and said, "Did you seriously just say 'posse'?"

"Yeah, I said 'posse' because I'm cool," she said. "Now listen. I really do need to go, but I think you're crazy if you don't go to New York tomorrow."

"Yeah, you might be right," I said, though still unsure what to do.

But when I moved on to the kitchen, my mom made the decision super easy.

She texted: Do you think you can do me a favor tomorrow?

Shit. I replied: What is it?

Mom: Daniel and I need a place to stay tomorrow night— it's a whole thing with our apartment management. Can we crash with you?

Now, even if I was at my apartment and critter-free, I would *want* to say no. But I struggled to ever say no to my mom because she was always helpless and in trouble.

I texted: My apartment is being fumigated, remember?

I knew I told her. I texted: I'm actually staying with a friend so I can't help you.

She immediately replied: Can we just crash where you're crashing? We won't be any trouble.

It never failed to escape my notice that she was the adult, the senior adult compared to me, yet I was always helping her out. She was *always* the helpless victim.

So it gave me great joy to be able to say: I'm so sorry but I'm going out of town tomorrow.

Mom: What? You didn't tell me you were going on a trip.

Me: It just sort of happened.

Mom: What do you mean? Is it a work thing?

I thought about that for a second. Technically Declan had just written a check to me for work that I performed, so it wasn't difficult for me to text: Yep.

But when I finished cleaning the apartment and went back to Dex's place, it was a little difficult for me to bring myself to text him that I was actually going. So I almost swallowed my tongue when I got a text that said: So have you decided yet?

I hated how hard he was trying to convince me, because it put dangerous thoughts in my head. He was a bored rich dude and I was his fun new friend *for now*—that was what I needed to remember.

I took a deep breath and squealed when I sent the text: I guess I'm going to New York tomorrow. Can you let me know when you book it?

He texted: I already did.

I laughed out loud—no, giggled like a tween—even though I was all alone. I sent: You were that sure I'd say yes?

He texted: I absolutely thought you'd say no.

I replied: That's right, you don't care about money.

He shot back: I told you I have a million frequent flyer miles from work travel, you judgmental dick.

I sent: Tell me everything I need to know.

He didn't tell me everything I needed to know, but he forwarded my boarding pass and told me he'd have a driver waiting by baggage claim, so that was more than enough.

I threw together some Edward pieces and a few of my own, packed up my toiletries, then spent a sleepless night wondering what the hell I was doing. Those thoughts kept screaming through my mind in the morning when I went through security before the sun was up, but then my mind was truly scrambled by business class.

He hadn't prepared me for this.

For starters, when I saw that it said *business class* on my ticket, I assumed that meant a level lower than first class. I thought it would just be seats closer to the front of the airplane, maybe with a little more legroom, which I would have absolutely appreciated.

But when I got on the plane and they told me to go to the left, I couldn't believe my eyes. The seats were all facing sideways, diagonally and kind of willy-nilly, little pods of privacy like the ones I'd seen in movies and FaceTime with Dex.

I found my seat and couldn't stop smiling when I realized I'd be spending the entire flight in this luxurious seat.

It took me a while to figure out which buttons did what, and before the plane was even finished boarding, a flight attendant approached and asked me if she could get me something to drink and if I would be eating.

Eating? On a three-hour flight?

I ordered a Diet Pepsi and a steak sandwich at six in the morning, unable to comprehend that this was my reality. The little pod had fancy headphones, a pillow, and a blanket, and my seat reclined until it was totally flat if I wanted to lie down and nap.

Of course I did not; I was way too excited to sleep.

I couldn't believe this was happening.

I was on my way to New York to spend a day there—one day—then go home. Just to get the vibes of the city for a few hours.

The plane took off and it was the *greatest* flight. I said no to the hot towel (hello, makeup) but yes to everything else, and after we landed, as promised, a man was standing by the baggage claim with a sign that read ABI GREEN.

Abi Green was one lucky girl.

"Hi," I said, impressed that he was dressed like an actual chauffeur with the black jacket and the fancy driving hat. "I'm Abi."

"Good morning, Abi," he said, sounding refined, as if he'd spent his entire life training to be a fancy driver. "I'm Leonard. Let me take your bag. The car is just outside."

"No, I can get it," I said, but he took the rolling suitcase from my hand, much to my chagrin. That bag was old and borrowed; totally embarrassing.

We walked outside and he led me to a black Mercedes with all the windows tinted. He held open the back door for me, and when I climbed inside the vehicle, I nearly jumped out of my skin when I saw Declan.

"Oh, my gosh, hi," I said, laughing in surprise. "I did not expect anyone to be back here."

He was wearing another beautiful suit, looking expensive and perfect as he sat in the back seat, and something about the way he smiled at me made a thousand butterflies go wild in my stomach.

"Yet here I am," he said, his eyes moving all over me.

All over me. The way he was looking at me was wreaking havoc on my sensibilities, and I wondered if this was a mistake. Could I handle this? Whatever this trip was, we hadn't really defined it, and that skewed problematic. We'd called it friendship, we'd joked about kissing, but if this wasn't part of our act, what in the world was it?

"Stop overthinking it, Mariano," he said, tilting his head like he was reading my mind. "Just have fun, okay?"

"Okay," I said, nearly jumping out of my skin when Leonard closed the door for me. "Well, then, what are we doing on this fun day?"

"Absolutely boring things," Dex said, "as per your request. We're going to drop off your things at my house, then walk around doing absolutely nothing. We'll eat food, maybe hit a play if we feel like it, and then we might just hang out in Times Square, eating ice cream and making fun of tourists."

"Don't you have to work today?" I asked, flustered by how *personalized* this day in New York was sounding.

"I worked a lot yesterday, so I'm going to play hooky today."

Honestly, that surprised me more than everything else about this impromptu trip. I didn't really know Dex, but I knew playing hooky was not a typical move for him.

"Does Warren know you're skipping out on work?" I asked, staring out the window as I took in new views.

"He's the one who suggested it when I said you were in town for the day."

"Oh. Warren," I said, not liking the slight dip of disappointment in my stomach. "So this *is* part of the—"

"No," he interrupted. "But I did mention to my good friend Warren that you were coming to see me."

"I suppose that makes sense," I said, not really believing this wasn't part of the ruse.

"By the way, how come you haven't cashed your check yet?" he asked. "I would've assumed you'd be cashing it before the ink was dry."

How flattering.

I hated that he'd brought up the money, mostly because I was starting to hate the fact that our friendship was born as a financial transaction.

"I just haven't had a chance," I lied. "I've been busy with work and being the perfect girlfriend for my fictional boyfriend."

"Yeah, that does tend to take up a lot of time," he said, smiling. "So how was your flight?"

"It was incredible, thank you," I said, deciding to move on from the things that made me uncomfortable. "I know you don't care about this stuff and you've probably never actually flown economy, but business class was unreal. I had a steak sandwich, four Diet Cokes, and a slice of chocolate cake."

"On a three-hour flight?"

"*Yes,*" I said, laughing. "It was ridiculous and insane and I loved every minute of it. I'm actually looking forward to leaving you tomorrow just because I can't wait to go on the plane again."

"You really know how to make a man feel special," he quipped.

I gazed out the window the entire drive to Dex's apartment, unable to look away from everything I'd always daydreamed about seeing. And when we pulled up in front of his building, which said 10 SULLIVAN STREET in cool lettering, I was met with yet another reminder of how rich Declan really was.

His building was shaped like a triangle, but with curved corners, looking like a tall, shiny island standing in between two streets. I mean, technically, compared to NYC architecture, it wasn't tall at all; it appeared to be fewer than twenty stories high.

But it was *gorgeous*.

Leonard opened my door and I stepped out, trying not to gawk like I'd never seen a city before.

But dear God, Manhattan felt the way I'd always imagined it would feel. Everyone walked down the street like they belonged there, and that thrumming energy of the city was virtually *pulsing* under the sidewalks. It smelled like garbage and delicious food, sounded like conversation and music and car horns, and I had no interest in ever going inside.

But then I felt Dex step out of the car behind me. I turned to see those green eyes all over me again, and my eyes flitted over his dark eyebrows and hard jaw and that mouth that I knew was capable of taking charge.

"Let's go up to my place, shall we?"

Wordlessly, I nodded and followed him into the building, feeling unbelievably nervous as we said hello to the uniformed doorman and took the elevator up to the seventh floor.

A week ago, the only thing I knew about him was what kind of shampoo he had in his shower, yet now I'd flown across the country to stay with him at his upscale New York City apartment.

He'd been so easy to text, so easy to talk to on the phone, that

I'd completely ignored the facts and now a very rich and powerful man was leading me up to his apartment, where I would be staying for the night.

Was he expecting some sort of sexual gratitude for this trip? *I don't even have pepper spray. Or money for a cab.*

I took a deep breath through my nose and forced those thoughts away. I wouldn't have come here if I sensed he was a bad person—I *knew* he wasn't. We were . . . friends. Plus, this was a once-in-a-lifetime free trip, something out of a movie or a dream, and I wasn't going to let my neuroses ruin that.

It was quiet on the elevator ride up, and when the doors opened on seven, we stepped out into Dex's private foyer.

Private because his apartment took up the entire floor.

I couldn't even manage words as he gave me a quick tour of his place, which had three bedrooms, four bathrooms, and a private terrace.

It was magnificent.

But it wasn't even about the size; that wasn't what made it magnificent.

No, it was that the unit had floor-to-ceiling windows, warm wood, and light colors. Unique artwork covered the walls, books were stacked on shelves, and the large leather couch looked worn and buttery soft. Somehow, Declan's beautiful apartment felt cozy. Like an actual lived-in house.

There was no marble on the floor or shiny golden accents, no sculptures or crystal chandeliers. It was exactly what I'd want to live in if I woke up in a dream and had my own ten-million-dollar condo.

I loved it.

"You haven't said a word," Declan said, looking at me with a wrinkle between his eyebrows. "What are you thinking, Mariano?"

I swallowed and felt a little overwhelmed, so I just said, "Your housekeeper does spectacular work."

 **26**

VANILLA

Declan

I was a relatively impatient person, so normally tourists in Manhattan kind of got on my nerves. They walked too slow, looked around too much while stopping in the middle of the sidewalk, and talked about everything way too excitedly.

But there was something about Abi's reaction to everything that was like freebased serotonin.

She'd seemed nervous at my apartment, when she was putting her luggage in the guest room and it was just the two of us, and I suspected she was second-guessing her decision.

Which I totally understood.

I'd been asking myself over and over again, since I got the damn tickets, what the hell I was doing.

Was this entanglement a good idea?

I was basically just following the urge to be with her, the enjoyment of being around her, but did I want it to go anywhere?

That was what I needed to figure out.

I'd been out of the dating pool for a long time because I had no patience for bullshit, but I liked the idea of Abi in my life. She was funny and smart and easy to be with, so having her in my life as a friend would be great.

But I couldn't deny the attraction and the chemistry, especially when the kisses we'd shared were always on my mind. Twenty-four-fucking-seven.

Dear God, the woman had gotten under my skin.

But I was also a practical person and could absolutely work around feelings even if they didn't make sense.

So I guess inviting her here was my attempt to make it make sense.

"If I lived in Manhattan, I would come here every day," she said, standing on top of the rock and looking out over the Central Park pond. "I mean, just look at that."

She pointed out in the direction of Midtown.

"Yes, I've seen it," I said, wanting to laugh. "And I run here in the morning when it's nice out."

"You do?" she asked, looking surprised. "It's nowhere near your place, though, is it?"

"No, but it's near my office," I said. "So Leonard takes me to the park early, I run, and then I head into work."

"Seriously?" she asked, her eyes all lit up like I'd just confessed to riding a golden unicorn to work each morning.

"Seriously," I said, nodding and letting myself imagine her going with me. "It's nice in the fall."

"God," she said on a sigh, shaking her head. "Running in Central Park in the fall; what a dream."

"We'd walk if you lived here, Mariano," I said, nudging her

with my elbow. "I'd only let you run in summer, when the rag-weed wouldn't torture your lungs."

Her smile went away, and she looked up at me with a wrinkle in her forehead.

"What?" I asked.

She shook her head. "Nothing."

"That's not me being controlling," I backtracked, realizing my words. "I know I'm not the boss of you."

"I know." She blinked fast a few times, like she was thinking, and then she said, "What are we doing for dinner?"

I had trouble catching up for a second.

"Wait. You've had a hot dog, a gyro, and a pretzel—are you still hungry?"

"Well, not yet, it's barely past lunchtime," she said. "But I'm always thinking about my next meal. Everything here smells so fantastic."

"In the park?"

"In the city," she corrected.

"Well, what are you in the mood for?" I asked, looking at her. I resisted the urge to pull my phone out and take a photo of her on the rock.

"Maybe we should just walk around over in that direction and think about it. Walk until we pass by the perfect place to have dinner."

"Well," I said, a little distracted by the way the wind was blowing her hair around her face and the way she looked in those huge sunglasses. "If we don't have reservations, we probably can't eat at a perfect place."

"Okay, so do you have a favorite restaurant that usually fits you in?" she asked. "Where the owner calls you 'Dekkie' and always says you're too skinny?"

"I'd never go back to a place where someone called me that."

She rolled her eyes. "Spare me the macho and find me a good Italian place, Dekkie. I'm kind of in the mood for spaghetti and meatballs."

"I'll think while we walk, Abster."

So we spent the entire afternoon walking around with no end goal. It sounded boring on paper, but I had a great time.

I took pictures of her in front of both the Simon & Schuster *and* Penguin Random House offices, helping her manifest her work being in print someday. And she took pictures of me eating an ice cream cone in Times Square because she found it to be hilarious.

I still wasn't sure why.

The day was perfect.

So perfect that I ended up accidentally kissing her.

She was standing beside me, laughing after I'd pushed her ice cream cone against her mouth so she had a vanilla smile, but when I looked down at her, I couldn't stop myself.

I needed a taste.

"Abs, you've got a little something right . . . *here*," I said, touching her bottom lip with my finger.

But as soon as my eyes focused on her mouth and she looked up at me with a question in her eyes, I heard myself ask, "May I?"

She started to nod and that was it.

I was *on* that vanilla, my mouth finding hers and going deep.

God, there was something about kissing her. It was like I'd never kissed anyone before, or like Abi did something differently.

Because the second our lips met, *every* time, I turned into a wild animal.

Her tongue was cold as it tangled with mine, her lips and teeth busy making me crazy. Nipping, grazing, sliding. Her hands found my face—I fucking loved that—and she went up on her tiptoes, kissing me back like *she* felt like a wild animal, too.

I pulled her closer, damn near groaning from the feel of every inch of her body pressed against mine. My hands were dangerously low on her back and they were shaking as I forced myself not to pull her even closer.

Obscenely closer.

"Fuck," I whispered into her mouth, then lifted my head. "Abi."

Her eyes slowly opened, and the look in them made me want to haul her to a bed and throw her down.

"Don't look at me like that," I said quietly, bringing up a hand to trace the curve of her face. *The softest skin.*

"Like what?" she said on a near whisper.

"Like you're as into this as I am," I said, watching my fingers moving over her skin.

"Is that bad?" she asked, lowering her hands so they were resting on my chest.

"It's distracting," I replied, wondering what she was thinking. "Kind of makes me forget where we are."

I wished we were at my apartment, because I was desperate to explore this further, but I was glad we weren't because sex wasn't going to make anything about our relationship easier to read.

She nodded. Her eyes roamed my face, and I could tell her mind was running wild.

"So what was that about?" she said, raising her fingers to touch her lower lip. "Did you see someone from Hathaway?"

"No," I admitted. "That one was just us."

"Just us?" she said quietly.

I swallowed and hated that our arrangement was even being brought up. But since I didn't know what she wanted, I admitted, "I kissed you because I wanted to. You look beautiful, I like your mouth, you kiss like a goddess—and we both liked it. That's it. So maybe let's not overthink it . . . ?"

That made her blink fast, like she was surprised.

I nearly shouted with relief when she gave a little nod and said, "Okay, I won't."

Because I didn't know what I would've done if she hadn't felt the same way about that kiss.

At around four thirty she declared she was famished, so I called my favorite little Italian place (the owner *did* tend to call me Dekkie when I only went in for a drink, but I wasn't about to admit that) and they squeezed us in at the bar.

But after the server brought us a bottle of wine, that nervousness appeared again on her face. She looked at me and said, "So what *is* this? I was trying to not overthink it, but I can't make sense of something I've never experienced. I don't have friends who fly me to New York to hang out for a day just because. It feels very weird that I'm not paying for anything, even though I know that all these expenses mean nothing to you."

She looked so stressed about it that I wanted to kiss her.

I wanted to stop her worries with my mouth on hers, but I knew she needed to get this out.

"It just feels strange to me," she said, the dim lighting somehow making her look even prettier. "It's not a normal situation that happens within a friendship. It gives it more of a relationship vibe, and I'm not saying that you want a relationship at all, by the way, I totally don't think that. But I just feel like I don't exactly know how I'm supposed to act because I don't know what this is."

It made perfect sense; nothing about the day had felt like *just* friends.

It'd been a perfect daylong date.

"What do you want it to be?" I asked, desperate to know the answer.

"Are you kidding me?" She laughed, shaking her head and looking at me like I was nuts. "Talk about your loaded question."

"Abi," I said, pausing to take down a little of my Manhattan because I felt like I needed backup. I swallowed the cold liquid, feeling the warmth of the alcohol in my stomach, and told her, "We're friends, and if you want it to stay that way, you say the word. I mean, I've done this for Roman before; I've flown him in out of boredom and he's hung out at my place for a few days."

"Really?" she asked, and I could tell it made her feel better.

"Sure," I said. "So if you want to be another Roman, that's absolutely fine."

I considered myself to be a self-aware person, and I had become painfully aware during the course of the day that my feelings for Abi were growing at an exponential rate.

But because of how we met, I wanted it to move forward organically—if it did at all. I didn't want her to feel pressured or like I had the upper hand in the power dynamics of our situation.

I just wanted to hang out with Abi and if it felt right, gradually move on to more.

"Another Roman," she said, smiling. "That's a new one."

"Right?" I said, praying to God she felt a fraction of what I was feeling because when I looked at her, I was a little overwhelmed. "For the rest of tonight and until you leave tomorrow morning, let's not define this. Let's just see where this goes on its own, okay?"

27

VIBES

Abi

I could tell he was interested in more.

I wasn't thinking that in a cocky way, like I thought THE Declan Powell wanted to wife me up, but we had good chemistry and it felt like he wanted to explore it.

Which terrified me.

Because I felt all the same chemistry pulls, *dear God so much*, and I was being swallowed by the urge to absolutely throw myself into it and not even worry about coming up for air.

But I knew my heart couldn't take him moving on. I knew my heart couldn't take him losing interest. It'd be bad enough to eventually lose my friend Dex, but the idea of completely falling into a relationship with him, something deeper, much more passionate—and losing *that*?

It was too much for me.

"Sorry, Dexxie," I said, injecting a teasing tone into my voice. "I get what you're saying, but I absolutely do *not* think we should do that. I like you a lot, but I have no desire to be in a relationship with anyone right now. So if we do this and find we're interested in more, that's a big fat fail because I don't want to be. So I'd prefer we just stick to being friends."

"Okay," he said, his jaw flexing and unflexing as he just watched me for a moment. My heart was in my throat until he said, "Well, if at any time you start to change your mind, you let me know."

"I will," I said, downing the rest of my wine. It was intoxicating, knowing this beautiful man would be interested in exploring something with me.

That was some heady shit.

Some heady shit I definitely could not handle.

We walked around the city after dinner, Declan totally humoring me and letting me walk for hours. I was obsessed with the way Manhattan really *was* the city that never sleeps. No matter what time it was, there were people everywhere and I didn't want to miss a minute of it.

And instead of being bored, like a local who didn't understand my obsession, he seemed into it, just like me.

And he opened up like an *actual* friend, telling ridiculous stories and laughing at mine.

"That doesn't even make any sense," he said, outraged for me after I told him a long, rambling tale about the time my mom thought it was a good idea for us to move in with the mother of a guy she was dating when I was twelve. "The old lady was a stranger, right?"

"*Yes*," I said, shaking my head. "And she had these birds that terrified me, in addition to making me sneeze twenty-four-seven.

I'm fairly certain my teachers thought I had a monthlong cold because of my red nose and swollen eyes."

"You only stayed there for a month?"

"A month exactly," I said, shaking my head at the memory. "Thank heaven for those god-awful birds or we might never have left."

He laughed. "So the allergies worked for good when it came to your mom's dating life?"

"Sometimes," I said, but then Doug's face popped into my head and I grimaced.

"Oh, dear God, what'd I say?" he said, bumping my hip with his and sliding his fingers through mine.

I looked at him, surprised that he was holding my hand, and he gave me the kindest smile. "Why do you look so sad now, Mariano?"

I gave my head a little shake. "No, it's a pathetic little story."

"Tell me," he said softly, looking at me like he really wanted to know. "Unless it's too much for you and still hurts."

That made something in my chest swell, or maybe grow, because what hurt a little bit was when he was so careful with me.

"Okay, so my mom dated this guy named Doug, right?" I said, clearing my throat and looking down the block in front of me, not at his face. "He was *perfect*. Good-looking, but more than that, he had a good job and was so incredibly nice to me. Like, he planted hydrangeas on his patio just because he knew I wasn't allergic to them. He was *that* kind of nice, right?"

"Right," he said, squeezing his fingers tighter between mine.

"He had a really great apartment, and I think my mom was

counting the days until we could move in with him. Doug was literally the answer to her prayers."

I could still picture the clean, bright apartment that always smelled like dryer sheets and sunshine. He used to let me play with the yoga balls in the fitness room when he ran on the treadmill, and sometimes he'd even take me to the apartment pool and let me splash around with him.

I *loved* Doug.

"Then he did something impulsive and sweet. He bought a puppy—a husky named Gaia. He said he'd always wanted one, and now I could play with her every time I came over."

"Oh, shit," Dex said.

"Oh, shit, indeed," I said, shaking my head. "My mother, being my mother, thought that perhaps since Doug kept his apartment so clean and I'd never been around a husky before, maybe Gaia wouldn't bother my asthma."

"Are you fucking kidding me?" he muttered, sounding incredulous, and it made me smile in spite of the shitty recollection.

"So we'd go over to his place, I'd love all over that gorgeous dog, and we'd have to leave because my eyes would almost swell shut or I'd have to take my inhaler too much. My mom was sure I'd just grow a tolerance to it—she wanted to see Doug but she also couldn't leave me at home alone. So, rinse and repeat until the time they had to call an ambulance because the inhaler just wouldn't cut it anymore."

"Dear *God*," he said, stopping me with the jerk of my hand, in the middle of the crowded sidewalk. He looked down at me with sheer outrage on his face. "Obviously you were okay, but holy shit, Abi. It could've gone so much worse."

My throat was tight and my eyes were scratchy as Dex raged for little Abigail. His reaction weakened my knees and made me feel kind of lightheaded, because even though he seemed angry, there was a softness in his eyes that told me he understood it was about so much more than a random allergic reaction.

It soothed something in me, the way he seemed to *get* it.

"It gets worse," I said, tugging his hand to start walking again.

"Worse than near-death asthma attacks?"

I nodded and swallowed. "Yep. When I went to sleep at the hospital, Doug was there, holding my hand among the balloons and candy bouquets he'd bought for me in the gift shop, but when I woke up, it was just my mother bawling in the chair by the window."

He stopped again, but this time he moved me closer to the building we were passing, out of foot traffic. "Why was she crying?"

I bit down on my lower lip, surprised this story still had the power to make me feel this sad. "Because Doug chose Gaia."

Dex's jaw moved back and forth, like he was grinding his teeth together. "What?"

"Apparently he'd just always wanted a husky since he was a little boy. He felt like he couldn't give her away because it would be like giving away his child. Gaia was like a child to him, like his baby . . . ," I said, trailing off because I didn't want to say the rest, that the man I'd wanted to call my father had chosen a puppy over me.

"I *hate* Doug." Dex looked down at me and said with ferocity, "He would've been the shittiest father, Abi. You dodged a bullet. Doug was never going to be good enough for you, and Gaia is the best thing that ever could've happened to you."

I blinked back tears and was surprised to feel myself smiling. "Gaia is the best thing that ever happened to me?"

Declan swallowed, bringing my eyes down to that strong neck, and then he said, "I'm sure of it."

As someone who didn't consider herself a hugger, it was shocking how natural it felt to wrap my arms around him and pull him into the tightest hug I had in me.

As if knowing another second of heartfelt emotion might break me, he murmured into my ear, "I cannot believe you're hitting on me like this, Mariano."

That made me laugh in spite of everything, so I pulled back and said, "You wish, Powell."

When we finally got back to his apartment building, just after midnight, he turned on *The Godfather* because I'd never seen it and he thought that was criminal. I went into the bedroom and changed into pajamas, and when I came out, he'd changed into sweats.

He looked so good in casual wear that it was a little distracting.

But once we started watching the movie, I couldn't stay awake. No matter how hard I tried, I kept falling asleep. I was exhausted from the day, and staying awake seemed nearly impossible.

But I refused to go to bed because too soon I'd wake up and it'd be time to go.

I didn't fight him when he shifted my body so I was lying on the couch with my head resting on his shoulder. He seemed comfortable in the corner of the huge sectional, and I was too tired to deny myself the pillow that was his body.

Apparently I fell sound asleep, because the next thing I knew, Declan was quietly saying my name.

"Wake up, Abi," he said, his deep voice soft and soothing. "Time to go to bed."

"Shhhhh," I said without opening my eyes, not wanting him to move because I was so damn comfortable.

He didn't say anything so I thought he was going to stay, but then I felt myself being gently lifted.

"Dex," I said, looking up at that face as he picked me up like I weighed nothing, like I was a sleeping toddler he was carrying off to bed. "What are you doing?"

"Shhhhh, sleepyhead," he said, carrying me toward the guest room where I was staying. I felt absurdly relaxed in his arms as he went into the room and set me gently on the bed.

"Thank you," I said, feeling sleepy and cozy as I nestled under the covers and pulled them up to my armpits.

"I kind of want those pajamas," he said, teasing me. "They've grown on me."

"I'm fairly certain they would never button over your chest," I said.

"That's probably true," he said, looking down at his chest. "Was your ex a weenie?"

"I don't know if I'd say 'weenie,' but definitely not as big as you."

"So I win," he said proudly.

"This is not a competition."

"Isn't it, though?" he asked.

"No, it's not." I laughed, mostly because we were only friends and we'd never even discussed the topic of my ex before.

Which was good because it was really a non-topic.

The last guy I dated was nice and we had a cordial time together and slept together twice before he said he was still in love with his ex, and I realized it didn't even matter to me.

His eyes roamed over my face, and I knew he was about to leave me alone.

And I didn't want to be alone.

"Can I just thank you again for this trip?" I said, because a hundred thank-yous weren't enough. "I had the best day with you today."

"It was a great day," he agreed, and I felt like he was speaking carefully, like he was purposely holding back.

I bit my lip. I should've held back, too, but the words came out anyway. "Do you ever think about our first kiss?"

He looked surprised at first, but then his mouth slid into a slow smile. "Hell, yes, all the time."

"You *do*?" I said around a laugh, shocked that he was being so honest.

"How could I not?" he said, stacking his hands on top of his head as he smiled down at me. "We both went in for this big Hollywood kiss but got completely lost in the realness of what a kiss is."

"'Of what a kiss is'?" I asked, almost breathlessly, my toes curling underneath the blanket.

His green eyes were hot. "I got lost in the softness of your lips and the smell of your perfume and the breathy little sound you made when I dared to use my tongue—all the physical magic of a kiss. I forgot about reasons and purpose and just wanted to stay in there and keep going, y'know?"

That made me grin. "I wanted to 'stay in there and keep going,' too, for the record."

"Listen, Mariano. Is there a reason why you're bringing this up while we're here in the bedroom?" He crossed his arms, raising an eyebrow. "Does this seem like a good idea to you?"

"Well, no," I said. "But if I was trying to seduce you, for the record, I'd want to do it in your big, fancy bedroom."

"Oh, do you have complaints about the guest room?" he teased, his eyes twinkling with boyish mischief. "Is it not big enough for you?"

"I'm just saying that your room is fantastic."

"You know you're welcome to it," he said, but not in a creepy way. He was literally talking about trading rooms. "I'm happy to swap and let you have it."

But it's like the mention of the kiss, sprinkled around the idea of his bedroom, instantly charged the air. The space between us suddenly felt like it was crackling with electricity.

I looked at his mouth, thinking a million inappropriate things, before forcing my eyes up to his.

I cleared my throat and said, "Thanks, but I have a wicked case of the night stabs and you don't want to get in the way of that."

"I definitely do not," he said, swallowing. "Night stabbings are overrated."

There was something about the way he was standing over the bed, smiling down at me, that amped the intensity.

I cleared my throat again and said, "Right. I always say that."

"You do?" he asked, his eyes all over me. "You always say that?"

"At least ten times a day," I managed, wondering if it was possible to spontaneously combust from the heat of a gaze.

"Yeah, same," he said, dropping his arms to his sides. "Well, good night, then."

"Good night, then."

I let out my breath when the door closed behind him, because I was having trouble breathing and it had nothing to do with my asthma.

I wanted him.

Holy, holy shit, I wanted him but not just for a good time in that wall-of-windows bedroom of his. No, I wanted him . . . *around*. Like, for an extended period of time, in my life and in my bed and on my phone when he was traveling.

I was head over heels in *something* with Declan Powell, damn it.

So what the hell was I supposed to do about it?

28

GOODBYES

Declan

Everything was different in the morning.

Her flight was early, so we walked down to the coffee shop at the end of the block at 6 a.m. to have an espresso before she had to leave for the airport. We sat on the terrace, drinking coffee as she rambled incessantly—like she always did, like I loved—but something had changed.

There was an awareness between us of something more.

And I couldn't gauge how she felt about it.

She was quick with the sarcasm and teasing, which was her way, but it felt like she was trying to avoid anything that could potentially become a serious conversation. Her gaze darted all over the place instead of just settling into normal eye contact.

Evasive.

I would've addressed it straight-out, because I didn't enjoy games, but there was a slight chance that *she* was completely normal and I was overthinking like a fucking teenager because I was way too into her, so I held off.

I had zero perspective when it came to us anymore.

So I was going to focus on the friendship. Until she brought it up, we were just pals with zero romantic interest. Because the longer I could keep her feeling relaxed by my side, the more time I had to show her she could trust me.

That what we had was genuine.

And worth exploring.

I couldn't take her to the airport because I had a meeting I couldn't reschedule, but it almost felt like she was relieved by that. She gave me a big friendly hug as she stood beside the car, and I didn't like the way it felt.

"Thanks for coming, Mariano," I said into her hair, wishing I could read her mind. "I had the best day with you, too."

A tiny crinkle formed between her eyebrows as she nodded and said, "Same, Powell."

And as she climbed inside the car and shut the door, I said, "Text me when you land."

"I will."

I didn't like watching the car disappear out of sight, and I didn't like the way I instantly felt emptier without her there.

As if watching from a window and knowing what was going on in my life, my phone rang. It was Roman. I answered, "Hey, what's up?"

"I was just curious how this morning went," he said.

When I'd told him Abi was coming, he said he was equal parts glad because he liked her and thought she was good for me, and

nervous because he thought it was way too soon for us to be flying to see each other.

He was right on both counts.

And last night, when I couldn't sleep so I spent a good hour
going over potential investments with him on the phone, I let him
believe that we were only interested in friendship. What was the
point in talking through possibilities with anyone other than Abi?

If things changed between us, I'd let him know then.

For now, it was none of his business.

"Good," I said, going back into the building and getting into
the elevator. "She's headed home, and I'm heading into the office.
Things are back to normal."

But as I stepped off the elevator and caught a whiff of something Abi-scented—her lotion, maybe—I hoped that wasn't the
case.

29

DOUG DAYDREAMS

Abi

My phone vibrated in my pocket.

Dex: Are we cool?

I looked down at his message and replied: I think so. Why wouldn't we be cool?

I was pricing the new bags of apples, and his text would've normally been a welcome interruption, but what was he after here?

I was overthinking every damn thing with him and a little stressed out about the entire friendship-relationship dynamic.

He was quick to respond with: You know why. Are you OK with how NYC played out?

Was I okay with the amazing kiss? Yes. Was I okay with him making me cry over long-forgotten childhood trauma? Yes.

Was I okay with a tiny trip to New York upending my entire emotional framework? *No.*

I texted: Yes. NYC = very good

He texted: I hope you mean that because I'm about to completely freak you out by throwing out another proposition.

"What the hell?" I muttered to myself, then sent: What can this even be?

"ABI, CAN YOU HOP ON A REGISTER?" Benny shouted over the intercom.

"On my way," I shouted toward the front of the store.

Dex: I don't know when they're done remedying your apartment situation, but how would you like to stay in my apartment for an additional week?

I stopped mid-step, almost running into a display of hemp lotion.

Because although I'd fallen wildly in love with his apartment, those eleven-foot ceilings weren't what I was picturing as I read his message. No, the only thing I could think of was *dear God, does this mean that he's feeling it, too?*

Because the kiss and the entire twenty-four-hour visit had wreaked complete and total havoc on my heart. I suddenly felt a *lot* toward Declan, especially when we were together. I'd been trying all day to calm my beating heart when it came to those feelings, so this message from him?

Not helping that.

He texted: Saturday is Dad's birthday party in KC. I thought maybe you would consider going with me in exchange for one more week.

The buzzing thrum of energy his previous texts had caused immediately dissipated. It felt like my entire body deflated as I read his words. Because when I saw the words *stay in my apartment for an additional week*, I'd foolishly thought he wanted to spend more time with me, or that maybe he didn't want our time together to end, either.

But instead of wanting to talk about our feelings, he was trying to pay me with real estate to extend this facade for his friends, colleagues, and family.

Then it got worse.

He sent: My family's gotten a little too attached to you, so I'm thinking we'll have the last hurrah at the birthday party and then I'll break the news to my family that we're taking a break. Hopefully I can string it along at work where people won't ask, but I feel too guilty to let my parents think this is a thing when it's not.

Everything he said made perfect sense, but I wanted to cry. After the weekend, he was going to end this pretend relationship and make Abi Green disappear from his life with a neat little bow. Did that mean us, too? I mean, he'd *said* in New York that he wanted to be my friend, but it was going to be way easier to forget me when everyone in his life no longer remembered my name.

"ABI!" Benny yelled over the speakers. "YOU COMIN'?"

I gritted my teeth and yelled back, "YES!"

And as irritation poured through me while I walked to the front of the store and saw the long line of unhappy customers watching me like I was ruining their day, I thought, *What the hell?*

Why *not* take another week of fancy living and have a blowout weekend in Kansas City before going back to the real world alone? But did I want to keep doing this and risk having things go terribly wrong between us and possibly his family?

When the rush slowed, I texted Dex.

I'll have to think about it. I don't know how much more
time off I can expect from Benny, and I've got a lot of
writing to do.

He replied: You can write in Kansas City.

I texted: I don't know.

Dex: What will it take?

I wish I knew what he meant by that. Did he think I was trying to bargain with him and make another deal, or was he just
trying to convince his friend to go with him? Were we back to
something transactional, or was it just a turn of phrase?

I sighed and sent: We're really busy right now—I'll text you
when things slow down.

My phone buzzed again.

Dex: Well hurry up, Mariano, because KC sounds a lot
better if you're in it with me.

Hmmm. I might not know the answer to *my* questions, but I
knew the answer to his. Fine—I'll go.

30

KC

Declan

I picked up Abi from work at noon on Saturday, and it was wild walking into the grocery store again. When I'd charged in there the first time, livid that some person was pretending to be my girlfriend, I'd seen a cute checkout girl who I assumed was a criminal.

But today when I walked in and looked over at checkout counter two, I saw a stunningly beautiful woman who made my heart feel lighter when I looked at her.

Who I wasn't sure felt the same.

I was respecting her boundaries, especially when I didn't know her feelings, but it was killing me not to be able to do anything about this situation.

I wasn't used to being patient.

She smiled when she saw me. I got in her line and said, "Are you ready?"

"Benny," she yelled over her shoulder, "I'm leaving."

"Did you get the produce stocked?" he yelled back.

"Of course I did," she said.

"Karen, have a good weekend," she said to the woman at counter one.

"You, too, Abs," the woman replied, and I still really liked that. *Abs.* I really liked everything about her, and I didn't know what to do with that.

My inner chaos only got worse when she gave me a full-on grin and said, "I'm so excited to go to Kansas City."

The hesitation I'd seen in her eyes the other morning was gone, and the tone of her "fine—I'll go" text was nowhere to be found. This was Abi in her full-throttle Abiness, and I could only agree. "Me, too."

I didn't know what to expect from a road trip with Abi, but I was looking forward to a few hours of just her with zero distractions.

As soon as we hit the road, she said, "I'm assuming you're good with us taking turns on the music selection?"

"Sure," I said as I merged onto the freeway.

"Perfect," she said, connecting her phone. "Let's play the music game, then, Dexxie."

"I don't think you can call that a game," I said.

"Hush until you know the rules," she said. "And my first song choice is 'Promiscuous' by Nelly Furtado."

I had to reach deep into the area of my brain where all the forgotten songs of the early 2000s lived to retrieve that gem. "Why is that your first song?"

"Because I thought of it the other day and feel like I haven't heard it in years, and I used to love it. Oh—also the important part of the music game is that you have to sing along to your song *perfectly.*"

"Still not a game, and no, thank you," I said, switching lanes.

"Well, it's a game if the person who sings along best, without missing any words, wins a prize," she said, obviously flying by the seat of her pants.

"Is there a prize?" I asked, glancing over.

"Um," she said, looking around.

"So there isn't a prize," I said, laughing. "And you're just making this up."

"There will be a prize," she said defensively. "And keep your eyes on the road, Powell. It's going to be the most amazing, wonderful prize, but the person who wins it has to be really good at singing along, so you probably shouldn't even worry about it. Not yours to win."

"How about the winner gets to *choose* the prize?" I suggested.

"That sounds dangerous," she said.

"Do we need to have parameters and limits? Rules to your prizes?"

"I don't think so," she said. "Because we're reasonable adults. We'll just each have veto power. If you demand I lick the concrete, I will veto that. But if it's reasonable, I will grant you your wish. But you won't win, by the way."

"Crank up that Furtado and get started, Mariano, while I think about what I want from you."

I hit the gas and she belted out the words, and I was obsessed with the way she was using a piece of paper to score the event, marking off a point when she missed something.

I chose "22" by Taylor Swift for my first song, mostly because what song was easier to sing along to than that? And I didn't give a shit about anything other than winning that prize; I sang my ass off.

But I quickly discovered that even if I lost, it was a win because Abi was having a great time. She cackled while I sang, which was the greatest sound in the world and I was kind of becoming addicted to it, leading to me going even harder the next time it was my turn.

She sang Olivia Rodrigo, Sabrina Carpenter, Maisie Peters, and Gracie Abrams, while I hit my stride with Metallica, Aidan Bissett, and Post Malone.

Abi was fantastic, by the way.

She sang full-out and was absolutely better than I was, far more performative and creative with her song choices.

But I was playing the odds, only selecting songs I knew I could nail.

Which meant I was the winner.

Abi sat in the car and tallied up the points when we got to the hotel while I took our bags out of the trunk, and when she finally came around to the back, she gave me a shy grin that I wanted to eat.

"So what do you want your prize to be?" she asked, squinting up at me in the bright sun. "And remember I have veto power."

"Oh, I remember," I said.

"So . . . ?" she asked, and the way she subconsciously licked her bottom lip, I swear to God she knew. "What do you think you deserve?"

God, she was pretty. I looked down into her eyes and felt like asking for every fucking thing. But I said, "I want to kiss you."

She swallowed, but then her lips kicked up into the cocky-ass grin that I was starting to think was her brave face when she didn't really know what else to do. "You've already kissed me *multiple times*, so does this mean it was so amazing that you need more?"

I was pretty sure she thought she had the upper hand by being mouthy like that, but she'd backed me into a corner where I had no choice but to be completely honest. I put my thumb on her bottom lip, my gaze stuck on the mouth that I couldn't stop thinking about, and I said, "That is absolutely what it means. So now the ball's in your court, Mariano. Are you going to veto?"

I was surprised when she went on her tiptoes, set her hands on my cheeks, and said, "That was going to be my prize if I won, too."

She pulled my head down to hers, and that was it. I guided her body against the car and devoured her mouth, exploring every corner while slowly dying every time I felt the flex of her fingers or the catch of her breath. It was hot and wild, frantic and hungry, the kind of kiss that would be accompanied by falling clothing if we were anywhere but a hotel parking lot.

I couldn't process time or anything else around us; every one of my senses homed in on the feel of her body against mine. It wasn't until I felt her pull away that my consciousness returned.

"So," she said, blinking up at me like she'd been lost, too. "Do you feel like a winner?"

I knew I was hiding nothing when a dipshit smile took over my face and I said around a laugh, "Hell fucking yes. Let's go check in."

31

ONE BED

Abi

So it had finally happened to me in real life.

I stood there in the doorway as Declan carried our bags into the hotel room—the hotel room with only one bed.

Elaine had booked all the rooms for the birthday party, and being a progressive sort of mother, she must've assumed that Declan and I would be staying in the same room.

Which made sense, of course.

But I didn't know what he was thinking at that moment, and I also didn't know how to bring it up. As much as I'd been sometimes honest with him about things and we'd handled everything so far together, I didn't know how to navigate this.

Because when I'd stayed at both of his apartments, there was a spare room. I was able to stay with him without muddying the waters.

But as I looked at the king-size bed in the middle of the room,

I didn't know what he expected. Had he known his mom was reserving one room? Was he just as surprised as I was?

I walked farther into the room and sat down on the bench at the bottom of the bed.

Of course it was a big, gorgeous room; this was the Powell family. The room was huge, with a massive desk and beautiful windows and a stunning balcony.

Everything looked pristine and the art on the wall didn't look like it'd come from some airport sale, which added to my stress and unease.

"So what time does the party start?" I asked, needing to break the silence. "Is it in a party room downstairs or something?"

"Didn't I tell you?" he said, but he looked distracted, like I'd interrupted his thoughts. He scratched his eyebrow like he was trying to catch up to the conversation and said, "It's at the bowling alley."

"What? Did you say *bowling alley*?" That was enough of a shock to break me out of my *what the hell am I going to do about this sleeping situation?* reverie.

"My mother rented out an entire bowling alley because my dad has always loved to bowl."

"Okay for starters, how would *your* dad have even ever bowled? I can't imagine Nana Marian taking him. Has he lived a life where bowling alleys existed?"

Dex gave me a half grin. "My mom grew up living a life a little less flashy than my father's. Her parents definitely weren't poor, but she went to a public high school. A very nice public high school, don't get me wrong, but she did cross paths with a bowling ball, so when my father asked her out and she was intimidated by him, she said she wanted to go on a bowling date. Y'know, to kind of level the playing field and have the home-court advantage."

"Sports analogies," I muttered.

"Yeah, but just keep with me."

"Fine."

"After that, my father fell in love with bowling. Not just because it was what his dream girl took him to do on their first date, but because he was naturally good at it. And he also loved the vibe. He loves the noise at the bowling alley, the fried food, the community shoes—everything about it. He forces my mother to take him bowling a few times a year, swear to God."

"This is hilarious," I said, unable to imagine Charles and Elaine tossing gutter balls.

"So when she found out they have this brand-new, really *nice* bowling alley in Kansas City, she decided to rent the whole place for a day so we could all celebrate his birthday."

"Well, this is absolutely unexpected," I said. "I filled my suitcase with fancy outfits Edward has zipped me into, but now I feel like they're all too nice for bowling."

"Sorry, I should have told you," Declan said sheepishly.

"No, I just assumed it would be something fancy, so I didn't think to ask."

I was genuinely excited to go bowling. For the first time since I'd met Declan, I felt like I would be somewhere that didn't feel foreign and out of my element.

"I brought jeans," I said, "but I wish I'd grabbed a sweatshirt or something. All I have are silk blouses and blazers."

"I have a sweatshirt," he said, gesturing toward his bag. "It's just an old Harvard sweatshirt that I've had for a million years and will be huge on you, but it's yours if you want it."

"You've acted so normal the past few times I've been around you that I forgot you went to Harvard."

"I could've bought the Harvard sweatshirt at Walmart, for all you know," he said, sounding defensive.

"But you didn't," I said. "I'd love to borrow it, though, if you're sure you don't mind."

"Of course."

"So we seriously get to eat bar food for dinner? I feel like you're going to tell me they're having canapes or lobster and I'm going to be so disappointed because no food is as good as bowling alley food."

"Abi—"

"And the french fries are usually made in a fryer that hasn't been cleaned in fifteen years, which makes them the best french fries that've ever been made."

"The snack bar will be fully staffed with inept chefs who know nothing about actual culinary science but are experts when it comes to a deep fryer," he said, dropping his keys onto the mini bar.

"Well, thank God," I said, thrilled that we were going to be bowling and eating normal food. "Do you care if I take a shower before we go?"

Working at Benny's always made me feel grungy.

"Yeah, no, for sure you should," he said, glancing at his watch. "I actually need to go call my mom and make sure everything is set, so I'll do that while I grab my charger out of the car and you can hop in the shower. Let me get that sweatshirt for you."

He unzipped his fancy leather travel bag and *of course* his clothes were perfectly folded inside. He'd probably die if he saw the mess that was inside my bag, but hopefully I could spare his genteel sensibilities by keeping it out of sight.

He pulled out a Harvard sweatshirt that was beyond perfect because it was faded and worn, like he'd been wearing and washing it on repeat since the day he showed up to freshman orientation, and I wanted to keep it forever.

Sleep in it every night.

Maybe that's what I'd ask for as payment for this weekend— the Harvard sweatshirt.

"Did you know the only reason Rory never went to Harvard after years of that being her main goal was because Harvard wouldn't let the TV show film there?"

"What? Who's Rory?" he asked.

"Rory Gilmore from *Gilmore Girls*."

"Oh." He looked at me like *I* was the crazy one for bringing up *Gilmore Girls* when he really needed to know that it was always right to bring up *Gilmore Girls*. "I never actually saw a single episode of that show."

"Well, you're lucky I'm not your girlfriend in real life, because I would totally make you binge-watch it with me. We'd spend an entire weekend in Stars Hollow, and you would thank me for it by Sunday evening."

His expression changed, and he looked serious and thoughtful as he peered at me.

"*Gilmore Girls*, huh?" he said.

I nodded and tucked my hair behind my ears, hyperaware of some sort of undercurrent blazing between us. Another unexplained moment of zipping electricity.

He cleared his throat. "Okay, go shower," he said. "I'm going downstairs, and then I'm also going to run over to the gas station across the street and get a candy bar. Do you want anything?"

I remembered his mom's story at the cocktail party about Dex and sweets; how did that already seem like so long ago?

"I would love a Milky Way," I said, wondering how long I had before everything changed.

"You got it," he said, grabbing his keys and heading for the door. "I'll be right back."

32

SCORPIONS AND SEX

Declan

I stepped onto the elevator and hit the button for the twelfth floor, a candy bar in each hand, knowing I'd become a ridiculous cartoon version of myself. *Go on a chocolate run because I'm catching feelings*—yes, that was what a reasonable, grown-ass man did.

But somehow, her mention of spending a weekend binge-watching some random show I had no interest in watching nearly dropped me. Out of nowhere, I desperately wanted it.

We'd done a lot together in such a short time, parties and dinners and events—all in front of hundreds of people—but I was hungry for the Abi at home. I wanted to see her curled up with a blanket because I knew she was always cold, and I wanted her to fall asleep on me again like she had in New York.

I'd thrown out the "gas station run" only because I knew a two-minute phone call downstairs wasn't going to be enough time away from her to get my head straight.

Abi was here, this weekend, as a favor to me. I knew there were feelings involved, but I also knew that when you added so much falsehood to a situation, it was nearly impossible to disseminate truth from fiction. I felt like I knew her, but was that just the her she'd been giving to me through the course of our arrangement?

I wanted to unravel it all and figure it out, damn it.

I wanted to dig in and determine what was real and what wasn't, who she really was and who she was pretending to be. *Who she wanted to be.* I wanted to pull apart every fucking thing and get lost in the truth.

If I were being honest, bringing her here to this party tonight was a lot more about that than the notion of wanting to make my dad happy on his birthday.

Yes, my parents liked her and it'd definitely make the weekend more fun if they saw us together, but I hadn't needed to bring her along. I'd spent a year pretending my girlfriend was too busy to go to these things with me, so no one was going to lose their mind if I showed up sans Abi this time.

But I hadn't wanted to.

I wanted to start to figure this out. I didn't necessarily need to tell her that's what I was doing, but I needed to start to unwind the knot that was Dex and Abi, all that was true and false, and see what was left when everything was undone.

And a *very* fucking interesting aspect of this thing was the fact that she hadn't said a word about the hotel room. My mother reserved one room, assuming my girlfriend and I would be staying together, and I expected Abi would immediately demand I get a second room.

Which I'd planned to do. Happily.

But she hadn't said anything.

I didn't know what that meant.

Was she nervous to broach the subject, or was she okay with this arrangement?

Asking her would be the smart move, but I was a dipshit who wanted to wait and see what happened.

Because I wanted to stay in the same room as her more than I wanted to breathe.

I knew I should be considerate, but the selfish part of me wanted to be around her all the time. I wanted to know what sounds she made when she slept and if she tossed and turned. Did she leave the TV on, or was it perfectly dark and quiet?

I'd book the second room in a heartbeat if she wanted it, no question. But the idea of sharing a room—and a bed—was really fucking appealing.

The *ding* of the elevator startled the shit out of me, and I cleared my throat and stepped out as soon as the doors opened.

Get yourself together, jackass.

When I got to the room, I could hear the shower running.

"Dex?" she yelled, almost like she'd been listening for me.

I stepped closer to the closed bathroom door. "Yes?"

"Can you please come in here *slowly* and help me?" Her voice was loud but calm. "There is a scorpion blocking my exit from the shower."

I slowly opened the door, thinking she was nuts because this was Kansas City, for God's sake; there weren't scorpions in the Midwest, were there?

But my eyes swept the room and holy *shit*, there was a brown scorpion on the floor right beside the walkout shower. That little fucker was resting right in front of the glass door that opened outward.

I had to suppress a shudder because that motherfucker gave me the creeps. Fuck. I had no idea how the hell you took out a scorpion. I desperately searched the steamy bathroom, looking for the best solution as I became very aware of how unprotected— and naked—Abi was.

She was standing frozen in the corner of the shower with a towel wrapped around her body. She wasn't under the spray of water—I was guessing she left the water on because she didn't want to freak out that little monster by shutting it off—but she was pressing herself against the back wall as if trying to make it move farther from the scorpion.

Oh, God, that thing was creepy as fuck.

I was wearing shoes, so my best bet was to try to stomp that thing, but I was pretty sure scorpions were super poisonous. I briefly wondered how quickly I'd die after getting stung by it.

But I looked at Abi's face, saw how terrified she was, and I knew I needed to act even though I had no clue what I was doing.

"Okay, honey," I said slowly. "No matter what happens, you stay far away from the scorpion, got it?"

"Well, I wasn't going to throw myself in front of it, but what is your plan?" she said without moving her lips.

"I'm going to stomp on it," I said calmly, even though I had a hardcore case of the willies and kind of wanted to hide as well. "But I have no idea how the thing will react. So your eyes need to stay on the scorpion and the second he moves out of the way, you need to run out of here, got it?"

"But, Dex," she said, sounding panicked. "Can the stinger pierce through your shoe? Do you even know?"

"No, it can't," I said, even though I had no fucking clue. The shoes were good Italian leather so I was pretty confident no stinger was going to be able to penetrate the soles, but what the hell did I know about a scorpion's range? "Now, if I fail and it runs away, keep your bare feet clear of him and get up on that toilet, you got it?"

Thank God the seat cover was down.

"Got it," she said, nodding. "Are you going to do a count-down or something?"

"Well, we don't want it to know our plan, do we?"

"What?" she said, and then I could see it in her eyes when she got it. "Do you really think this is a great time for jokes?"

"I'm not sure there's ever been a better time for jokes," I said, my eyes moving to that *thing*.

"True," she said, her voice almost a whisper. "Well, if you're about to die, and I'm sure you're not, I just want you to know I had fun with you."

"Wow, that's really quite an amazingly vanilla proclamation. I've adequately filled your time."

"I'm trying to be speedy in this perilous situation."

"Okay, let's do this," I said. "You ready, Abs?"

"Yes," she said, nodding again.

"One, two—"

"Oh, my God!" she yelled, and I let out a very embarrassing screech as the thing started moving across the bathroom floor.

In my direction.

"Shit!" I scanned the area, looking for something to drop on him. He wasn't running, but the fact that he was moving felt like he had an armory of guns pointed at me and he was about to fucking take me out.

A vacuum was moving out in the hallway, so close to the door that I heard it bump, and I wondered if that was what triggered that fucking monster to move.

Shut the fuck up, housekeeping!

"Stay in the shower," I yelled at Abi as I sidestepped over to the door and pulled it open, hoping that guy would leave on his own. The little fucker was still moving in my direction, *come on, buddy*, but suddenly I realized that I was going to send a killer out into the hallway in the direction of an oblivious housekeeper.

"Damn it!"

Without thinking, or even looking at the woman, I wrenched the vacuum from her hand and rushed back into the hotel room.

It was a Dyson, so maybe it would work.

I drove that vacuum over it, and holy fucking shit—it sucked up the scorpion.

Or did *something* to it, by the sound of it.

My eyes frantically searched the floor, but it wasn't there anymore.

"Did it work?" I heard Abi ask by the bathroom doorway.

"Was that a scorpion?" I heard from the housekeeper in the hallway.

"Did you get him?" Abi asked from where she was crouched.

I looked up and we stared at each other in disbelief, almost as if we each expected that thing to come creeping back out, even though the sound inside the vacuum made it clear that thing had been good and truly shredded.

I turned off the vacuum and literally threw it out into the hallway with both hands, yelling, "Sorry and thank you!"

And then I shut the door and locked it, as if that'd keep any
future scorpions from coming into our room.

"Holy shit, you very effective man, did you seriously just utilize your brain and save our lives?" Abi asked, holding onto the
top of her towel as she came closer.

"I did." My heart was racing and I was still breathing heavily;
that'd been fucking scary.

Abi came closer, grinning as she impressively secured the top
of her towel.

"Did that seriously just happen?" she said, starting to laugh,
and I couldn't help it.

I joined her and we lost it over the whole ridiculous thing.

"Did you actually," she cackled, "throw a scorpion-occupied
vacuum at housekeeping? Do you not remember my vocation?"

"The twirling canister killed that thing," I managed. "Probably."

"Are you sure?" she asked, her smile dropping just a little.
"What if it crawls out and stings her?"

God, could she be right?

I opened the hallway door and the maid, who was staring at
her vacuum, looked over at me.

"You should call maintenance to double-check it's dead," I
said. "And keep your shoes on."

"Why would I take off my shoes?" the woman asked, looking
at me like I was nuts.

"I have no idea. Sorry."

I closed the door and turned around to find Abi was laughing
again.

"Thank you," she managed to say through her giggles.

"I didn't do it for you, Mariano. I'd just never forgive myself if I killed a maid by throwing a scorpion-filled vacuum at her."

She lost it again, her face tilted up to grin at me when she said, "Is that really a sentence we can use?"

"I can't believe it, but yes," I said, laughing.

That was the thing with Abi. We were both cry-laughing over something that should've been traumatic. But instead, it was refreshing and freeing.

As I looked down at her, wiping her teary eyes, I noticed everything. The smell of her wet hair, all that naked skin above and beneath her towel, the dip of that little bow on the center of her top lip.

I swallowed and tried to think of something else.

Anything else.

But my brain wasn't budging. I was locked in on her and I couldn't break free.

She blinked in awareness, our situation coming into focus.

I watched her throat move around a swallow, my eyes tracking her exposed neck like a predator looking for a vulnerability.

"You've got to help me, honey," I said, leaning down toward her mouth, struggling to make my voice sound like anything other than a rasp of wanting as her big amber eyes looked up at me.

Those eyes.

Suddenly my hands were underneath the back of her wet hair and I wasn't sure how they'd gotten there.

"Help you with what?" she asked, her voice a near whisper.

"To remember why this might be a bad idea," I confessed,

nipping at the full bottom lip that was suddenly the greatest temptation I'd ever encountered. I wanted to consume it, consume her, as the softness of her breath became my new oxygen.

"I can't," she said, her voice more air than sound as she nipped me back, electricity shocking through me at the feel of her teeth on my lip. "I can't help you because I can't remember, either."

33

LFG

Abi

What should I do?

Our breaths were mingling, his hot green eyes my entire universe, and my brain was at war with my body. Because dear *Lord*, I'd never wanted anything as much as I wanted to give in to this. To follow these sparks and set the world on fire.

But what did it mean?

Was it part of one of our deals, the genuine progression of our relationship, or straight-up chemistry?

It seemed like this was my constant inner monologue when it came to Declan now—*what does it mean?*—and I was getting tired of it. I wanted to *know* what it meant without worrying. I wanted to turn myself over to the feelings and let it burn.

"So where does that leave us?" he asked, toying with my mouth as I set my palms on his chest. I swear to God I could feel the heat of his skin under my fingers as the tiny bites of his teeth on my lips drove me nuts, like an appetizer that was perfection but not nearly enough.

It just made me hungrier.

"Giving in," I said, and suddenly it was like those two words served as the flash point.

His hands brought me closer and he dove in, opening his mouth wide over mine and going deep. His lips, teeth, and tongue were hungry, fucking everywhere with me as we devoured each other beside the hotel room door.

Technically it was just kissing, but it was feverish and frenetic and somehow more intimate than any sexual act I'd ever experienced before this moment.

"Your towel," he said, lowering his face to taste my neck, my shoulder, the hollow underneath my ear, "is about to go, Mariano. You good with that?"

Was I good with that? I was losing the ability to form words entirely as Declan made me weak.

"Your shirt," I breathed, my head falling to the side to give him better access. "Lose it first."

Suddenly I didn't care what it all meant because I knew.

It meant everything to *me*, and that was enough.

"Fine," he said, biting my neck in a way that made my knees buckle as he pushed me against the door with his hips like he was unwilling to lose contact with my body to remove his shirt. It was gone in a second and his hands were reaching for my towel, but I batted them aside because I was greedy to feel every single square inch of him first.

Oh, God.

My hands slid over his chest, hard and wide and solid and warm, and he looked at me with eyes on fire. His jaw was rigid, his nostrils flared as I dragged my fingers down over the muscled ridges of that perfectly toned torso.

"Nope," he said through gritted teeth, setting his hands over mine.

"Nope?" I repeated, my voice barely there.

"I need you in that bed, Ab." His gaze was all I could see, all I *wanted* to see, as he said in a near growl, "Now."

I'd never felt more inclined to listen to an order than right now with Declan looking at me with a wild hunger in his eyes.

34

BED POETRY

Declan

I lifted her and carried her over to the bed, muttering a curse when she wrapped her legs around me, hell *yes*. I was back on her lips, tasting every drop of their sweetness as my knees hit the mattress and a second later, I was stretched out over her.

"Is this okay?" I asked, lifting my mouth just enough to lower it to her neck. I was oddly into the smooth column of her throat, that graceful strip of skin that smelled like sweets and tasted like promise. I'd decorated it with chocolate diamonds at the jewelry event, and I was no less entranced than I'd been that night. My tongue was everywhere and I was a mess, an unhinged man whose only focus was the soft skin laid out in front of him.

I wanted to pen poetry about the slide of my tongue against the slip of her skin.

"*Yes*," she said on a hot breath, driving her hands into my hair and holding my head in place as I dragged my teeth over her. There was a shake to my fingers as I inhaled the scent of her clean skin, and a shiver rocked down my spine as she slid her feet up the mattress and arched her back.

"Kill me, Mariano," I said, raising my head to look into her eyes. "You fucking *kill* me, honey."

She looked up at me through heavy-lidded eyes that humbled me, because I didn't deserve a look like that, and I was no longer capable of going slow. I grasped her towel and pulled it loose from her body.

My hands trailed all over her skin, dipping and sliding, tracing and teasing, and my mouth followed, doing everything possible to make her writhe and arch. I was sick with the need to draw out every moan, distracted by the trembling in her legs, *obsessed* with the way she whispered my name over and over as she got close.

And the way she cursed when she was there?

It was intoxicating, a high like I'd never experienced.

I was blackout drunk on her body and had no plans to sober up anytime soon.

I kissed my way back to her mouth, capturing sighs on the way, but the breath in my lungs got a little stuck when I returned to kiss her slightly swollen lips.

Because the sight of her face made it hard to breathe.

Her eyes were closed, her hair a damp curtain on the pillow, and it pinched my heart, how beautiful she was. The sight of her soft face stung my eyes and my throat, and I might've broken down and started speaking in poetic tongues if she hadn't chosen that very moment to reach for the button of my jeans with her very capable hands.

I sucked in a breath and froze, every muscle in my body becoming stone as those very capable hands touched me.

It was the sweetest torture, holy *shit*.

She opened her eyes, blinding me with hot amber orbs, and it was over.

We exploded into action, moving fast, a mad rush of hands and limbs and wrappers and frenzied kisses until I was over her, panting, swallowing down emotions I couldn't express as I met her eyes.

Do you feel this, too?

Are you as terrified as I am?

Can you kiss me for the rest of your life?

I swallowed again and managed, "Are we good here, Mariano?"

35

WE'RE GOOD

Abi

"Are we good here, Mariano?"

I looked up at Dex, his face a tight mask that I would've described as a glower if he hadn't just chanted cursing praises of me the entire time he'd worshipped every inch of my body.

No, he didn't look mad, he looked intentional.

Intense.

I watched his strong neck as he swallowed and I could feel the tremble in his arms as he held himself above me. He was poised and ready, a hunter about to go in for the kill, and I'd never wanted anything more than I wanted him at that moment.

His green eyes looked dark as he waited for me to say yes, and nothing could've stopped me from trailing my nails down his long, muscular back and saying, "So good, Powell."

Then he was there, we were there, and everything else in the world—the room, the lights, the air—disappeared from our universe. It was only Dex and me as he held my hips and went deep, only us as he licked my skin and made me whisper his name on repeat, only Powell and Mariano as he flipped me around on the huge mattress, biting down on the back of my neck while I screamed into the pillow and he groaned my name on a string of profanities.

But everything returned, soft and muted and lovely, as our fuzzy surroundings came into focus again. He pulled me into his body, turning me to face him, and dropped a kiss on the tip of my nose.

My eyes were burning alarmingly as he gave me the sweetest smile, pushed my damp hair back, and said, "Is it weird to say the scorpion was worth it? That I'm sort of glad that little fucker cornered you in the shower?"

I coughed out a laugh and raised a hand to touch his cheek, reveling in the feel of such soft skin on an unyieldingly chiseled face.

A *beautiful* face.

"Well, I mean, it seems kind of wrong when they're apparently poisonous," I said, tracing his dark eyebrow with my index finger. "But I feel the same way."

He swallowed, and I wasn't sure why I was always so obsessed with that.

With the movement of his Adam's apple.

Probably because I liked to think it was some sort of emotional tell, a sign that he was feeling things that his mouth wasn't saying.

"So you're saying you feel the same way," he said, his voice low and rumbly, where I could feel it in my chest. His eyes moved all over my face, like he was searching for something, and then he kissed my forehead. "Good to know."

36

BOWLING

Declan

"There are definitely scorpions in Kansas City."

I looked at my dad and wasn't sure whether to laugh or mock him because at this point, I didn't need his confirmation. Obviously there were scorpions in Kansas City because Abi and I had seen one up close and personal.

"That was definitely a surprise I didn't expect to enjoy on your birthday," I admitted.

"I'm really impressed by your idea to suck that thing up," Roman said. "Good thinking."

Abi popped up beside me and held a basket of fries in front of my face.

"I thought we were going to share fries," I said, though not really hungry.

"You did say that," she said, "but I don't like to share my fries so I got you your own."

"Is that right?" I said, obsessed with the teasing glint in her eye.

Obsessed with everything about her, actually. If I'd been into her before the scorpion, I was over-the-top, out-of-my-head into her now.

I would've been happy never leaving that room. I'd actually begged her to let me call in sick to the birthday party, but she wouldn't hear of it.

"Yeah, but if you can't finish yours, let me know and I'm sure I can help," she said with a grin.

"You have quite the appetite, Mariano," I said.

"What is that?" my dad asked.

"Fries . . . ?" I said, unsure of his confusion.

"No, you just called her Mariano," he said, his eyes narrowed in confusion. "What's that all about?"

Oh, shit. I scratched my chin, looking for a way out. I'd gotten so used to calling her that that I didn't even notice when it happened anymore.

"It's a quote from a show we like," Abi said, smiling like it was a cute story. "Have you ever seen *Gilmore Girls*?"

"Can't say that I have," my father said, and it made me laugh, the idea of my dad watching *Gilmore Girls*.

"Well, Dex hadn't either, but now he loves it. Anyway, Jess Mariano is one of the characters. And he really loves french fries."

I looked down at her and quietly said, "Does he?"

"I have no idea," she muttered around a laugh, her eyes dancing, "But he's smart, so probably yes."

"Okay, time to bowl," my mother said, putting an end to a conversation that could've blown our cover.

Everyone except for my parents looked stunned to be wearing community bowling shoes and like they didn't quite know what to do with themselves. The whole business-in-the-front, party-in-the-back thing was going on with these designer outfits that were now paired with bowling shoes.

"Ready for a beatdown?" Abi teased, and every time I looked at her, I felt utterly transfixed.

Even if we hadn't just had mind-blowing sex in our hotel room, the sight of her in my faded favorite sweatshirt and jeans, with her hair pulled back in a ponytail and glasses on her nose, made me feel like I was in love already. She was fucking adorable, and hilarious, and suddenly I didn't really care about anything else, much less winning a game of bowling.

"Don't be cocky, Green," I said anyway, giving her a look. "You've got no shot of beating me."

"What do you think a nerdy asthmatic kid did with her Saturday mornings?" she asked with her eyebrows raised. "I played in a bowling league. The Saturday Strikers kicked ass and you're about to see evidence of such."

"'Evidence of such,'" I said, shaking my head. "Maybe we should make a bet on who's going to win."

"Enough with all your little bets and deals," she said, shaking her head.

"Yeah, I suppose it's not necessary now, right?" I said quietly, leaning down because I wanted to bury my nose in her hair. "What more could I possibly want?"

I heard her suck in a breath, like she was surprised by my words, but Abi couldn't let me have that.

She looked up at me with a smile and said, "To beat me at bowling."

37

LOCKET

Abi

I found it to be totally unfair that since Declan was so much stronger than me, his ball hit the pins harder—when he knocked a few down, they knocked all the others down easily. I stood by the fact that I was better at the sport of bowling, but he managed to beat me in all three games.

His entire family had been wildly entertained by our competition, because all three games were close; he only beat me by a total of ten pins.

But it was, without question, the most fun I'd had in years (aside from New York with Dex). With the few boyfriends I'd had in high school and college (and I could count those short-lived relationships on one hand), I'd never experienced that partnership feeling, where it felt like it was the two of us against the world.

But somehow, I had that with Declan.

And as someone whose family had always pretty much consisted of just me and my mom, it was overwhelming—in the very best way—to be surrounded by all these people who seemed to love one another.

Dex's aunts teased him, Nana Marian doted on him, and he had inside jokes with, like, ten or eleven cousins.

I didn't have *any* cousins.

It felt like the smile never left my mouth for the entire night, and I seriously got a little misty when his Nana Marian kissed me on the cheek before she left.

I was terrified to put my trust in him, in this, but it was too late for me to do anything but.

My heart was already his.

I wasn't saying I was in *love* with him, but I really did like him a whole lot and there was no turning back from that.

Especially after the sex.

Could it be called sex? It'd been so good, so . . . like nothing I'd ever experienced with another human, that I wasn't sure it could be referred to as such.

When he'd pulled me into his arms and kissed my nose, it'd taken all my strength not to cry. Seriously. And what was that all about? It'd been hot and steamy and toe-curlingly wild.

So why had I felt a little pinch that was similar to homesickness when he'd done that?

After bowling, and after saying goodbye to his family, Declan drove us to a shopping area where we walked around. It was a perfect fall night and the streets were all lit up; it belonged in a rom-com montage. He told me childhood stories about the family members I'd just met, I told him stories about my favorite books while he held my hand, and when my legs got tired, he gave me a piggyback ride to the car.

It was a fantastic night.

But then he did it—he *actually* made me cry when we got back to the hotel.

I stepped outside on the balcony, looking out at the gorgeous night, and he followed me.

And pulled a black box from his pocket.

Now, there was no misunderstanding—we definitely weren't in any place where I would somehow think it was going to be a ring.

But I was shocked to see him hand me a box that clearly held jewelry, with a shiny satin bow tied around it, and a soft smile on his mouth.

"What is this?" I asked, taking the box from his hand.

"Nothing important," he said, almost looking embarrassed. His green eyes seemed brighter than usual as he said, "Just a trinket that reminded me of you."

I pulled off the ribbon and opened the box. I felt like I'd been struck when I looked inside.

It was a gold bracelet with a tiny, delicate gold book charm, the spine covered in what looked like diamonds.

"Oh, my God, it's so beautiful," I said, blinking fast as I looked down at the gift. It was nicer than anything I'd ever received (aside from the necklace he'd given me), but that wasn't what made it hard to breathe.

It was the fact that he'd seen a book charm and thought of me in particular—and felt compelled enough to get it for me—that made me feel like my legs were going to give out.

"Open the book," he said, nodding toward the bracelet with his chin. "It's a locket."

"It is?" I whispered, barely capable of speaking.

Dex held the box so I could use both hands to open the book, and when I pried the sides apart, there was a tiny folded piece of paper inside.

I unfolded it, expecting a printed fortune, but instead found a book quote.

In the prettiest handwritten font.

You have bewitched me, body and soul

"Dex," I managed, unable to say anything else when he looked at me. I was immediately crying, and I couldn't even put my finger on why his gift made me so emotional. Was it because he remembered what my favorite book and movie were? Was it that he secretly bought me a gift when I wasn't looking?

Was it the fact that he bought me a gift at all and was giving it to me on a balcony after a perfect night together?

Was it because he'd sucked up a scorpion for me and then proceeded to make me feel loved in a way I never had before?

"Well, I'm never buying you anything again if it makes you cry," he said, looking a little uncomfortable. "I bought it because I wanted it to make you happy."

"I am happy," I said, sniffling and wiping at my eyes. "Can't you tell?"

"No," he said, shaking his head. His eyes were all I could see when he took out the bracelet, carefully put it on my wrist, and said, "I don't want to steal lines from your movie Darcy, but my brain can't help but plagiarize when I look at you. It seems that you have bewitched me, little Abi Mariano."

38

HEADING HOME

Declan

I never wanted to see her cry again.

I knew they were happy tears, tears that meant she liked the gift, but I hated them.

Abi Mariano should always be smiling, twenty-four-seven.

And what the hell had I just said to her? Had she manifested that I would become a sentimental poet with her stories? Is that what was happening?

Because I'd just laid down some mean-it-to-my-toes, *very* sentimental words.

"You cannot say things like that," she said, looking up at me with an amused little grin that made not smiling back impossible, "and not expect to be attacked."

"Attacked good or attacked bad?" I asked, even though I recognized the look in her eyes. My fingers were clenched in preparation of the Harvard sweatshirt tear-off.

"I suppose that's your call," she said, walking me backward

until my back hit the sliding door. I loved the way she was handsy with me, those palms flat against my pecs as she went up on her tiptoes and raised her mouth.

I was hooked, lowering my head and dipping into those honey lips. It was inexplicable, how into her I was already, because it felt like I vibrated around her. My nerves *crackled* in her presence. As she lifted her face, I was on her like we shared a connection, like an I-move-you-move type of thing.

"Why are you wearing those ridiculous jeans?" I growled, running my hands up the back of her legs, wishing she wasn't wearing anything so I could feel her skin on my fingertips.

"Why are *you*?" she replied, her hands sliding down my stomach in a way that made every muscle in my torso tense.

"We're fools," I said, licking the corner of her lip before grazing it with my teeth. "Because we could've had balcony sex if we'd dressed right."

"Balcony sex is off the table now?" she asked breathily, her hands still moving.

"We have to go in to get these off," I said while I slid my hands underneath her sweatshirt. "And once they're off, we're in."

"I feel like that doesn't make sense but you're right," she whispered before a moan overtook her as my fingers flicked open a clasp and she was in my hands.

"Dear *God*," I whispered, feeling almost overwhelmed by how good it felt to be with her, to have her hands wreaking havoc on my sanity while my hands returned the favor.

We fell all over each other, stumbling back into the room in a race to wear less, to feel more. Her mouth kept me on a tight leash, her kisses so hypnotically good that I refused to stop kissing her as we tumbled onto the bed.

"I like the way that bracelet looks," I said as I trailed kisses down her body, "when you aren't wearing anything."

"I like the way *you* look when you aren't wearing anything," she teased, but her giggle turned into a different noise when I found a spot where she *really* appreciated the touch of my tongue.

Things turned frenzied then, the kind of frenzied that was like an extended-cut, stretched-out, high-impact version of sex, strung up on the tautest of intensities. I gave her everything I had, loving her without holding anything back, and her responses made me wild with the way she matched mine.

She fell asleep in my arms afterward, wearing my sweatshirt and nothing else, but I spent the next few hours wide-awake in the dark. Not because I *couldn't* sleep, but because I didn't want to.

Abi was snuggled against me, her breathing soft and her legs tangled between mine, and I just couldn't bring myself to close my eyes and miss out on soaking her in.

It was perfection that I couldn't bear to walk away from.

We met my family down in the restaurant for breakfast before heading home, and I might as well not have been there. Everyone loved Abi so much that they were acting like she was part of the family, exclusively talking to her and taking up her attention.

Which kind of put thoughts in my head.

Thoughts that were way too premature, but everything about her just fit somehow.

And that *wasn't* the great sex talking.

No, the great sex was just the world's biggest bonus.

She was up at the buffet, grabbing a glass of juice, when Roman came over to me and said, "That girl is so good."

I glanced over and remembered that he knew about our fake plan. I wasn't in the mood to discuss my feelings, so I generically agreed, "Yeah, she is."

"Seriously, if I didn't know better, I'd think you guys were madly in love. Bravo—very impressive acting on both your parts."

"Can we not talk about this now?" I said, my voice low because I didn't want anyone to overhear. "We can discuss it later."

"Yeah, sure," Roman said. "I've got some stuff I want to bounce off you, anyway."

"Work?" I asked, wanting to shut him up about that, too. We *did* need to go over some things, but not around my family.

"Are you two talking work?" Abi asked as she walked up beside us.

"We are," Roman said, giving her a smile that told me he genuinely liked her. "Your man is relentless. I've never met anyone so hell-bent on making sure their company's making as much money as it possibly can."

A wrinkle formed between her eyebrows and I wanted to smack him.

"Are you still eating, or are you ready to go?" I asked.

"I couldn't eat another bite," she said. "And I'm sick of your dad trash-talking the Cubs, so let's take off."

My dad was a huge Cardinals fan, which made them sports enemies.

Of course, the fact that she loved baseball made him her biggest fan.

The drive home was just as fun as the drive there had been, and when we got to my apartment, something new happened.

I slept in my bed, *with* her, and it felt like all was right in the world.

And when she woke me up in the morning with her tongue on my neck, telling me I had to go to the airport in an hour, I suspected I would never want to return to this room if she wasn't in it.

39

ROMAN AT BENNY'S

Abi

Going to work sucked a lot less when you woke up in a fabulous apartment.

There was just something about the billion-thread-count sheets, the shower that could fit four people, the enormous kitchen stocked with everything I could ever need to make a delicious breakfast; I did not hate starting my days at Declan's.

But as amazing as those luxurious things were, the fact that it was Declan's home was what I loved. Even though he was out of town, I could *feel* him in the details of the place.

The soap that smelled like him in the shower, the orange juice he loved in the refrigerator, the random pair of his glasses that were sitting on the end table.

Lauren texted just as I was putting away the orange juice and cleaning up the kitchen.

Call me—I think I've got something on the Roman/Declan business (nothing bad don't worry).

I deleted the message and put my phone away. I totally regretted snooping and felt like trash about it, because I definitely didn't have any doubts about his business dealings anymore. Whatever she'd found was confirmation that they were on the up-and-up, and I didn't need to spend an hour texting her about that.

I'd much rather pretend I'd never snooped.

That way I wouldn't have to feel guilty.

The sun was coming up when I pulled his car (he'd insisted) out of the garage, the city waking up in the way only downtowns came to life, and every cell in my body was infused with happiness.

I hit ninety-five on the freeway while cranking the Cult, so I was buzzing with adrenaline when I got to work. I was in the most ridiculously good mood as I rang up groceries, humming under my breath to the terrible piped-in music that played on repeat in the store.

I wasn't even annoyed by all the snooty people who didn't care to say thank you or answer my questions when I asked if they brought a bag or if they wanted to use a box. I spent the entire morning very nearly whistling while I worked, pretty sure nothing could ruin my good mood.

But then something did.

Because after lunch, when I was back at the register, I was met with a man who looked familiar. He was buying supplements, which was normal; a lot of health-conscious people bought their supplements at Benny's because we had such a big supply.

"Abi!" the guy said, smiling. "I didn't know you worked here."

I realized it was Roman, Declan's friend.

"Hey, how are you?" I said, surprised to see him. I instantly felt wary, seeing someone from Dex's life at my real job, but I pushed that feeling away as I remembered Roman knew about our scheme.

"I didn't realize Benny's was the grocery store where Dex found you," he said around a grin. "It's my favorite."

"Nice," I said, sliding his electrolyte caps over the scanner.

"Did he tell you that I'm the one who convinced him to bring you to the cocktail party?"

"You were?" I said, grinning as I manually punched in the barcode for the chia energy gels. For some reason, they never rang up right.

"Yes, ma'am. I was the genius behind the Abi plot."

"'The Abi plot,'" I repeated, not liking the sound of that, but it was what it was. "I guess I'd assumed it was all his idea."

"God, no," he said, shaking his head. "Think about it—Dex? Does he really seem like he'd engineer a let's-just-see-what-happens kind of plan?"

I laughed, because he was so right. "Yeah, no—you're right. He would never."

"He was pissed and ready to just get you fired until I suggested he borrow you for the shareholder weekend."

"Well, then, thank you," I said, surprised how much I genuinely liked Dex's friend. The fact that he seemed obsessed with work and making money, calling Dex at all hours of the night, should've made me dislike him on sight, but he was impossible not to like.

"I kept my job and got to dress cool for a weekend. I am forever in your debt."

"Okay, so, remember you just said that," he said, looking toward the sky with his eyebrows raised like he was thinking through something. "Because I might have a proposition for you."

"What is it?" I asked as I hit the total button and pointed to the credit card machine.

"I hadn't thought of this," he said as he tapped his card, "but as I stand here in your line, I'm realizing you could be the answer to all my problems."

"Well, I'm sure I am, because that's just my role in the world, but you might want to explain."

He grinned and nodded while his receipt started printing. "Okay, so I have to go to a wedding in Ashland this weekend and I'm dreading it because since my girlfriend and I broke up last month, my mother is convinced I am depressed and dying inside. She doesn't know that I'm having the fucking time of my life, because that would only worry her if I told her I've been going out a lot. But if I showed up with a new date, well, that might really ease her mind."

A little knot formed in my stomach, even though I wasn't exactly sure why, but something felt off. I ripped off his receipt and held it out to him.

"It's my mom's side of the family, which is all super farmer-type people so it won't be anybody that Declan knows. Would you consider being my fake date for the wedding? I don't need what you gave Declan—hell, I don't even have the kind of money to get that sort of a deal," he said around a laugh. "I just need somebody to pretend to be my date. We can even say it's our first date and you know nothing about me. But I can totally, like, buy you a hotel stay if that's what it takes. What do you think?"

What did I think?

What did I *think*?

I think I want to die right now.

My brain tried to fully process everything he just said.

As if it wasn't bad enough that Declan's friend saw me as a business transaction, as a benefit he could also utilize for the small price of lodging, his comment made me wonder if Dex had told him we'd slept together.

Is that what he meant by not *needing what I gave* Declan and *not being able to afford . . . that*? Did he think Declan paid me all that money for me to throw in sex as part of our deal?

Did Declan think that was part of our deal?

We'd discussed that it wasn't, but in his head did he think that it was?

My cheeks were burning and I knew they were bright red. I wanted to throw up. It was hard to swallow around the knot in my throat, because I wanted to cry. All this physical trauma was happening as this asshole looked at me with a hopeful smile on his face, waiting to see if I could be bought yet again.

"I'm so sorry," I managed, trying to sound like I was very funny and cool about this. "But I am out of the business now."

"Oh, come on," he said, and I could tell he wasn't a jerk. He was a nice guy, just like Declan.

A nice guy who was rich enough to think I could be bought.

Which obviously I could.

God, I was such a fool.

"You're sure?" he asked. "There isn't anything I can give you so you'd help me out here?"

"Nothing in the world could convince me to do that again," I said.

"Okay, well, let me know if you change your mind," he said, and I smiled and nodded mechanically as he walked away.

I didn't realize until he was out of the building that I was shaking.

I don't know that I'd ever hated myself as much as I did at that moment.

40

WTF

Declan

It had been hours since Abi had responded to any of my texts, and it was driving me crazy. I knew she had her own life, and a few weeks ago I hadn't known she existed.

But her silence was stressing me out.

And I *missed* her, damn it.

I hit the FaceTime button, knowing it was kind of a dick move to not text her first before doing it, but I also knew she was off tonight so she was probably at home. Hell, she was probably baking in my kitchen or binge-watching something on my TV.

It rang and rang, to the point that I almost hung up, but then she answered.

I was immediately grinning like a total chump because I loved her face. I loved her stubborn chin and freckle-sprinkled nose and those brown eyes that I could stare at for hours and never tire of.

"Why have you been ignoring me all day?" I asked. "Too busy joyriding in my car to talk to me?"

"No, I was just really busy," she said, and I realized at that moment she looked more serious than she ever did.

And she wasn't really looking at me, she was looking down.

"Something wrong, Mariano?" I asked, unease settling into my gut.

"No," she said, lifting her chin. "Everything's fine."

But the fact that she wasn't saying anything else meant everything was definitely not fine. And then I noticed the background.

"Where are you? I assumed you would be lounging around my place."

"Yeah, I actually started moving back home this afternoon," she said, like it was no big deal.

"Why?" I asked, dread settling into my stomach. "You still have time left on our deal, remember?"

"Yeah, our deal," she said around a weird laugh that was a hundred percent artificial. "Since we're pretty much done with pretending and my apartment's finally ready, I figured it was time. I left your car keys on the counter, and I just need to run by in the morning for the last of my things. On that note, you should probably go public with our breakup soon, don't you think?"

My head was spinning and I didn't know what the fuck was happening. Yesterday she'd been all over me, and today she was telling me to publicly end our fake relationship. Was that it—had *everything* been fake to her?

"Is that what you want?" I asked.

I had a million other questions I wanted to ask, but my pride wouldn't let me say any of them. I was scared to ask, scared to hear her answers.

She looked into the camera then, holding my gaze for a split second before looking away and saying, "That was always the plan, right?"

"I guess it was," I said, hearing a roaring in my ears.

"Well, thanks again for everything," she said, still looking everywhere but at me. "It was all really wonderful and I promise I'll never crash your fancy apartment without permission again."

She gave me a fake smile as she referenced what'd started everything, but it felt like a big proclamation that I fucking hated.

Abi Mariano was out.

"Great," I said, feeling like I couldn't get enough oxygen in my lungs. "See you around, Abi."

"Yeah, you, too," she said, and instead of saying goodbye or waiting for a response, she disconnected the call.

I sat there staring at my phone for what felt like hours.

What the hell?

Was I seriously the world's biggest chump? The negotiated time we were to spend together was over, so now she was gone?

What about New York?

What about Kansas City?

The more I thought about it, the more I just couldn't accept it. Something must've happened, or there was some detail I was missing, because there was just too much between us for it to disappear like this.

It consumed me all night, and I flew home the next morning.

I damn near went straight to Benny's from the airport, but

then I remembered she had class. I went to my apartment instead, which suddenly felt depressing as fuck when I walked in.

I'd really gotten used to the sound of her being nearby.

I grabbed an orange juice and went out on the balcony, hoping the fresh air would do something to lighten the heaviness in my stomach as I waited for her. But it didn't because her notebook was sitting there, under the umbrella on the table. It immediately brought back the image of her on that first night, writing in that notebook when she was supposed to be waiting for me by the door.

I grabbed it and took it inside, but when I dropped it on the counter, a piece of paper fell out. I bent down to retrieve it, but the sight of my name scribbled among an entire sheet of words caught my attention.

My name was at the top, followed by random notes everywhere, like someone jotting down recipe ingredients on every inch of a recipe card.

Declan Connor Powell
—arrogant, wealthy, careless, soulless, easy to charm with "normalcy" because it's a novelty to him, takes calls from billionaires at all hours of the night because it's the only thing that's important to him, "I will not be blackmailed by a maid," "reminds me of the freckles on your shoulder," "You are stunning for a felon"

Well, shit.

I dropped the paper like it was burning my fingers because, what the fuck?

I felt like I'd been punched as I stood there in the kitchen, staring into space as her words kept coming at me again and again.

Easy to charm with "normalcy" because it's a novelty to him.
Soulless.

What the fuck?

I rubbed the back of my neck, trying to convince myself that this had something to do with fiction but failing because she'd written quotes of things I'd actually said to her.

Was that what she really thought of me? Had she thought that the entire time?

I looked down at her notebook and I couldn't help myself. I knew it was a gross invasion of her privacy, but I picked it up and opened it to the first page.

Chapter One

Connor

The first thing I noticed about Connor was that he didn't smile. Ever. He was far too important to be bothered with things like emotions. Pleasantries. Those were things experienced by people beneath him.

The second thing I noticed was his watch. It ~~looked~~ was ~~impossibly~~ absurdly expensive, even though I wasn't sure exactly what it was that made me think that.

You could just tell.

And he glanced at it constantly, as if every ~~one of his moments~~ moment he breathed was so valuable it must be tracked, recorded for posterity by the gentle ticking of the feather-fine golden second hand that surely cost more than my car.

So it was no surprise that when his green eyes landed on me, the only thing they expressed was boredom.

I couldn't stop reading, even as every word she'd written begged me to throw the notebook across the room.

41

DAPHNE VIBES

Abi

"Abi, these are fantastic ideas. And Daphne's story is already my favorite, even though it's only been outlined," my MFA advisor, Anna, said, smiling as we sat in her office. "I just have a feeling it's going to be the centerpiece."

"Yeah?" I hated that story now, even though I knew she was right. I felt like that story had the most promise to be something really unique, but it was kind of becoming too gutting to work on. The story was fiction, of course, but the characters were being played in my head by their real-life counterparts so it was a bit of a mindfuck, picturing Declan's face as the one who betrays Daphne.

Especially now that we were over.

"I thought so at first," I said, "but now I'm not so sure."

Anna stared at me for a long moment, so long that I fidgeted in my chair.

"*You* are wrong," she said, taking off her glasses. "Writing is

MAID FOR EACH OTHER 299

subjective, but I'm confident on this one. Think about it. The plot is interesting, the way these wealthy people suck her in and then spit her out without a care; very Daisy Buchanan and I love it. But to me what's far more compelling about this piece is watching Daphne get sucked in until she sees that these are really great people, right? She goes from harshly judging them to ultimately considering them to be the most amazing of people, people she suddenly feels more than just an admiration of their wealth for; she can envision them being her family. Throw in all the feelings, and the reader will be absolutely heartbroken along with her when those characters turn on her in the end."

"God, that's terrible," I said, my brain superimposing all of Declan's inner circle onto my characters. It made my throat hurt.

"It's fiction," she said, giving me a pointed look as if to remind me that this wasn't actually a story about me.

And she was right. The thought of writing it was harrowing, but it was by far the most thought-provoking of all my ideas.

After the meeting, I headed for Declan's apartment to retrieve my notebook. I'd carefully packed all my things so I never had to return to his place, but then remembered last night that I'd left my notebook on the balcony.

Which was terrible. Awful. The last thing I wanted to do was return to his building.

But at least he wasn't in town.

Somehow, I just couldn't bear the thought of seeing him. I needed a clean break, and the thought of being anywhere near him felt like too much.

Overwhelming.

I let myself in when I got there, melancholy settling under my breastbone as I closed the door behind me. Somehow the apartment looked the same and different, all at once, because it wasn't the place I cleaned for money and it wasn't the place I'd stayed at . . . for money.

It was just . . . Declan's home.

And I missed it so much already.

I started across the room, needing to get the notebook and get the heck out of there before I melted into a sobbing puddle in the living room. I was just about to open the patio door when I heard, "Are you here for this?"

I jumped at the sound of Declan's voice—*ohmygod he's here*—my heart in my throat as I set a hand on my chest and turned around. "You scared me."

He was standing in the doorway of his office, wearing an impeccable gray suit, and he looked a lot like he had the first time I met him. Gorgeous, rich, perfect—and angry.

He was frowning—no, glowering—as he held out my notebook. *Oh, God.*

"Y-yes," I said, feeling unbalanced as my feet started moving in his direction. I managed a breathy little, "I can't believe I left it here. Thank—"

"You're a talented writer," he said, raising the notebook. "I'm impressed, even if it isn't the kind of literature I usually read."

A thousand thoughts screamed through my mind as he looked at me, but the words that came out of my mouth as I grabbed it were, "You read it?"

I remembered him teasing me about the way I treated the notebook like it was top secret, and I also remembered him assuring me I didn't need to worry because he would never read it without my permission.

I'd never do that, Mariano, come on.

"I did," he said, his jaw flexing and unflexing as he watched me. "Since you left it here I thought perhaps you wanted me to."

I wasn't sure what was happening, but my cheeks were hot as I said, "No, I definitely didn't want you to."

The notebook was full of random thoughts and ideas and the initial first chapter I'd come up with for Daphne before I started drafting it on my laptop. I was mortified that he'd read it, so shocked and angry that I didn't even know what to say.

"I'm glad I did, though," he said, his voice entirely lacking in emotion. His eyes were flat when he said, "It's nice to know what you *really* think about everything."

If he'd said it in a different tone, I might've been compelled to explain that what he'd read was an early version of something very fictitious. I might've felt the need to clarify that I didn't think he was anything like Connor.

But as he looked at me like *that*, distant and angry and like the grumpy millionaire I'd once thought he was, I realized it was the perfect excuse. There was no reason to discuss real feelings or my genuine heartbreak when everything was already over, so who cared if he thought I'd written a lot of trash about him?

It wasn't going to work out anyway and he didn't actually care about me, so why not let him walk away pissed off about what he considered an inaccurate portrayal?

"Well, it's nice to know you felt entitled to read it," I said through gritted teeth. "Although I *am* surprised you didn't pass it around to your little friends."

"Yeah, it's not exactly the kind of thing I'm inspired to share," he said, his jaw jumping as he watched me.

"Declan—"

"Abi." He inhaled sharply through his nose, his eyes impossible to read. "I have to go. Lock up when you leave."

And then he was gone.

I had been dismissed.

I held it together until I went home to my crappy apartment—which felt way crappier now that I'd lived on the other side—and sat down at my desk to write. Once I started, I couldn't stop. It was gut-wrenching and terrible, and I cried the entire time I wrote it, but when I finished, even though it was a first draft, I knew it was fucking good.

Daphne deserved better than those assholes, but she also didn't, because she'd let herself hope.

What a foolish, foolish thing.

42

PLAN

Declan

"What the hell is wrong with you?"

"What do you mean?" I said, looking at Roman like I had no idea what he was talking about when I knew a thousand percent what he was referring to. I picked up my beer and played stupid. "Am I not eating fast enough for you?"

"Don't pretend to be obtuse, asshole," he said, shaking his head. "We both know I'm not talking about the food."

"If you have something you want to say, just say it," I said, glancing over at the wall of TVs and regretting my decision to meet him at the sports bar for the Chiefs game. I wasn't in the mood to talk.

Or watch football.

Or drink any more than I'd already been drinking lately.

"Well, for starters, you've spent the last month working in Omaha."

"So?"

"So that's not normal behavior for you," he said, jamming a handful of fries into his mouth. "And every time I ask you about portfolio selections, you tell me to make the call."

"So now it's bad that I trust your judgment?" I said, raising my empty glass when Carol, our waitress, walked by. "Should I not let you make the call? Do you need me to help you form your opinions?"

I knew I was being an asshole, but I was in a bad mood.

I had been for weeks.

"I need you to act like a grown-up, not a pouty, lovesick piece of shit."

"I'm not—"

"Yes, you are," he said, grabbing the ketchup and squirting it all over his plate. "You've been a colossal dickhead since Abi disappeared from your life. And I don't think that's a coincidence."

"God save me from this bullshit," I said, wishing he'd drop it. "This has nothing to do with her."

"Really? Are you seriously going to deny it to my face?" He scowled. "At least be honest."

"I *am* being honest," I said.

"No, you're not," he said, badgering me like he was my therapist. "Try again."

"Why don't you fuck off and tell me what it is *you* think is going on, jackass?"

"I will, thank you," he said, grinning like he'd been waiting for this opportunity. "I think you guys were pretending and it became more. Your little project ended and you miss her but you're too much of a Declan Powell to swallow your pride and go to her and tell her how you feel. So you're miserable."

"Shows how much you know," I said, pissed because he was making me think of her when I'd been doing a great job all day of not picturing her face. "You might be right about the feelings part, but Abi is the one who wants nothing to do with this. She walked away with her intentions very fucking clear."

"What does that mean?"

I couldn't mention the story because it still made me sick. The idea that she'd seen me that way, or had been inspired enough by me to write such an insipid character, was far too depressing for me to put into words.

So I only mentioned the other shitty part.

"It means she didn't take the money, okay?"

The day after our last encounter at my place, I came home and saw it next to the bed.

The check for $40,000.

The necklace from the jewelry event.

The fucking bracelet.

She'd left them all behind.

I'd walked over and picked up the bracelet, remembering how hard she'd cried when I'd given it to her.

Why the hell would she leave it behind?

And the money? It didn't make any sense, since that was the whole point of this arrangement.

But as I sat there with the golden trinket in my hand, I realized what it meant.

She wanted no connection to me.

It was a massive severance of ties.

Abi would rather walk away from all those "valuables" than keep me—the real-life Connor—in her life.

"She fulfilled her part of the agreement, and then she left the money behind because she wanted to wash her hands of this *that* badly."

"Wait a minute—she seriously left the money behind?" he asked, shocked. "Like, she didn't cash the check?"

"Didn't even take it with her," I said, my gut churning as I pictured it sitting there with the jewelry. "She left it on the side of the bed, and if that's not a message, I don't know what is."

"Are you fucking serious?" he said, his voice almost a yell as he looked at me with wild eyes.

"No, I'm making up the whole story. Of course I'm serious."

"Oh, my God, you're so stupid, Dex," he said, digging his hands into his hair as he continued staring at me like I was insane.

"Thanks. This definitely helps my mood."

"No, you fucking moron," he said. "Why would she leave the money—think about it. You two had an agreement and she fulfilled it. If she had zero feelings for you, she would've taken the money because it was just like a job. The only reason somebody would change their mind and not take the money, especially that much money, is if they *did* have feelings for you."

I frowned. "Wait. What?"

"Think about the girl you met. You needed a favor and she demanded money. You guys shook on it and boom—*that* girl would take the money. Now think of the girl you spent time with in New York. That is the girl who *didn't* take the money. And the only reason she wouldn't take money, in my opinion, is if it felt gross taking money from someone she had feelings for."

My head started pounding and I rubbed my forehead, feeling off-kilter.

Because I didn't think he was right, yet I also felt like there was something there. Something to the question of why she wouldn't take the money.

It seemed like, now that Roman had said it out loud, if Abi just wanted to wash her hands of me, she actually *would've* taken the money and dipped, right?

But the story.

"I couldn't have gotten it this wrong," I said, looking at him. "Could I?"

"I think you could. And remember the day I ran into her at Benny's and she had zero interest in being my fake girlfriend for Kennedy's wedding?"

"No," I said, trying to recall. "What are you talking about?"

"I told you I went to Benny's, didn't I?" he said. He obviously thought he'd already told me about whatever the hell this was.

"What were you doing at Benny's?"

"I always go there for supplements. Their prices are way better than everywhere else. I think they get them whole—"

"Are you serious right now?" I interrupted, desperate for him to get to the actual story.

He rolled his eyes. "Oh, I forgot who I'm talking to; you probably don't have to bargain shop for your supplements like the rest of us."

"Shut up about the damned supplements—what the hell are you talking about 'fake girlfriend'?"

He looked at me, shut his mouth, then crossed his arms over his chest, like he was reconsidering telling me.

"Fucking *go*, Roman," I said. "Come *on*."

"Okay, but you can't get pissed because I didn't have time to think it out. Like, it was a spur-of-the-moment idea, and I really thought she was in it for the money, no strings attached."

Shit, shit, shit. "I'm going to hate this, aren't I?"

"I think maybe yes." He sighed, dragged a hand through his hair, then proceeded to tell me a story that made me want to hit my very best friend.

"Are you serious right now?" I yelled, staring at the world's biggest idiot. "You straight up insulted her with that offer."

"You're probably right," he said, shaking his head. "I swear I was just dreading that wedding."

"*Shit.*" She probably thought I told him about everything as if it was all transactional, and then he came to her, trying to get in on it. "What the hell were you thinking?"

"I was thinking I wanted to get my mom off my ass."

"You're such a pain in *my* ass," I said.

"Yeah, maybe," he agreed, looking apologetic. "Do you want me to talk to her for you? Clear it up?"

"*No.* I need to talk to her," I said. I was still pissed when I thought about her notebook, because it was impossible to forget she'd written the words *careless* and *soulless* underneath my name in her loopy handwriting.

How was I ever going to not feel attacked by that?

But it *was* fiction, and I *had* been reading without permission, so maybe it was time to at least clear the air about that.

"Even if she's moved on and wants nothing to do with me," I said, "I don't want her to think we thought we could just pass her around."

Was that what she'd meant when she said she was surprised I hadn't shared her notebook with my *little friends*?

"Yeah, God, I'd hate that, too," he agreed. "I'm so sorry—this is totally my fault."

I sighed. "This *is* your fault, but it's mine, too. Mostly yours, though."

I picked up my phone and tried texting her, but I got no response, as expected. I tried FaceTiming her, but of course she didn't answer.

Maybe she blocked me.

"You are hilarious," Roman said. When I looked up from my phone, he was grinning. "The look on your face is so intense that I kind of feel bad for Abi."

"Don't feel bad for her, just help me find her," I said, gesturing to Carol that I was ready for the check.

"Didn't you just order another?" she barked from two tables over.

"Changed my mind and need the check."

"Maybe go to Benny's," Roman suggested.

"It's already poured—I'm gonna have to charge you, hun," Carol said.

"Fine," I said, distracted, then said to Roman, "She only works three days a week, and I don't want to be the creepy guy who shows up at her job."

"Why not? It works in the movies."

"Yeah, it also works in real life for women with stalker exes who show up at their places of employment. I don't want to put her in that situation."

"It's already been poured," Carol said again from where she was leaning on the bar, probably shit-talking me to the bartender. "Sure you don't want it?"

"Just the check, please," I bit out.

"Okay, so then what do you do?" Roman asked.

"Does your friend want it?" Carol yelled.

"I don't give a *shit* about that beer," I yelled back, needing the world to shut the hell up so I could think.

But the entire bar shut up then, as it seemed every eye in the place was on me.

Looking at me like the asshole I truly was.

"Sorry, Carol," Roman yelled, pointing at me. "This one's in love and losing it. Please forgive him."

That made her laugh, and the killer glares from around the restaurant softened just a bit. I was grateful for my idiotic friend's quick thinking.

"So," Roman said, grinning like he was having the very best time. "I think I have a plan."

43

THERE HE IS

Abi

I knew it had to happen sometime.

Still, it felt like a gut punch when I checked the schedule and saw I had to clean Declan's apartment that night. *He must be in New York*, I thought, which I couldn't let myself think about because even though I was healing, anytime I thought of our trip, or pictured his beautiful SoHo apartment, it was impossible to keep the emotions at bay.

I hadn't heard a word from Declan.

Not. A. Word.

Because I'd blocked his number.

I knew hearing from him wouldn't be great for me.

Because as I wrote the Daphne story, filling in all the gritty details that made it work, I realized I needed to be stronger. Daphne had been susceptible to the charms of Connor and his family because she was weak and lonely. She let them in because she'd been hungry for love and attention.

And I suspected I'd been the same way.

But Daphne's ultimate failure had been her inability to learn once things started changing; she'd been incapable of even considering that Connor and his family weren't worthy of her trust.

The brief dalliance with Declan had weakened me momentarily, like Daphne, because before him, I didn't have delusions of romance or daydream about love.

That was something my mother did.

I was more of a work-my-ass-off-and-make-things-happen person. I was working two jobs and going to school because I was going to be a college professor, own my own home, and depend on myself for the things I wanted.

I'd seen my mom spend her entire life being reactive, moving about the world in hopes of something—or someone—giving her the things she wanted, and that was bullshit.

But I'd become a version of her—and Daphne—when I was with Dex, daydreaming and begging for heart crumbs, and that was unacceptable.

I mean, I'd almost walked away from a great story idea because I'd lost the ability to disseminate truth from fiction. Somehow, Daphne's story had felt a lot like mine, so much so that I couldn't think about it without crying because it'd made me feel empty inside.

The brief Declan chapter in my life had been self-indulgent, where I'd allowed myself to absorb him into every empty hole and crack in my life, taking them and expanding them but filling them more in turn so that *after* him—when his existence in my life quickly disappeared—my aloneness felt more amplified than it ever had before, and the holes left larger and empty once again.

MAID FOR EACH OTHER

So now I was trying to remember how to get back to the old me.

Which was why I hated that I had to clean his apartment that night; no way would that *not* set me back a few steps.

Before we met, I'd been able to enjoy how gorgeous his place was when I cleaned it. I'd imagine what it'd be like to live there, but when I thought of the person who actually lived there, this stranger I didn't know, I mocked the idea of him.

The idea of somebody who was never there but spent a fortune on a gorgeous condo.

It had to be someone with zero respect for money and all the wrong values, right?

And now I knew that was absolutely true.

I was filled with dread as I took the service elevator up to his floor. I knew his place was going to look different to me now than it had before. I was going to remember making food in the kitchen, watching TV with him, dropping my raincoat and having him tell me I was stunning.

It was like my movie had been filmed in that apartment, my favorite rom-com in the entire world that I'd rewatched a hundred times.

But now it was over, those characters weren't real, and the apartment was just another set. Abi and Dex were people who'd been playing their parts and now they'd moved on to their next show, leaving this set vacant and ready for whatever the next act was going to be.

I used my key and let myself in, ready to concentrate on work and nothing else. I was going to scrub surfaces without really *seeing* the place; that was the plan.

Eyes down, mops up.

But as soon as the door closed behind me, I heard Declan's voice, and it shook me to my core. It felt like the worst déjà vu.

"Abi, is that you?"

Shit.

Shit, shit, shit. I didn't know what to do.

Part of me wanted to just run out the door like I hadn't been there, yet there was another traitorous part of me that was hungry for the sight of him.

But I didn't want him to see me, not like this.

Somehow the thought of him seeing me with a cartful of janitorial supplies, not to mention my bird's-nest bun and *I LOVE NEW YONK* T-shirt and shredded jeans was too much.

"Abi."

It wasn't a question this time, and he walked out of the office, his unwavering gaze on me. He was wearing black slacks and a button-down with a tie, and my favorite watch.

He looked so beautiful it made me want to cry.

"What are you doing here?" I asked, wishing I was anywhere else. "It looked like on my schedule you were going to be gone. I can clear out of here and just have them reschedule when you're—"

"I'm here because of you," he interrupted.

"What?" I asked. "What do you mean?"

"I've been trying to reach you and couldn't get a hold of you, so I lied to Masterkleen and said I was going to be out of town on the off chance you'd show up."

"What do you want?" I asked, feeling like the rug had been pulled out from under me.

Did he need another weekend? I wanted to puke at the thought.

"I want you to tell me why you didn't take the money."

Oh, he's here about the money.

"Because I realized it was ridiculous," I said. "It was madness that someone would have to pay a small fortune for a weekend companion. It wasn't difficult work, so it was ludicrous to take money like that."

"Bullshit," he said, his face unreadable.

"I'm sorry?" I managed, hating him for how much he'd made me like him, for how much I missed him.

For how much the memories hurt.

"That's bullshit," he repeated. "It's what we agreed upon and you knew it was going to be easy money; you said that the day we agreed upon it."

"So you're mad I didn't take your money?" I asked, unsure of what exactly he seemed irritated with me about. "I'm not going to sue you if that's what you're—"

"Roman told me he saw you at Benny's."

"Oh." I wasn't sure what to say to that. "Yeah. He was buying supplements."

"I know," he said.

I waited for more, but he gave me nothing. He didn't say a word, so finally I said, "We get wholesaler prices, so we're able to sell them for way less than every—"

"I don't care about Benny's supplemental price points," he said, throwing his hands up in frustration. "I care that my friend stupidly suggested something that might've made you feel like a commodity."

"He—" I stopped myself from saying more, because I didn't know *what* to say to that. He'd just explained exactly how Roman had made me feel. "You didn't know he was going to do that?"

"I would've fucking destroyed him for the proposition," he growled, looking straight up pissed now. "And if you'd said yes, it would've destroyed *me*."

I blinked fast as his words crashed into me, jump-starting the heartbeat that'd been frozen since I'd walked in. Suddenly my heart was racing and my face was hot and my hands might've been trembling because what did this mean?

"It, uh, it would've?" I asked, my voice coming out sort of husky. "Why, exactly?"

"You're going to make me say it?" he asked, stepping closer, closing the space between us.

And suddenly, it was too much. I could smell his cologne and see his Adam's apple and hear the ticking of his fancy watch and I couldn't get sucked back in again, I couldn't.

I wasn't Daphne, goddammit.

I cleared my throat and shook my head, stepping back. "You don't have to say anything. It's cool."

His eyebrows went up and he frowned. "It's *cool*?"

I couldn't do this. I was finally starting to not think about him incessantly, to throw myself into my writing, to force myself to find my own happiness. I needed to get away from him. I said, "It's all water under the bridge and we're good."

"It's 'cool' and now 'we're good.'"

He was air-quoting me again, damn it.

"That's right," I said, nodding and giving him what I hoped was a carefree smart-ass smirk. "We're 'good.'"

I air-quoted myself.

Or I was air-quoting him air-quoting me.

Whatever.

I said, "It was really good seeing you, but I've got to get to work before I get fired. Obviously they got it wrong and you're in town, so just let me get my stuff out of here and I'll be—"

"What if *I'm* not good?"

His words hung there, in the air between us. He swallowed and I saw his jaw flex before he said, "I'm the opposite of good. I'm fucking *miserable* without you, Abi."

I wanted to run to him, to kiss him, to bury my face in that strong chest while he wrapped his arms around me—I wanted it so badly I could almost feel his warmth—but that would only make things worse. I wouldn't survive when he eventually got bored and shrugged his shoulders at me like I'd seen him do with cars and money and jewelry.

No, this was simply a boy not accepting he wasn't getting something he foolishly thought he wanted.

"That's only temporary," I said, a weird part of me feeling bad for him. "You'll find someone shiny who makes you forget all about the one that you thought you wanted."

His eyebrows screwed together. "What the fuck does that mean?"

"It means," I said, trying to keep my thoughts in order when his presence was messing with my emotions and making it hard to process anything, "that you live in a world where you get every single thing you're ever remotely interested in. You might enjoy it for a while, but eventually you end up just giving it away or not caring for it because it no longer matters to you."

"Careless?" he said, and we both knew he was referring to what I'd written. He stared down at me, his eyes everywhere on my face, and I had to force myself not to fidget.

Then he said, "Tell me why you think that."

"I mean, you *did* offer me your car multiple times, you didn't blink over my demand for a small fortune, you didn't care about the diamond necklace—you have so much that nothing retains its value. You buy things that you ultimately just walk away from because you're done with them."

His eyes narrowed and he said, "Those are *things*, Abi, possessions with actual price tags. You can't lump yourself into that."

"I think I can, actually," I said.

"No, you can't," he growled, dragging a hand through his hair. "Because I'm not Connor. I *don't* give a shit about possessions— I'm happy to give them away because it's just stuff. Material bullshit. I work my ass off so I *can* give things away. But you aren't a possession."

I sucked in a breath when he reached out a hand and pushed my hair behind my ear. "I can't walk away from you."

I wanted, so badly, to close my eyes and rub my cheek against his big hand. But instead I said, "You'll get over it."

"I won't. I can't." As if reading my mind, he stroked his fingers against my cheekbone and said, "Because I'm in love with you, Mariano."

44

CHAOS

Declan

I don't know what I expected, but it wasn't for her to laugh.

It wasn't a genuine laugh, but she gave me a sarcastic little cough-laugh as she stepped back from me and said, "No, you're not."

"Yes, I am."

"No, you're not!" she said loudly, her voice filled with agitation. "You don't even really know me or my life. You know the version we curated for our show, the version who wore the right clothes and held your hand while you gave speeches and played with you in SoHo as if she belonged in an ten-million-dollar apartment. *That* is not me, Declan."

"I know that," I snapped, terrified that I wasn't going to be able to change her mind.

"Do you?" she asked, her fiery brown eyes on mine.

We heard a noise erupt at the entrance.

"Holy shit," Roman said as he walked into the apartment

with boxes piled up to his nose, oblivious to the scene in front of him. "Sorry I'm late but this was a bitch to—"

"*Yes*," I said to Abi, ignoring Roman and wondering how it was that we were yelling at each other when I was trying to convince her I was in love with her. "I liked that version of you, but that's not who I'm in love with. I'm in love with the girl who buys stupid T-shirts because they're a good deal, whose hair sticks straight up in the morning when she runs around in pajamas with her own face on them, and the idiot who risks her fucking life to run in a 5K because she made a commitment."

She furrowed her eyebrows, her eyes unreadable.

Roman bumped into the wall and dropped all his boxes.

"I'm in love with the girl who would rather enjoy her job than make a fortune in finance. I'm in love with the girl who only cooks noodles and worries about a scorpion stinging me through my shoe. I'm in love with the girl who creates backstories that have me falling off a treadmill for her, for God's sake."

"Oh," she said, her perfect mouth forming a perfect O.

"Oh is right. I'm in love with *you*, damn it, and it's really pissing me off that you refuse to accept that." I hadn't meant to yell at her, but I couldn't get her to hear me. To understand how badly I wanted her in my life. "I don't know how to convince you. Tell me what I can do to show you. *Please*."

"He bought you all this," Roman said, kneeling down beside the mess of boxes he'd just dropped on the floor. "Cost a small fortune."

"Shut up, Roman," I muttered.

"Yeah, no offense," she said sarcastically, sounding exactly like the Abi I'd met in Benny's the first time, "but Dex spending money actually proves *my* point."

She gave him a look like she wondered why Roman was even there.

"But on *these?*" Roman asked, holding up one of the small boxes. "He spent a fortune on inhalers, which I was supposed to help him weave into the bouquets in his office, but I was too slow and you showed up earlier than we'd expected. You really should've called."

I sighed, wondering how he was so good at so many things when he could be such a bumbling jackass about others. "Roman. Stop."

"What, um . . . ," she said, her eyebrows crinkled together in that way that I loved, "bouquets . . . ?"

Oh, God, please let that be interest in her eyes.

The doorbell buzzed and I heard, "MISTER POWELL?"

Fuck, what now?!

"Hold that thought," I said to her, holding out a hand, terrified she'd leave. I yelled to the intercom, "Yes?"

"LAUREN SMEARHAVEN HERE TO SEE YOU. SHOULD I SEND HER UP?"

Lauren who? I didn't know—

"No!" Abi yelled to the intercom, her eyes wide.

Her cheeks were pink as she turned to Roman and me, blinking rapidly as she said, "That's my friend."

Her friend? At my apartment?

Then she yelled to the intercom, "I'm coming down!"

Roman raised his eyebrows at me as if to say *what the fuck?*

"She's welcome to come up," I said, desperate to make Abi stay.

"No," she said, shaking her head. "This will only take a second."

"You're coming back?" I asked hopefully, realizing how pathetic I sounded.

"I mean, I have to clean the place and I need this job," she said as she headed for the door. "So yes. I'll be right back."

As soon as the door closed behind her, Roman said, "Holy shit."

I shook my head and dragged my hand through my hair. "Holy shit, indeed."

"No, I mean holy shit—Lauren Smearhaven has been an investment. I think she was July, maybe."

What? "Are you sure?" I asked.

"Think about it—Smearhaven? Not a name I'd forget."

I looked at Roman and shook my head, wondering what in the hell *else* could be thrown into this scene that was supposed to be ending with Abi in my arms.

Lauren fucking Smearhaven.

"Ho-*ly* shit."

45

REVELATIONS

Abi

"What are you doing here?"

I grabbed Lauren's arm and pulled her into the lobby restroom, because I was very aware of how big Carl the Doorman's gossipy ears were. I'd benefited from countless entertaining stories since I'd started with Masterkleen of all the things he'd overheard from his desk.

"You haven't responded to my texts," she said, scowling. "I was worried."

In spite of the chaos of the day, my heart got a little warm as I looked at my irritated friend. She'd been worried about me.

"Awww," I said, pulling her into a hug. "Thank you."

She pulled back and scowled even harder. "You don't hug—what the hell is wrong with you?"

I shook my head. "Forget it. Nothing. Now why are you really here?"

"I was worried, but also I've been dying to tell you what I think I discovered about your friends."

My friends. I had no idea at that moment *what* they were. I was stuck between (a) desperately wanting to believe Dex because he'd just said everything I wanted him to say, and (b) knowing he might feel that way today but it was surely fleeting.

"Why couldn't you have just texted it to me?" I asked.

"Because," she said, lowering her voice even though we were the only ones in the bathroom, "it's *hugely* a secret. So secret that I didn't even want to send it over a phone."

"*What?*" I said, a little too loudly because she put her hand over my mouth.

"Shut *up*," she hissed, her eyes wide. "I'm about to go all first grade on you and whisper as quietly as I can into your ear. So you're going to need to keep your mouth shut and just listen, okay?"

"You sound bonkers," I said, wondering why she was acting so bizarrely. "Just tell me quietly, there's no one else here."

"My way or the highway," she said, and sighed. "Fuck it. Just shut the fuck up and listen."

Lauren grabbed my head, pulled it to her face, then cupped her hands around my ear.

"There is a thing online called RestWell—you've probably heard of it, I don't know. It's this anonymous drop box where people can randomly ask for money, basically. Like they fill out their name, their request—how much they need and why—and their Venmo or PayPal info, unless it's over a certain amount and then there's other requirements, I think. But no one knows who runs it or how it works—and people have been trying to find out for *years*—but this modern-day Robin Hood literally gives away millions of dollars every year. Like, *millions*. To random users on the internet."

"You guys okay in there?" Carl yelled from outside the door.

"We're fine, Carl," I yelled back, knowing he was champing at the bit to flirt with Lauren because he loved brunettes. "It's girl stuff."

"Carl out, then," he said, and I heard the click of his shoes walking away.

"So," Lauren whispered. "A few months ago when my mom fell behind on her mortgage and was being eaten alive by the interest, I thought, *what the hell, why not try it?* I submitted it just as a last resort, and they paid off my mother's fucking house."

"What?" I yelled, which made her slap me in the arm. I lowered my voice to a whisper and said, "Are you serious?"

"Of course I am, you idiot, why would I make this up?" she said. "But here's the thing. When you sent me that picture of the email on Declan's desk, something felt familiar about it, and I couldn't figure out what. But I finally figured it out, Ab. The six-digit number that was in brackets beside the list of names? There was a number like that on my payment memo."

I leaned back to look at her, trying to figure out if I was getting this straight. "What?"

She nodded, pulled my ear back to her face, then whispered, "And the email addresses they were using were for a company called RWDR. Could that be an acronym for Rest Well Declan Roman?"

I blinked and stared at the paper towel dispenser. *Could this actually be a thing?*

"No," I said, shaking my head. "That's a stretch, don't you think?"

"I would," she whispered, "except that I found a recent social media post from one of the people on that email, Camille Johnson. She posted that RestWell gave her the $76K that she needed to pay for her son's cancer medications—the exact amount listed on that email message."

I gasped. "Oh, my God."

"Right?"

"So you're telling me that Dex and Roman—"

"Don't you dare say it out loud!" she whisper-yelled, looking at me like I was ridiculous. "Have a little respect for the lore, will you?"

I stared into the mirror above the sink and tried to wrap my head around how wrong I might've been about him. If this were true, he wasn't a rich guy who gave things away because he didn't care about them.

If this were true, he was a rich guy who cared enough to give them all away.

46

FINALLY

Declan

I stopped pacing when I heard the key in the door.

I turned, and there was Abi.

And a brunette.

Who was grinning from ear to ear.

I tried reading Abi's face, but I had no idea what was going on there. She no longer looked mad, sad, and closed off. No, she looked . . . mysterious. Like she was *trying* to be mysterious.

"This is my friend Lauren," Abi said, pointing to the only other person in the room.

"Hi," the woman said, smiling so widely that it was almost alarming. She looked fucking insanely happy to see me. "It's so nice to meet you."

"You, too," I said, glad that Abi's friend didn't seem to hate me.

But I felt like something was going on, like some sort of gotcha was underfoot.

"Where's Roman?" Abi asked, looking around me.

"In my office," I said, a little annoyed by all the extra company. I just needed to talk to Abi alone, damn it. "Why?"

"Roman," she yelled, and I really hated not knowing what was going on. I felt like I had zero control of this situation.

The office door opened and Roman walked out, carrying one of the finished bouquets that I'd told him not to bother with because it was too fucking late to pull off that romantic gesture. "Yes, Abi?"

"Can you keep—"

She stopped talking, her eyes on the bouquet of hydrangeas.

Holy shit, Roman did a great job.

"Are those . . . *inhalers*?" Lauren asked, looking at the flowers through squinted eyes, like she was seeing something offensive.

"And EpiPens," Roman said, grinning like it'd been his idea. "Perfectly placed by yours truly among these lovely hypoallergenic hydrangeas."

"You're kidding me," Lauren said.

"There are three more bouquets just like it in the office," he said proudly, the little shit. "Romantic as fuck, am I right?"

"Can you two leave?" Abi said, those brown eyes on me as she said it. Her face was impossible to read, but that gorgeous amber gaze held me in place like a vise grip.

"*What?*" Lauren asked. "I just got here. You brought me up with you, remember?"

"She doesn't mean me," Roman said to Lauren. "I mean—"

"Please leave us," Abi said.

"Don't *Pretty Woman* me," Lauren whined, and I had no

fucking clue what she meant but I was glad to see her turn toward the door. "Come on, Roman."

"I don't think she means—"

"Get the fuck out of my house, Roman," I said, feeling like I might die if I didn't get to talk to Abi alone.

Roman and Lauren were talking over each other, thankfully taking the chaos with them as they exited my apartment. Once the door clicked shut behind them, it was quiet.

Until Abi started moving. She walked toward me until she stopped only inches away, setting her hands on my chest. At her touch, I felt a spark of hope spread through me and my whole body was buzzing as she moved both of us until my back was against the wall. *Just like Kansas City, praise Jesus.* Her voice was low and husky when she said, "Before we were interrupted, you asked me what you can do to show me."

My arms wound around her so fucking fast. "I'll do anything. Just name it."

"Forgive me," she said, looking up at me with so much seriousness on her pretty face that it hurt a little. "Please forgive me for assuming the worst about you."

"What, uh . . . ," I said, torn between wanting to know what changed and wanting to shut the hell up and just go with it. "What changed?"

She bit down on her lower lip and tilted her head, watching me like she was trying to figure out her next words. "I know about RestWell."

"*What?*" That was the absolute last thing I expected her to say. I was shocked and didn't even try to deny it. I just asked, "How the hell did you find out about that?"

"So it's true?" Abi looked up at me like she couldn't quite believe it. "It's actually you and Roman who do all of this . . . Robin Hooding?"

"It is," I admitted, wondering if she knew that she was the only person in the world besides me and Roman who knew.

"I definitely want to talk about that, but first will you forgive me for being a judgmental asshole?"

"Done," I said, sliding my hands up to cup her face. "Forgotten."

"And the things I wrote were not about you," she said, speaking quickly like she was in a hurry for me to know. "They were inspired by your lifestyle, but never about you, Dex."

"Never?" I teased. "I mean, your asshole character's name *is* my middle name."

"Mostly never," she corrected, a giggle in her voice. "He was created in the image of who I thought you were the first day I met you."

"Ah," I said. "When I promised to get you fired and maybe arrested."

"That's so Connor," she replied. "Right?"

"I love you," I said, feeling like I couldn't go another second without saying it.

"I love you, too," she said, and something about hearing her say those words made me weak.

I kissed her mouth, a small kiss that would've been appropriate all the times we attempted to pull that off, but I quickly pulled back. Because I needed to hear her utter those words one more time. "Say it again, Mariano."

"I love you," she said, her face glowing in complete happiness that I fucking adored.

"Again," I said, lowering my mouth, and I knew what she was going to say before she even said it.

"You're not the boss of me," she said, biting my bottom lip. "But I'm saying I love you because I *want* to say I love you."

"Fucking thank you for that," I said, then I went in for everything.

I kissed her with everything I had, trying to make her feel what I felt for her. Her fingers gripped my cheeks, her tongue licked into me in a way that made every muscle in my body tense, and her lips were fucking wild.

We were fucking wild for each other.

I maneuvered her into my office, wanting to work fucking hard on Abi on top of my large mahogany desk. I lifted her, in love with the way she felt in my arms, but when I reached for her idiotic *NEW YONK* shirt, she pulled back.

"What are you doing?" she asked, a snotty little grin on that addictive mouth.

"Oh, you want mine off first?" I teased, reaching over my shoulder to grab the back of my shirt.

"No," she said, pushing my chest a little and climbing off the desk. "I mean, we can't get naked, are you kidding?"

"Why not?"

"I have to work," she said, her eyes narrowed like I was the one saying nonsensical bullshit. "I've already wasted too much time, to be honest."

"Are you talking about cleaning my place?" She couldn't be

serious. "It looks great and I don't care. I'll tell them you scrubbed the place all night long."

"*No*," she said, her eyebrows furrowed. "Masterkleen is paying me to do a job, so I'm going to do it. You need to leave or, like, retire to the bedroom."

"Abigail Mariano," I said, grabbing her shirt and jerking her back to me, "so help me God, I am going to call Ken Adams and get you fired, just so you have to stay here all night."

"You wouldn't," she said around a laugh, and I wasn't sure how I'd gotten lucky enough for her to choose my apartment to squat in.

"Try me," I said.

"What if we made some sort of a deal," she said with a grin. "You agree not to get me fired if I . . . ?"

"I thought you didn't want me to make any more little deals."

"I *don't*," she said, groaning. "I was trying to be sexy."

"Oh, is that what that was?" I asked, even though her watching paint dry would probably be sexy to me.

"It *was*. You were supposed to suggest something overtly sexual, to which I would agree, and then I could go scrub your damn windowpanes while we both suffered from raging need. Now . . . you ruined it."

"I ruined it?" I said, laughing my ass off.

"*Yes*," she said, laughing, too. "Now you're just going to have to keep me company for the next few hours while I clean. So much more boring."

"And after that . . . ?" I asked, giving her an obnoxious eyebrow waggle.

"After that, I go home to my place," she said, and disappointment settled into my belly. After a month without her in my life, I didn't want to be apart from her for a minute, much less a whole night.

But before I could argue, she added, "If you're good, I might just invite you to join me."

"You sure I won't get infected with anything?" I teased. "If I go to your 'slumlord jackass' apartment?"

"No," she said with a grin. "But don't worry. When I got an infestation, it ended up being the best thing to ever happen to me."

❦ Epilogue

ONE YEAR LATER

Declan

"You're serious?"

"Of course I am," Abi said, rolling her eyes at me as she wheeled her rusty old bike into the guest room. "I've always wanted to ride a bike through Central Park, so why wouldn't it make the move?"

The movers were at my apartment with Abi's stuff, and each thing they hauled in brought up a new topic of conversation. My adorable fiancée refused to part ways with any of her things, even though they could easily be replaced with newer, safer models, so the apartment was starting to have an eclectic, very lived-in vibe.

Which I didn't hate.

The place on Sullivan had Abi all over it now—the smell of her perfume, the cabinets full of noodles, the closet full of stupid T-shirts—and I was fucking pinching myself that we'd made the leap to living here full-time.

We hadn't planned it, but every time we visited, we hated leaving. Somehow it felt like *our* place, as weird as it sounded, so when she secured a teaching job at a community college in Westchester after she graduated, it seemed like fate.

Especially when I'd accidentally proposed the week before.

I'd had a lunch meeting with Warren at Immersion, with no ideas of marriage in my head, but then he had to stop in and say hi to Susanna at Jaques.

And while they'd chatted it up about the diamond market, I'd somehow found myself standing in front of the ring Abi had selected at the private event. I'd remembered how she'd looked in that black outfit as she laughed with the jewelry team and flaunted the heart-shaped diamond ring like we were a real couple.

As I stood there remembering, I'd never wanted to buy any *thing* more.

So I did.

Totally without a plan.

But when she came home from Benny's that night (she'd fucking schooled me on the realities of prescription med prices and the absurdities of health insurance when I tried convincing her to quit) and informed me that she'd seen Nana Marian at the store, it felt even more meant to be.

Because apparently my grandmother had always purchased her supplements from Benny's, which was how she'd recognized Abi the first time they'd met. So we'd been *this close* to being found out on our very first date, but somehow the stars had aligned and we'd made it through.

I strongly suspected Nana Marian had known all along and chose to simply watch and wait.

She'd barely finished the story when I think I blabbed something like *I bought this for you because you became my heart that weekend, and I couldn't leave the store without it. I promise if you say yes, I'll plan a romantic proposal worthy of you and we can redo this whole thing but I just couldn't wait another minute to give you this.*

Whatever embarrassing nonsense I said worked, because she said yes and refused to consider a second proposal.

So now we were engaged, though neither of us were in any hurry to get the wedding planned because we were so damn happy with our new life. Professor Abi was obsessed with her job, I'd finally gotten promoted, and the two of us were disgustingly smitten with the newest member of our household.

"Look who was asleep in the spare room," she said as she walked out of the bedroom, looking cute as fuck in my tattered old Harvard sweatshirt, leggings, and her hair piled on top of her head. She was grinning down at the fluffy-ass cat that she adored more than anything in the world, including me. "Little Dexxie."

I still couldn't believe, after our massive monthslong allergy-test manhunt to find a pet for Abi that wouldn't make her wheeze, she'd named her beloved Siberian kitten *that*. I walked over and scratched his belly while he purred but looked at me like I was an asshole.

"How is it that I love someone who's such a pain in the ass?" I asked, leaning forward to kiss her forehead.

"You made a deal with the devil," she said with a grin. "For the price of $40K."

"No, I made a deal with a devilish *maid*," I corrected, "and it cost me my whole entire heart."

ACKNOWLEDGMENTS

First and foremost, thank you, God, for giving me so much more than I could ever deserve.

Thank you, Kim Lionetti, my incredible agent, for making my writerly dreams come true. And Maggie Nambot, you are the wind beneath all our wings. And shout-out to Samantha Lionetti for being just so freaking cool.

Angela Kim, I'm not sure how I got lucky enough to land you as my editor but I'm so happy I did! You make my stories better, and I'm so grateful to be on your team. And thank you to *everyone* at Penguin Random House and Berkley, including the amazing Chelsea Pascoe, Elizabeth Vinson, Kalie Barnes-Young, and all the publishing people who make the magic happen.

Random thanks to random people for bringing me random joy: Taylor Swift, Aidan Bissett, Gracie Abrams, Noah Kahan, my Berklete pals, Lindsay Grossman, Daniza Jeanne, and Abi Griffin, "my faves (taygracie's version)," Emma, Diana, Sude, Eva, the other Emma, Colleen, my Omaha bestie Jenn, the lovely team at

Postscript in Ashland, Joyful Chaos Book Club (aka idiots who STILL think that tater tots are good but I forgive because I adore them), the supremely talented @belltcvia, the supremely talented Annika @dunderperks, LizWesNation, Diana, Cleo, Allison Bitz, Chaitanya, Mylla, Becca, Anderson Raccoon Jones, Lori Anderjaska, Clio, Aliza, Tiffany Fliedner, Wes Bennett's Entourage, Carla, Caryn, Alexis, Ally Bryan, Anna-Marie, Katie Prouty, Jill Kaarlela, Brittany Bunzey, Shaily, Steph Bolan, and Marisol Barrera.

Ooh—also Larissa Cambusano, Haley Pham, and Elyse Myers! Your book content gives me such joy, and it's amazing to see how many readers are inspired by your wildly entertaining content. I am your biggest fangirl.

As always, thank you to my amazing family for being amazing.

Mom, thank you for EVERYTHING. The happy childhood filled with books, the ability to laugh at myself, the obsession with rom-coms—all this began with you and I love you more than words can express.

Dad, I miss you every day.

And what can I say about my offspring? Cass, Ty, Matt, Joey, Kate—I adore you and think you're my favorite band of humans. Terrance, Jordyn, and Emily—I continue to be amazed at how much Kirkle nonsense you're willing to put up with. Thank you for going along with hypercompetitive Wiffle Ball games and a long list of absurd traditions; we appreciate your tolerance and begrudging acceptance.

And finally—KEVIN. I feel like it's getting nauseating, the way I gush about you in the backs of books, but I cannot help myself. I think you're cool, okay? I think you're cool and I love you more than I love popcorn on a weeknight. And how is it that life with you keeps getting MORE fun? I'm positive I should be getting sick of you by now, but you make me cackle every day and I might even like you more now than I did the day we played Nintendo at work while the front desk (unbeknownst to you) held your calls so I could take advantage of the time and make you see how cool I was. Obviously my scheming worked because you're still here . . . #mastermind

KEEP READING FOR AN EXCERPT
FROM THE NEXT ROMANTIC COMEDY
BY LYNN PAINTER,

First and Forever

Duffy

"Are you ready, Ms. Distefano?"

Was I ready? I kind of wanted to throw up and my entire body was shaking, so yes—I was as ready as I'd ever be. For someone who hated public speaking and avoided it at all costs—*my career choice is tax accounting, hello*—it was surreal that I was about to willingly go onto a stage and be interviewed in front of an audience.

My entire *life* had become surreal as of late.

"Yes," I said, nodding and getting out of the greenroom chair, ready to follow the intern to my idea of hell on earth. "I'm ready."

"Wait!" my dad said in a rushed panic, stopping his nervous pacing to hold up a hand and speak like he was trying to convince a hit man to spare his life. He'd insisted on accompanying me because he was certain without his guidance I would "sink us even deeper," and his face was so serious it was almost comical when he leaned in close and said, "Duffy Distefano, this moment is of the utmost importance. I don't care how much it hurts, you gotta dig deep and conjure up *sweet*. Pin on a smile and pretend to be

freaking perky, you got me? You know I love you, kid, but don't
be yourself this time—there's too much at stake."

"Oh, that's really nice, Dad," I said, my heart beating out of
my chest as the studio audience applauded something on the
other side of the curtain. My father was the only reason I was doing this. If it were just me, I'd accept my fate as a pariah and go
underground forever, but being excluded from Sundays was killing him.

Coyote football—and being a season ticket holder—was part
of his identity.

The man had proposed to my mother at a Coyote game while
buzzed and wearing face paint, for God's sake.

So when someone from the *Kel and Kell in the Morning* show
called the house a few days ago and offered me the chance to tell
my side of the story, my dad called them back (without asking me
first) and accepted on my behalf.

"*Don't be yourself* is exactly what every child wants to hear
from a parent during a stressful moment," I said, trying to take
deep breaths through my nose. "Very reassuring. Thank you so
much."

"Come on, you know you suck at people," he said with a
smirk.

He wasn't wrong, so I just kissed his cheek and said, "Get out
of my way so I can do this, old man."

I went around him and followed the intern, shaking out my
numb fingers while desperately hoping I wouldn't fall down or
pass out or get struck in the face with another hot dog, because
that shit was getting old.

And yes, the word *another* was actually applicable in this

instance. I'd been pelted with so many concession snacks over the past two weeks that I could probably nail a blindfolded test where I had to name which treat was bouncing off my forehead or which beverage was being thrown on me.

That's a corn dog. That's popcorn. That slime is the butter from a super pretzel.

Not only is that beer, but it's the fall seasonal IPA that they only serve at the north-end concession stand.

We stopped at the edge of the curtain and waited, and as soon as Kel said the words "Please welcome Duffy Distefano," the intern gestured for me to move and I was walking out onto the stage.

Surprisingly, I didn't hear a single boo as I went straight for one of the two stools sitting beside the sports talk show duo; I'd gotten used to being booed everywhere I went, so this applause was refreshing (but still terrifying). So far, I'd been booed on the bus, booed at my cousin's high school hockey game, and I'd even been booed by some rando at Sunday mass, although my dad gave the entire congregation his slow-searching *I-will-find-and-destroy-you* scowl, which made the boo-er go radio silent.

The guy probably started praying my father—and my three brothers—wouldn't find him.

So why does the general population of the Twin Cities hate me, you ask?

Because they'd witnessed me "brutally attacking" Coyote Carl, the NFL team's beloved mascot, on national TV.

It was such bullshit.

Had I knocked him down? Yes.

Had I meant to? Also yes.

Had he deserved it? *Hell* yes.

The oversize furball had stopped right in front of my seat to *dance* when the pivotal game was in overtime. I couldn't see around him and it was third and one, for the love of God. Our playoff possibilities hung in the balance while his costumed ass did the Macarena and blocked my view, and when I tapped him and asked him to move—three times, for the record—instead of moving, he *hugged* me.

Which did nothing to improve my ability to see what was happening on the field.

And as I struggled to break free of Carl's suffocating clinch, one of his gloved hands grabbed my ass.

Hard. As in, *not* an accident.

So I pushed that mangy pervert, which was a completely appropriate response.

Unfortunately, he lost his balance and toppled over backward, tumbling down quite a few of the steep stadium stairs. Like, a *lot* of stairs.

And he took out a popcorn vendor on his way down (which led to the crazy-viral meme of his barrel roll set to "Rollin'" by Limp Bizkit).

Yes, the Jumbotron cameras captured my "violent outburst" just as it happened (though they missed the ass grab), so I was now the villain.

Especially because we went on to lose that game.

Our star tight end who never made mistakes dropped a perfectly thrown pass just before time expired, but instead of blaming *him* for the loss, the entire city of Minneapolis was blaming *me* for giving the team "bad mojo."

Apparently I'd cursed the Coyotes.

It was absurd and ridiculous, but I was slightly terrified to think what could happen if Minnesota didn't make the playoffs.

We might have to move states.

"Welcome, Duffy," Kel said with a blindingly white grin, crossing her legs as I sat down. "You've had an interesting couple of weeks, yes?"

"You could say that," I said, and *of course* the microphone squawked in that way that made everyone cringe and cover their ears.

Fabulous. The way to Minneapolis's forgiveness is definitely to damage their eardrums.

"Well, we want to hear all about it," Kell said, his bright smile matching that of his cohost wife's. "But first, we're going to bring out another guest so we can discuss it together."

Oh, God. Were they going to bring out Carl? I'd memorized all the nicey-nice things my dad wanted me to say in hopes of making us marginally less hated, but I had no idea how to play a conversation with the mascot who'd ruined my life.

"Who is it?" I asked a little too intensely, wondering if I'd be able to deny the urge to push him again if he dared to show his snout in front of me. "Who's here?"

Kel shot me a weird look, like she hadn't expected me to respond like someone on the edge.

Am I sweating?

"You're about to find out," Kell interjected through his cheesy smile, his eyes a little big and fake, like he was worried—or excited—that I was about to have a meltdown. "Friends, can we give it up for Coyotes tight end Connor Cunningham?"

My mouth dropped wide open—I caught a glimpse of it on one of the many monitors mounted around the studio—as the crowd went wild and Connor freaking Cunningham walked out onto the stage. Kel and Kell stood, so I stood, too, and I watched in disbelief as the man who'd single-handedly delivered my fantasy football championship last year grinned and shook Kel's hand.

Connor Cunningham was a massive human. Six-five, two hundred sixty pounds, with size 15 feet and a hand size of 9.63 inches. I'd seen him on the field at every single home game since he'd been drafted by Minnesota, and on our TV for every away game, yet he somehow looked even more enormous as he stood there within point-blank range of my eyeballs.

He was wearing a red Coyotes pullover and dark jeans, very casual compared to his usual suited-up high-fashion pregame 'fit, yet he appeared wildly stylish compared to my Amazon Basics black cardigan, long black skirt that I borrowed from my neighbor because my dad thought all my pants looked too "dodgy" (whatever the hell that meant), and three-year-old black flats that I'd Sharpied on the way to the studio to cover all the scuffs.

My dad and I had loved him since he'd signed with the Coyotes—the guy was a beast of a tight end—but we'd become superfans after he'd been the only person to *sort of* defend my actions.

At the press conference after the loss, when they showed him a clip of my "attack" on Coyote Carl and asked him about it, he'd laughed his ass off.

But when he stopped laughing, he said the most amazing thing.

"Kind of makes you wonder what ol' Carl did to deserve it, though, right? I didn't see him ask for consent before the hug, so he might've deserved to get laid out."

I would never forget those words, because it felt like there was at least *someone* in the city—in the world—who didn't want to murder me for pushing down an oversize man-dog.

My breath caught in my throat when he looked at me, when he moved to shake my hand. *Dear Lord, that is a handsome man.* His hazel eyes were all I could see as his big hand wrapped around my sweaty palm, and my breath was coming too fast as I attempted to speak but instead just moved my gaping mouth like a fish gasping for air . . . or water . . . how did fish breathe again?

The noise of the studio suddenly sounded far away, like I was in a bubble, and I felt lightheaded and dizzy as Connor released my hand.

"I can't believe your hands actually *are* nine point six three inches—" I said on a breath, unsure why I was saying it out loud—*is the audience laughing?*—but unable to stop my woozy self because his hand was ginormous.

"Hey, are you okay?" he interrupted in that deep voice of his, his dark eyebrows furrowing together as he looked down at my face.

"—yet you still managed to drop that pass against the Raiders," I continued, wondering why I sounded like I was slurring. "How is that even possible?"

He looked surprised, and then he disappeared as everything went dark.

Photograph by Jackson Okun

LYNN PAINTER is the *USA Today* and *New York Times* best-selling author of *Better Than the Movies* and *Mr. Wrong Number*, as well as the cocreator of five obnoxious children who populate the great state of Nebraska. When she isn't reading or writing, she can be found binge-watching rom-coms and obsessing over Spotify playlists.

VISIT THE AUTHOR ONLINE
LynnPainter.com
LynnPainterBooks
LAPainterBooks
LAPainter

Ready to find
your next great read?

Let us help.

Visit prh.com/nextread